The Fortress

Apr 17

# BY THE SAME AUTHOR

(AS J. M. MCDERMOTT)
*Last Dragon*
*Maze*
*Straggletaggle*

THE DOGSLAND TRILOGY
*Never Knew Another*
*When We Were Executioners*
*We Leave Together*

COLLECTIONS
*Disintegration Visions*
*Women and Monsters*

# THE FORTRESS AT THE END OF TIME

## JOE M. McDERMOTT

A TOM DOHERTY ASSOCIATES BOOK

NEW YORK

This is a work of fiction. All of the characters, organizations, and events portrayed in this novel are either products of the author's imagination or are used fictitiously.

THE FORTRESS AT THE END OF TIME

Copyright © 2016 by Joe M. McDermott

Cover illustration by Jaime Jones
Cover design by Christine Foltzer

Edited by Justin Landon

All rights reserved.

A Tor.com Book
Published by Tom Doherty Associates
175 Fifth Avenue
New York, NY 10010

www.tor.com

Tor® is a registered trademark of Macmillan Publishing Group, LLC.

ISBN 978-0-7653-9280-0 (ebook)
ISBN 978-0-7653-9281-7 (trade paperback)

First Edition: January 2017

*For my father,*
*who taught me from a young age to read science fiction,*
*and to wonder*

The Fortress at the End of Time

We are born as memories and meat. The meat was spontaneously created in the ansible's quantum re-creation mechanism, built up from water vapor, hydrogen, carbon dioxide, and various other gases out of storage. The memory is what we carry across from one side of the ansible to the other, into the new flesh. My memories are as real to me as the hand that holds this stylus, though the flesh that carries them did not, actually, experience them.

Knowing the self is vital to clones, psychologically, and more so at a posting like the Citadel. If we perceive no origin, and there is no place but the Citadel, and all else is just a story, then I would prefer not to uncover the truth.

Therefore, I will confess the name I remember from Earth as my own, and tell the story of my sinful transgressions, to seek from you, my mysterious confessor, an appropriate repentance.

Ronaldo Aldo is my name. There are as many of me as there are colonies. My cloned brothers are undoubtedly punished for the crime they remember, though none of them committed the act. This is a compelling argument in favor of memory being our only truth. They are guilty for what they remember but did not do. I did it, alone.

I do not deny my guilt, and will never deny it.

I pushed a shiny red button. I pretended to be screaming of an invasion in a final, dying act along the securest ansible line. There were no intruders; it was all a sham. In the space of time between the admiral's results from a scouting patrol, and the filing of official reports about that patrol, I exploited a hole in the network emergency protocols. It was such a simple hack in a procedural gap that I can only imagine what all the networks of the universe will do to prevent it from happening again.

But let me begin my confession of sins from the very beginning. God will measure all my sins, not just my latest. I hope that He holds me up against my sins and not my sins against me; I hope, as well, that my final sin be held up against my life as the triumph it was. I was pushed to this great act by the station, the military protocols, and the lies I was told about transcendence. I sinned against the devil and beat his game. By grace of God, my sin against the devil is the triumph of my life.

———————

Back on Earth, I was no worse than any other child of my place and position. Certainly, I was rude to my parents on the boat we called home, drifting across the Pacific Rim for my father's contract work on sea mining rigs and port factories. On our cramped boat, I threw things overboard to get my revenge. Once, I threw my mother's purse into the gyre. I was beaten with a stick and locked in the closet that passed for my room for two days without toys or dessert. I was allowed out only to use the toilet. I do not recall how old I was, but I was very young, and it seemed like the greatest punishment imaginable, to sit in a tiny room alone, with nothing to do, for hours and hours.

I had many venial and vaguely mortal sins, I'm sure, of the usual sort. I confess freely to being unexceptional in both my virtues and vices. I was part of a cohort school over the network lines and did student activities at whatever port we found, with whomever else was around at that working station. I had friends that I saw with the drifting regularity of work on the platforms, where our parents' boats washed ashore. I recall my only real fight, when I was thirteen and we were in Hokkaido. At a public park, I got in a fight with a little Japanese boy whose only crime had been speaking with an accent at me, to tease me. I spit on him. He took a swing, but it glanced off me, the larger boy. I bloodied his nose and didn't stop hitting him until he outran me, crying for his mother away down the street. I don't remember any consequences for that sinful deed. I returned home to the boat, and washed my hands. I was alone, and made a cup of tea. I hid my bruised hands and never spoke about it to my mother or father.

I stumbled into military service, in part, because I could not think of anything else to do upon matriculation in a position that would liberate me from my parents' boat. I did not wish to be a passing contractor technician, mining or recycling or tinkering in one place or another until the resource dried up, where all the oceans looked like the same ocean, and the whole world was rolling in waves beneath my bed. I joined the military and tested well enough, but not too well, and managed to secure a place as an astro-navigation specialist at the War College outside of San Antonio. I was to be a pilot and navigator of starships as far from my mother's boat as I could possibly be in the solar system. Perhaps it was sinful not to honor my father and mother, but it did not feel sinful. They were proud of me and encouraged me to go find my fortune in the stars, and to make something of myself in the colonies. Part of me would always remain behind, after all, on that side of the ansible, and that version of myself could worry about honoring them. I have tried to keep in touch with my mother and father, though our dwindling letters have little bearing on my life. I mourn the space between us because there is so little to discuss now. I do not consider gently falling out of touch with them to be a sin.

Perhaps my greatest sin, before I was born again on the Citadel, was the night before my journey here. After all the tests, all the preparations, and just before we received the announcements of our first postings, we feasted. The colony worlds are all unevenly resourced. Nothing is so well established with farms and water and stable atmospheres that we will ever eat like we can on Earth. Graduates spend the whole day drinking fine wine and expensive Scotch, eating all our favorite foods, and we go out to a fancy restaurant at night for the culmination of our orgiastic eating of all the things our clones would never have again. I had gone out with six of my fellow classmen, including my roommate, Ensign James Scott, and Ensign Shui Mien, a beautiful woman for whom my roommate and I had both fallen. The other three who had come with us had already surrendered their livers and gone home to bed. I had been trying to stick close to Shui Mien, pacing myself, and waiting out to be the last with her, or to leave with her. She was easing her way through the ecstasy of food and drink, slowly savoring everything a piece at a time, as if intentionally slowing down time. Ensign Scott was doing the same beside her, talking and cracking grumpy jokes and frowning at me. We were in competition to be the last with her, he and I; at least, I had thought.

The thought that a part of me would enter the cosmos somewhere far away and never see her again made my heart ache. Worse was knowing that soon we would receive our solar postings. Even in the Sol, we'd drift years apart among the asteroid colonies' shipping lines. That night was the last chance.

Ensign Scott had it worse than me. He couldn't contain himself around her. He often tried to touch her hand, which she inevitably pulled away to touch the golden cross she wore around her neck, anxiously. She had to know we both wanted her. As students, relationships were against the rules, and could get us kicked out of War College. We had to be ready to drop all our worldly commitments to extend ourselves to the stars. We could not be burdened with the weight of unfulfilled romance. We had to be free men and women, ready to embrace a colony of limited resources and limited opportunities. Many colony worlds had fewer people in them than a college campus. Even the established colonies had only a few million people, yet.

Ensign Scott and I were both there, and she was there, and the whole city was below us. We were on an ancient platform that spun slowly, high above the city, with a distant view out across the horizon. We were the last three. We sat beside her mercurial smile, sipping fancy cocktails and staring out at the city, exhausted and trying to speak about anything to keep this alive a little longer, to be the one to walk her home and request a single, impossible favor: just one night together before we were all cloned.

I was angry, and tired, and a little drunk—which is no excuse, rather it is only an explanation of what had weakened me—and I committed a grave sin against my friends, and I destroyed not only my relationship with Mien, but also my relationship with James. I proposed a contest. I proposed that we should toss a coin and see who would cover the bill. The loser would stay behind and pay, and the winner would escort the glorious and lovely Ensign Shui Mien to a hotel for a wondrous night that would carry in our memories through time and space.

She choked and scowled. "Why not you both pay, and then you both have your way with me. You could take turns. Or, even better, why not you two could have your memorable night of lust together without me." She said this with clear disgust on her face, and her arms. "I am not a trophy, Ronaldo."

"Seriously, Aldo?" said Ensign Scott. "I should punch you right now. You understand that I should punch you very hard in the face?"

"Come on," I said. "Why not? A part of us will never see each other again. What's the harm?"

"We still have to live with ourselves in this solar system," said Mien. "You could have tried actually seducing me, you know. It wouldn't have worked, but you could at least have tried." She stood up. "Good evening, gentlemen," she said. She went to the waiter machine and paid for her own ticket.

Ensign Scott glared at me. "Now neither one of us is getting laid tonight," he said. "Good job, Cadet."

"I don't understand," I said. "It was just a game . . ."

"No," he said. "You clearly don't understand anything at all." He got up, too. "You're paying for my food. You lost the toss and you didn't even know it. You owe me now."

"What do I owe you?"

"I'm not punching you very hard, and repeatedly in the face with my angry fist," he said. "This is a favor I'm doing to you because you are my friend."

He turned and left me alone. The city was there, spread out before me, and I did not understand what I did that was so wrong. This is the nature of sin: Often, we do not understand the terrible consequences of even tiny failures of spirit.

I paid my bill alone, and went to leave. Ensign Shui Mien was waiting for me near the door, and I was breathless seeing her there.

She had her arms crossed. "Tell me you never knew about Ensign Scott and me."

"What?"

"You have to have known," she said.

"I didn't."

"You had to know. You were his roommate."

"I guess I'm . . . I don't even know what we're talking about."

"That's really pathetic," she said. "It was right in front of you and you didn't know?"

"No!"

She uncrossed her arms. "You're serious? That's very sad, Ronaldo. The stars will be yours. I will never be. We are still friends. Good-bye."

Ensign Scott was hidden back beside the coat check line at the elevator doors, watching us. She and he left together, with their arms around each other.

I felt like such a fool.

Abashed, I walked alone to the bus station, still tipsy, but sober enough to make it into a seat by myself. Back at the dorm room, Ensign Scott was nowhere to be found. I knew where he was, didn't I? I didn't want to think about it. I showered and dressed and checked my messages. My assignment came in over the wires, along with a special summons.

The pit in my gut was vast. I opened the message and saw my posting and cursed to myself.

———

*The Citadel,* this hellish rock and the miserable station spinning above it, undersupplied and out far on the edge of the Sagittarius dwarf galaxy, a listening post for the empty places of the Laika cluster. This is the deepest human station in time and space. It was spontaneously created by the remnants of the last great battleship of the last great war, when the ship was too broken to go anywhere but farther out. It was like stepping back in time.

The ansibles run precisely entangled at the quantum level, but time is ever relative. The generations on the planet surface of the Citadel move as they do, and have reported back that some seeds won't even grow because the shift in time, though subtle to us, is too much for the delicate seed. The gravity is slightly off everywhere, a bit heavier than Earth.

We make do where the last battleship collapsed chasing the last enemy fleet out of our corner of the known places in space and time. All the soldiers, back then, knew there was no way to travel home. So much time had passed with near lightspeed travel. It had been a thousand years since they left, or thirteen, or time isn't even real to be measured except as an illusion of man's cosmic folly.

The ansible rings true and through it all. The planet called Citadel is the farthest colony of man from Earth. The station called Citadel placed herself above the only desert rock they had in range with enough magnetic fields to sustain a planetary colony against the stellar winds. They gathered ice comets and liquid moons and hurled them upon the surface to inject life into the ground before the damaged battleship's supply ran out, but it is not enough to sustain a complex economy like Earth's. It is described as a desert in its lushest places, a wind-blasted moonscape where man has not begun to change the ground. Terraforming is always slow, and as distant as they are relative to the center of cosmic gravity, the speed of terraforming seems even slower to the solar system. Every year, Earth is three weeks faster than us on the Citadel. It is Sisyphean to consider a place like this, and it is Sisyphean to sit here in my little cell and write about what is obvious to everyone: This is a terrible posting at the edge of the human space and time, and everyone here knows it, even you.

I remember the oceans of Earth, staring out into the empty sky above the water, knowing always that below my feet swam giants. I had no love of deserts, or of God. These dreams I have, these memories of deep water and whalesongs through the walls, only make me long for something I will never have. Perhaps this is my call to faith now.

The children born here must feel cursed. The generations to come will wonder that anyone called this blasted hell a home, a place of peace. Whatever sins I had accumulated until the day of my posting, the cloned version of myself paid for them at birth out here, in our infernal home.

---

The morning after my gluttony and failure with Shui Mien, I had gone from feeling terrible because of the previous night's rejection to feeling worse than ever before because I had been given the least desirable assignment in all of space and time, a distant world removed from everything, sparse and barren, staring out into the void between galaxies on the cusp of the Laika cluster's blackest edge. My whole life would be spent watching for the return of the enemy that would likely never come, and if it did, we would be ill prepared to stop it for centuries and more.

Shui Mien texted me. *Are you awake?*

*Yes.*

She called me. "I'm going to Lacaille Station. I will be working with the whale colonies on the moon over Planet Che. What did you get?"

"Citadel at the edge of the Sagittarius dwarf galaxy," I said. "Farthest inhabited star of the whole Laika cluster."

"That one? The emergency colony from the damaged warship? The listening post?"

"Of all the hundreds of potential postings . . ."

"I'm sorry your clone will not fare better. I hope that he promotes and transcends quickly. Do a good job, and you will clone out to a second colony in three years."

"The commandant wants to see me, too. I have no idea why. Am I in trouble for something? Am I being punished?"

"I wasn't asking for you to be punished, but I cannot speak for James. I doubt he said anything about your morals violation. We'd be in just as much trouble as you. He is still asleep. He would be upset that I called you at all, in fact, but I told you, we are still friends. I have seen his message. He will be stationed in Sirius A, the Ancient Aregosa. Part of me will never see my beloved again. I am glad I don't have to make peace with that here."

"Peace . . . You both have amazing postings in well-established ecosystems, and you'll have the memory of love. I have nothing, Mien."

"That's not true," she said. "We'll talk again, someday, when you've stopped being so selfish. We're going to need you to stop being a jerk before the wedding, you know."

She hung up on me. I was slow to leave. I had a headache from the day of gluttony; I had a pit in my gut from reality. I truly didn't know, or I preferred my ignorance subconsciously. I felt so stupid, and so impossibly defeated by fate. I sat out under a mesquite tree in the courtyard and gazed up into its sweeping, feathered limbs. I saw the sky beyond the ragged green tatters of leaves, blue and clear as an ocean with white foam clouds. I was going to have to start again, and I took great comfort in knowing that the me that was on Earth was going to be a lift runner to Jupiter's moons and back. My clone had a terrible posting, but there, my original self would be free in eight years with an AstroNav pilot license, and there would be other beautiful women, a cosmos full, and at least I was cloning at all. Beneath the mesquite, the reaching branches thick and gnarled, I looked up at the sky and swallowed my shame and my heartache and saw a future where all these terrible things would be behind me forever. I saw resurrection in the sky, and I felt the promise of transcendence. The commandant's office's order to meet was a strange command. I stood up from beneath the tree and went to his office on the other side of the school. I was early but the assistant waved me back. I stood at the yellow line like a good cadet, though he wasn't there yet.

I heard him before I saw him. He was a big, physical man with oddly bushy silver hair for a military man where cueball was the standard style. He had kind eyes. He looked me up and down. "Are you prepared for transfer, Ensign?"

"Yes, sir!"

"You passed. You don't have to stand on the line like a cadet anymore. At ease, Ensign."

I relaxed only a little.

"Citadel Station is your posting. It is a tough posting, and everyone knows it. There is still occasionally very strict rationing. The station lacks many amenities. Many cadets complain about this posting and request a transfer before they get quantum cloned. Are you going to be rushing to file a complaint after our little meeting, Ensign?"

I could do that? I didn't even know how, and I had maybe an hour to file the forms. Still, they would only find a way to make it worse, with a punishment post, if it was even approved. It would hang over my record and prevent transcendence to new colonies. "No, sir!"

"Good soldier, then? Going in to your posting proud and strong?"

"Yes, sir!"

He nodded at me like a proud father. "Humanity thrives across the Laika because of dedicated men and women like you, Ensign. You're ready to brave the hardships of far space to stop the enemy's return into our heart system. I salute you." He did, just that, on his feet and firm. Then, the commandant reached into his desk and pulled out a leather briefcase. He had it not only locked, but sealed with 'Top Secret' tape. "You are to take this through, and leave it sealed. After quarantine hand it to the station admiral and only the admiral. I don't need to tell you not to open the goddamn briefcase wrapped in 'Top Secret' tape, do I?"

"No, sir."

"Good man, Ensign. Get going. You need to clear medical before you can cross the ansible. If they give you any flak about the briefcase tell them to call me. Bring the briefcase back here after transfer and return it directly to me and only me."

I saluted and left. The briefcase was heavy. It was more than paper, and seemed to rustle like a rattle if I swung it while I walked, and there might have been something liquid inside too. In the courtyards of the college, I stood out with a top secret briefcase. People stepped back and stared.

It made me feel important after all my humiliations.

Across campus, to the ansible attached to the space elevator, I looked up at the distant top, where ships drift away into sky. At the tip of the elevator, a signal line reached out across space and time with quantum entanglements. The binary signals of matter itself could be used to send data and create matter out of the chaos of hydrogen gas and ions and electrons. Inside, I was prodded with shots and immunizations against the spectrum of known biota I would face on the new colony. I was even partially inoculated with some in a drink, to prepare my intestines for the impending shifts. There, on Earth, I would be flushing out the foreign bacterial gut organisms I had just been inoculated with for a few days with minor indigestion. On the station, I would be repopulating my body with wave after wave to get in line with the diet and native microscopic flora and fauna on the distant station. They pretended to ignore the briefcase, but the nursing tech kept staring at it. I held it across my chest while my body temperature was being taken. I kept hold of it while my fingernails were being scrubbed and sanitized, moving the briefcase from one hand to the other—never putting it down.

"You're going to be overweight," he said.

"What?"

"Your transfer weight was prearranged, and the briefcase puts you over by almost twenty-five pounds. That's a lot of mass to account for."

"What am I supposed to do? I have orders from the school commandant to take it with me."

"What's in it? Can we take out some of it?"

I pointed at the tape. "Do you have clearance for that? I don't. Call the admiral."

He got on the horn to his bosses. An old doctor came in and looked me up and down, looked the nursing tech up and down and nodded. "He will be fine. It happens from time to time. It is not our concern. We will call ahead and warn them of extra mass. Usually, they already know about it, unofficially."

Without even waiting for a salute, the doctor moved me to the next room. His face was smooth and clean, but he smelled old, and he had the lightly trembling hands of extreme age. He was kind, though, and wore admiral stripes on his collar. "Try to relax," he said. "Everything will be fine. We do this every day. We haven't lost anyone yet. It's safer than going to the Day of the Dead Festivals, statistically."

The room was large with a high ceiling and had all sorts of tubes and wiring in the rafters. There were different sizes of glass funnels above, ready to descend, with rubber sealant sprayed onto them. The tanks of gas were overhead, too, nestled like eggs among the coiled tubes.

"I'm relaxed, sir," I said. I tried not to look up again.

"Good. So, we're going to stand you in the center of the room, right inside the yellow square painted there. A glass tube will descend. For just a moment, you'll be in vacuum, but you're young and strong and you can handle it. Then, the ionized gas will fill the vacuum in an instant, and the glass will come up once transfer protocols lock in. You'll be done in less than a minute. Okay?"

"Yes, sir."

"Take a deep breath and hold it on my signal. Keep your mouth closed. Best thing to do is just hold still, try to relax, and let it happen. It will be over before you even start to hurt."

"Got it, sir." I stood firmly in the center of the yellow square, but I looked up at the glass tube above me.

"It will hurt. The ionization process is not a pleasant one. But it will be no worse than getting a shot in the arm, except over your whole body."

Lights went on in another room behind a glass window that was darkened before. I saw technicians there looking in, and working at terminals, securing their connections and focusing the data lines into the proper channels for my transcendence.

"Hold still, Ensign," he said, speaking calmly. "On my count, take a deep breath. Three . . . two . . . one . . . Hold."

Air held still inside my lungs. The glass came down from above surprisingly quickly, but not so fast that I couldn't jump out from under it if I had the nerve. It separated me from the room, and the vacuum seal hissed. I couldn't hear anything, then. The air filled with a blue gas that emerged in spots and lines like a grid of flowers in the air itself. It was dazzling and sudden, like getting punched and seeing lights. The gas filled out the air, and swirled and then I was through. In fact, I had been through for a few moments already, and the gas was actually an optical illusion of my body and brain trying to process the sudden shifts in my vision and orientation.

The glass came up and I was born here, on the Citadel.

The moment I had seen gas, I was already here, and the images in my retinas of the place I had been is proof to me that it was real. Once upon a time, there was a place called Earth, and a young cadet named Ronaldo Aldo who had lived at sea with his mother and father, until he went to War College in the ancient Mexican city, and he stepped into a glass tube that quantum cloned him, creating me.

I was born, then, and I was reborn with all the sins still in my heart, my failure with Shui Mien, with my terrible pride.

---

The room I entered was darkly lit, gunmetal gray, and loud. The station is always spinning to maintain gravity, and I actually stumbled and had to catch myself when I attempted to move a little, in the suddenly changed g-forces. I was alone in the room; there wasn't even a chair.

"Ensign... Where's the personnel file, Tyrell? Okay... Ensign... Aldo. Ronaldo Aldo. That's right, I hope?"

The memory of my first words, and my mother is the military, and I cry out for her. "Reporting for duty, sir!"

"I'm Captain Oyede Obasanjo. I'm the ExO. A full briefing will be on your tablet." Captain Obasanjo managed all ansible transfers, and he had allocated the hydrogen and helium and carbonaceous resources from storage that had been re-formed into my self. "Welcome to the Citadel. You are in quarantine for forty-eight hours. I have other transfers to make this cycle, so I need you to step aside and let me get the rest of the stuff into the room."

I stumbled across the room, and lost my grip on the briefcase. I left it where it fell against the wall. The floor was slightly curved. Every floor would be, here. I leaned back and clutched the top secret briefcase close. An even larger glass tube descended from the ceiling, and after the hiss of a vacuum seal, a huge slab of stone appeared. It made no sense to me, at first, because the angle that I saw was undecorated. On the sides, it had crosses carved into the rock. It was an altar table for the monastery, from Earth, and blessed by the pope. It was an antique, as well, from an old monastery in the deserts of central Africa.

"Ensign," said the voice from the intercom, "can you help me and move the altarpiece out of the way of the cylinders?

We can't go in there and break your quarantine to move it ourselves."

I stood and leaned over to the altar, which was half a meter thick and three meters wide of solid stone. The edges were smooth and damp with moisture from the sudden shift in humidity from wherever it was to where it is now. I pressed my fingers down and attempted to push. It was far, far too much for one man to lift. I looked around me toward the cameras and shook my head. "Can you hear me, sir?" I said. "I don't know why you think I can move that." I leaned back against a wall.

There was silence for a little while.

Then it came on again. "You're not even going to try?" said a new voice.

"I'm sure you are aware how much that weighs, sir. I can't even push it over."

"See if you can roll it, Ensign. Man up. *Hoo-rah.*"

I pushed and pushed, assuming I was both the victim of a terrible prank, and being commanded to do so by an officer of rank. I pushed like I was a raw recruit, squirming through basic. I broke a deep sweat and ached and stopped, leaning against the altar like the wall that it was.

"How did you plan on getting this thing out of the room, at all? Do you have anything that can lift it that's small enough to get through the door?"

The intercom buzzed on, again, and it was a grizzly, old man speaking. "Okay, we're going to need to move you, Ensign. We've got a room prepped for you down the hall outside. I've hung a tablet from the door for you, and there's some rations in there. We're going to send scrubbers through as soon as you're in, so stay inside."

"Yes, sir!"

"I mean it, Ensign. We're breaching protocol just to get you out of the room. We're falling behind on our transports, and Obasanjo needs the room clear. When you're in the room, you don't leave the room until we come and clear you."

"Yes, sir!"

I was ecstatic to leave the room. No one had arranged a re-stroom, in here, that I could see. I saw no sign of a doorway, and waited for one to be revealed to me by my benefactor in the other room.

I waited.

"Hello?" I said. "Where's the door?"

A different voice came on the intercom. "Hold up, Ensign. NetSec is working around the protocol breach."

I sat back down after a few minutes. I closed my eyes and wondered what they were doing, but I couldn't picture it. I had no context for this situation. I was supposed to remain here for forty-eight hours, before being transferred to a medical facility for isolated observation while the biota inside of me and the biota that had developed in the station interacted. I was very likely to become ill. Very occasionally, these illnesses could be serious. I also had a good chance of carrying something across that might infect the crew. Quarantine, then, until my biota could stabilize, was the law of quantum transfer.

Eventually, a door attempted to open. The door creaked out from the sealed room, where it was a seamless piece of wall. It slid open from the center, but made terrible groaning noises in its servometrics and smelled of smoke.

Over the intercom, Obasanjo gave his orders. "Push it the rest of the way. We had to disable part of the system. I'll need you to shove the door closed on the other side, okay?"

The door was stiff, but easier to move than a stone altar. I grabbed the briefcase and pushed through the hole. I was able to shove it closed manually with just one hand on the other side. The hallways, here, curved gently up. We lived inside an eggshell, spinning to make gravity with centripetal force. We always walk uphill, on the stations. Gravity changes subtly with the level we walk on. The lower levels would be heavier than the upper levels. Both the top and bottom were used for storage, but I wasn't completely clear on that, at the time. When I was sitting in the quarantine chamber, the tablet was preloaded with forms I needed to work through. Until I filed as an official quantum clone with central processing, I didn't officially exist. I was just an accumulation of spent resources—mostly water—in a distant system, and a record of ansible usage at a very high rate. The world did not know me or my name or who I came from until I plugged it into the boxes on the form.

The room was clearly for storage. Shelves were stacked with cardboard boxes of cleaning supplies. A cot had been set up for me, and I sat on it uncomfortably. I had so many forms to file. I had to request a new soldier ID number, a new government identity tag, and forms to distinguish my banking in the massive financial network separated from the Ronaldo Aldo in the solar system, so far away.

Outside, the hallway filled with sound. Scrubbers blasted through, fumigating as they went, clearing out as much biota as they could with heat and bleach. I felt the extreme heat of the water emanating through to my side of the wall. Down at the bottom of the doorway, which was supposed to be a clean vacuum seal, a little bit of the steaming bleach leaked through. I snapped a photo of it with the tablet and saved it for maintenance.

I wrote my original self a note, too.

*Dear Ronaldo Aldo Number One,*

*I have arrived safely. It's very strange, so far, and I don't know what to think about the place, and I am still in quarantine, but on the whole, I have decided to be hopeful. I hope you and I both keep in touch and consider each other like brothers, for we are closer than brothers, while also much farther apart.*

*Sincerely,*
*Ronaldo Aldo the Second*

When it came time to find food, I looked around and saw nothing obvious. The packaged items were labeled in a Cyrillic alphabet, and appeared to be varieties of cleansing products dated as if they were antique heirlooms, not viable supplies. I scanned them for any Mandarin or Japanese letters. I could recognize what kind of product they were, if I could recognize the language. Finding none, I continued to search through the boxes.

My sin, upon arrival, was probably pride. I was too proud to pick up the tablet and ask for help. I was too proud to admit that I had no clue what I was doing there, and needed guidance. It took me a long time to find food, and it was not the food that was intended for me, which was placed under the cot just out of sight, thoughtlessly. I reached into old storage and found hard food bars, like sea tack made out of amaranth seeds and red dates. It had the mineral-taste of too many vitamins and it was not meant to be eaten dry, but I did my best.

When I couldn't stomach any more of it, I went back to my cot and finally noticed the lunch box underneath the cot. Inside, it had the food I was supposed to be eating, with a rich slurry of biota that would populate my intestines. I waited a bit before attempting to drink it. My belly ached from the expanding tack. When the pain subsided, I choked down the disgusting slurry, and nibbled on the food as I could. There was a restroom facility inside the room, according to my tablet, but it was hidden behind boxes that needed to be moved, and I had no time for that. Fortunately a bag was provided for emergencies in my little lunch box. On the cot, after being successfully sick into the proper receptacle, I leaned back and attempted to finish all the forms. I had opened a retirement account through the military service, and refiled my pilot's license. I had to recertify in training modules, and start over with zero hours, but it was good to know exactly what I would be doing first upon clearance. I also had to familiarize myself with the astral navigation maps that would fill most of my time at a listening post. I was the one who did the most listening.

The scrubbers passed through the hall outside, again, spraying a warm goo that I knew was biotic.

Life on a station was a carefully managed yogurt. Six full-time technical specialists are dedicated to monitoring the evolution of biotics, and quelling anything truly harmful. The quartermaster nominally oversaw their actions, but the tech sergeant ran the show, and the post required advanced degrees and training just to show up on day one. For all the difficulty and training, it was odd that they had no prestige or pull on the station. They could not access the outside universe. They were too high-risk to transfer out, with all the biota during their career. For this reason, even though they are highly trained and very skilled, they are rarely promoted up to officers, and then never promoted off-station through the ansible. They retire planetside, and remain in quarantine for a while when they do. During my career, the first Tech Sergeant Hwong died of cancer not long after my arrival, and Sergeant Adebayo Anderson was promoted up to full tech sergeant until she took over the whole quartermaster crew. I had little interaction with Hwong, and was surprised at news of his passing. Mrs. Anderson and I, however, had much interaction, particularly after her husband was retired from service. But I shall save our sins for another page. At the time, we hadn't even met. Let us remain, at present, with my early days.

I heard the work crew come back through, after the goop was splattered everywhere, scrubbing with brooms and mops.

I banged on the door.

"Hello!" I shouted. "Hey, wait, I need to let you guys know something important!"

My shouting and banging did get someone's attention.

"Stay inside. Don't open the door. We're in the middle of an iodine sweep."

"No, listen," I said. "The door has a busted seal. I can show you a picture of the bleach leaking through. How do I send it to you?"

"Shit," said a woman's voice. "Just stay inside. We're incinerating everything in there as soon as you're out."

"Why'd you put me in a storage room if you're burning it all?"

"I didn't put you there," she said. "Just stay inside. We're going to clear that room out, too, once you're done. A little leak won't bother the gel, and we can fix it later. Where is the leak, on the top or the bottom?"

"Bottom," I said.

"Okay, well, hold tight and we'll handle it. She's a leaky old tub. What's your rank and name?"

"Ensign," I said. "I'm Ronaldo Aldo, from the Pacific gyre. I'm your new AstroNav."

"Welcome to the Citadel, Ensign. I'm Tech Private Ann Watkins. It's a shit assignment on a shit world, but it's our shit," she said. "Uh . . . sir."

I didn't feel bad about exploring the different boxes, then. It gave me something to do after the forms were all filed. I found lots and lots of soaps and ration bars. I found a few boxes of towels, way in back of the storage room. There were all sorts of strange chemicals and packages, and I opened none of them to investigate. Eventually, this grew dull and I returned to the cot to lean back and investigate the tablet. The data treaty with the monastery and the clogged arteries of the ancient ansible meant very little of what I saw was up to date, if it wasn't located directly in the Citadel system. I recognized old planetary designations in the database, where newly formed stations were still demarcated by their old number and letter codes. Once I had access to navigation computers, I would push an update through the queue. The long quarantine ended when I thought it would be eternal. How appropriate to begin my life on the Citadel imprisoned. Eventually, my release came when the door alarm pinged, the door opened, and Obasanjo on the intercom buzzed me out of my stupor.

"Still alive in there, Ensign?"

"Yes, sir!"

"Report to MedTech for clearance. Sixth floor, room six."

"Six and six, yes, sir!"

Outside, in the hall, I had no idea what floor I was on.

I looked around for signs of direction. Finding none, I checked doors for stairs or elevators. All I found was storage. For almost an hour, I walked uphill, opening doors. Soon, I remembered that much of the station used to be a warship. I checked between doors for the invisible seam signals, designed to make boarding parties difficult early in the war effort, when we thought the enemy would board ships, and immediately found a stairwell. Inside, the floor was listed as AB-23. I had no idea whether six was up or down. I guessed down because gravity seemed light up here, and medical was usually a little heavy. The blood flow likes weight. I went down a level, looking for a sign of the sixth floor. The floor levels were named after the old warship levels on this side. Memory of old schematics glanced at while in training did me no good. The ships did not spin the way that stations do, and they did not name their floors the same way, as a result. AB meant I was Aft-Bridge, and 23 meant I was that many floors separated from it. In the station, the sixth floor would be in relation to just the livable spaces, up from the bottom. Gravity was only Earth-like in a certain shell of the spinning ball. Much of the ship's space was dedicated to protecting the ansible at the core, and building up around it with storage and machinery and engine parts. So much of what was the ship was a series of moving parts, and so much of the crew of enlisted were highly skilled mechanics for the advanced machinery. The officers were really the only warfare-certified specialists on board. If war actually came, we would reserve space in the ansible for far more, but it had been a hundred years since the enemy was in our corner of the Laika, and, at the moment, there was no organized piracy and no crime on this remote station meriting any sort of strong military presence. On the planet surface of the Citadel, there weren't even a thousand people yet.

Down, I climbed, and down and down, falling into heavier and heavier gravity. I felt the weight of my body. I felt the way my feet steadily got heavier and heavier. I checked the door signs for the numbers, and found none. When I felt I was reaching the edge of useful gravity, I opened the door and started to look for a terminal that might point me in the right direction.

I was far lower than useful gravity and didn't realize it right away. Going down, and disoriented, without understanding the numbering system, I had allowed the weight of things to fool me. I had gone down too far, into the storage tanks where light gases are compressed into liquids in huge tanks, and water is recycled in open vats that released oxygen from the algae in the pools, though it stank like a sewer. I knew right away that I had gone too far, but I saw no terminal. I did see exoskeletons for high-gravity work, and drifting plates that could lift objects and tanks. I thought I should be able to find a terminal relatively easily. Every schematic I had ever seen for stations had terminals dispersed every twenty yards. Even an old station like this one ought to have terminals around for workers on the level.

The gravity weighed me down, and made the top secret briefcase far heavier than I expected. It was not so heavy that I couldn't be fooled, but it was heavy, and I should have taken an exoskeleton. Again and again, my early steps on the station were marked with mistakes. The first impression I gave was not of a promising, young officer, but of a bumbling newcomer with no clue how to function on board. The only good thing was my briefcase was intact, but it was heavier by the minute and my hands ached from carrying it.

Soon, I was so exhausted, I stopped to rest near one of the bubbling algae tanks. I was breathing hard, and my joints were aching. I put the briefcase down and tried to rub life back in my hands.

I heard a ring, and a booming voice.

"Ensign, are you down here?"

I shouted. "Hello! I'm lost!"

"Yeah, you are. Did you not see the directions on your tablet?"

"No," I shouted.

"Why did you leave your tablet back in the room?"

"I don't . . . I assumed it would all be destroyed after quarantine."

"Why would we . . . Listen, where are you?"

"I'm next to an algae tank. I don't know which one."

"We're not going to mount a search party. Can you knock on the tank with something? A button, or something? Make some noise without losing your voice?"

I tapped the pipes with the handle of the briefcase and it made enough resonant noise to be heard by the intercom.

"Okay, we're going to send Corporal Adebayo Anderson down to get you. Keep tapping so she can locate you. You need to stop trying to move around on your own."

"Yes, sir," I said, continually tapping on the tank.

The intercom cut off. I listened to the sound of my own tapping, echoing up through the tank. I listened for footsteps. I heard, instead, the low hum of a lifter driving through the halls on wheels that needed to be serviced.

I kept knocking, and sat up. I turned to look, and saw her floodlights on, driving toward me in the fluorescent halls. I called out to the soldier behind the lights who was only a silhouette. The lights dropped away and it rolled to a gentle stop. The soldier there was a beautiful African woman with an accent from somewhere I couldn't place. "Ensign Aldo, is this where the devils led you, sir?"

"Afraid so. Nobody said to keep the pad. I heard the room was going to be liquidated."

"Welcome, welcome. If you are on a floor with braces, wear them. The heavy gravity is a devil on knees and blood." She threw braces to me that clattered on the ground at my feet. I slipped into them clumsily, until the machines locked in and took over. Standing up was much easier, then.

I noticed she wasn't wearing any, but moved as nothing. She trained in high gravity to build tolerance and strength. She was very fit, even compared to Wong, whom I hadn't met yet. Certainly, a raw graduate was outmatched by her exceptional strength.

"We are small enough to only maintain habitation on three floors. The rest is storage. Down this low, there are nothing but water tanks and algae. If it wasn't for PT, we wouldn't even maintain an oxygen cycle down here." She helped me up onto the lifter and took off with a playful lurch. The braces caught me.

"My husband is the warrant officer pilot, Sergeant Anderson. Jon. He will be happy to get a break from flying with a real AstroNav around. He is out on supply now."

"I can't wait to get to sky," I said. At this point, I would say anything to distract from my embarrassment. She talked about the volleyball team and their training regime. They have won the last fifteen tournaments on the planet, and will win the next one, too. Anyone may join. "Are you an athlete, Ensign?"

"No more than usual. I am a good swimmer."

"These tanks are the only ones large enough to swim in for light years around. You think you swim in these, huh?"

The algae made slight bubbling noises. It stank of an open sewer even as it cleaned the air of toxic gases. "I might some-day, if I keep messing up. The admiral will throw me in."

She didn't laugh. "The admiral would never, never do that, sir."

It was the last thing she said.

When we reached the lift, I stripped the braces, and felt my weight sink into my knees and shins. She left the lift to park itself and chose a floor far above us on the elevator, not the stairs.

"I'm sorry if I offended you," I said.

"I am not offended. Sir, I should not be so friendly with officers. It causes trouble."

"Is that really what you're worried about, Corporal? You have been on this station longer than I have and I am the one who inconvenienced you by getting lost."

"Ensign, forgive me for being philosophical. Few will greet you with a warm heart. We are 16.3 percent more likely to commit suicide at the Citadel in our first year. Almost one in four will commit suicide before retirement, on the Citadel. The regular service on most other stations has only between two and seven percent, between all postings. Ergo, the philosophy is to try and keep distance until new clones are here awhile. Let us leave it there, yes?"

"I did not come here to commit suicide, Corporal."

"I hope not, sir."

"When was the last suicide?"

"Your predecessor, sir. It was not long ago. We actually lost two in the same week, but biotic technicians are much easier to replace than War College graduates."

In silence, then, we ascended, and I enjoyed the silence. The more I communicated with her the crazier I felt. I was separated from her and the station. And in my separation, aloof to this place, my pride held me up. I stood with soldier pride, back straight and head high.

In the hallway, gravity was light as silk after the depths with the tanks. In the hall, I heard the sound of muted laughter. From behind some doorway, men were laughing. I ruffled. I could only assume I was the butt of some joke.

She gestured to the door ahead, nondescript and unmarked. "You will learn the way around soon. Here is the admiral's office. Good day, Ensign."

Day, she had said, as if there were such a thing here. We were not meant for starships and stations. Even the ghosts of language long for the summer sun.

Only after she left did I realize that she was the first person I had ever seen, despite my memory of before. Shade of quantum lives not mine, illusions to me, newly born—if I were a duckling, she would be my mother. I could not have asked for a better one.

The briefcase was heavy as if with child and I was glad to be rid of it. Upon entry into the admiral's chamber, I expected a secretary or reception or at least an ExO, but the door opened upon his tiny room. A gruff, dusty man looked up upon me with alarm and disdain. "Who the hell are you?"

"Sir?"

He wore the uniform of an admiral. He was bald and steely-eyed like one. His name was Admiral Antonio Diego, and he was not my friend. "In or out," he said. "Don't be a cat." His teeth were black and brown, some missing. It gave his words even more menace to see his diseased teeth.

I shut the door, straightened my uniform, and tried again, this time knocking first.

"Enter," shouted the admiral. I opened the door.

"Sir," I said, stepping in and saluting.

"You have wasted a lot of time and resources, Ensign Ronaldo Aldo."

I said nothing.

"What were you thinking when you ripped into our stockpile?"

"Sir?"

"You were not instructed to open boxes."

"Sir, the tech said the room would be incinerated."

"And you believed him? Were you instructed to open boxes?"

"No, sir."

"You were instructed to keep your tablet with you. Where is your tablet?"

"I don't know, sir."

"You don't?" He reached into his desk and threw it across the room at me. I caught it, at least. I did not drop and stumble. It was difficult with the briefcase in my hand, and for just a moment, I was proud of my dexterity, I admit. Even there, being dressed down by my commanding officer, I felt my pride swelling over my successful catch.

"Ensign, are you aware why you are here on this pimple at the edge of God's fart-nozzle, instead of some other colony unfortunate enough to earn your inadequate services?"

"No, sir."

"You are not aware? Really?" He stood up and touched

the wall and a video started. A man in a space suit stood alone on the side of a station wall. "This is the last AstroNav we had."

The man in the suit was not responding to the shouting in the video. Voices were shouting questions, orders, alarm. He stood unmoving. He reached briefly and swiftly for the helmet, but stopped and hesitated. I heard his long shout, and his hands rushed in a dart to the helmet seal, releasing the glass with a sudden, sucking zip into silence. The helmet floated away, and the head exploded under sudden pressure shift. Blood and liquid brain matter floated in a corona. He had put his pressure setting painfully high on purpose to blow his skull out in the shift.

The video stopped. "Ensign, you are here to replace that man. He is the third consecutive AstroNav to end his life. You are not permitted to kill yourself. I will not have them send me an officer less competent than you. I get sent flunkies that no one ever wants sitting in a cockpit. Your test scores are mediocre. If you kill yourself, they will just send me someone worse. You understand, Ensign?"

I said nothing but yes, sir. Admirals only ever liked to hear themselves, anyway.

"You will obey. You will train to improve your excremental flight rating. If the enemy returns, you will lead the charge to distract their weapons long enough for someone else to save the day. You will likely fail at that, too, because you have proven to me that you are not worth the water and hydrogen we used to create you. Try to improve yourself, and maybe you might prove me wrong, someday. Understood?"

"Yes, sir!"

He pointed at the briefcase. "That's mine," he said. "Give me my briefcase, Ensign. If you broke the seal, I'll court martial you."

In a flash, I saw the commandant's face in this bald, surly, black-toothed admiral. One clone had handed me a briefcase to give to another. The admiral snapped the briefcase away and cut the tape with a long pinky fingernail that was sharpened to a point. He opened the briefcase and showed me what was inside. It was seed packets, all corn and bean and other things labeled and unrecognizable, plus two sturdy bottles of very fine bourbon. He produced a single, small glass tumbler from behind his desk and poured out a small finger of the bourbon. He smelled it like he was about to drink it through his nose. He slowed down, and savored the smell, his hard face breaking into a crazed fervor. Sweat broke out on his forehead.

"Get out of my office, Ensign," he said. "And don't forget your goddamn tablet again."

"Sir," I said. I left. Anyone only ever got alcohol if it came over the ansible, or made it in some sort of illegal fermentation. It was a rare and legendary commodity on the highly regulated Citadel Station. On the surface, no food-based sugars were ever left over enough to permit fermentation and distillation. There simply wasn't enough water to grow materials that were not for immediate consumption on the ground below, and what illegal distilling the Biotics attempted were rumored to be mostly undrinkable swill. I was never brave enough to try.

The admiral's original copy at the War College apparently had been sending over illegal briefcases every time anyone was cloned across, in total disregard for the law and order and the resources available to be used for the raw material of transfer. The admiral's legendary treasure trove of alcoholic beverages has been the source of much debate on station. We spent many hours over cards speculating the hidden location, and not even a lowly tech managed to stumble upon the precious bottles while sanitizing a closet. Sometimes, the admiral was drunk or hungover, and this was the only clue that the mysterious treasure still existed, at all. Even after his death, his legendary treasure is hunted, but has never been found. I theorize that it was all consumed before he left us.

———————

The tablet was my master and commander for the days to come. It guided me to the quarters. It pointed to the mess hall and the physical therapy room for exercise. I was led to the quartermaster's warehouse to train on piecemeal equipment like a raw pilot recruit. I had to prove I understood the drive mechanics and could troubleshoot in zero gravity. Then the tablet would run me through small simulations. Then, I would sit in a simulator made out of spare cockpit parts and certify flight maneuvers. The quartermaster, Captain Quiswanathaa—Q, we called him—was my official direct supervisor in chain of command. He was far too busy repairing our ancient station to supervise my recertification. Q was a thin, brown man with close hair as rough as if he cut it himself with utility scissors. He had no humor, at all, and reviewed my reports with a stoic indifference to my scores. "You need to score perfect," he would say. If I did score perfect, he'd say the same in the same tone of voice, as if he didn't notice that I had achieved the desired outcome. At the time, I assumed he was just another overworked quartermaster, in the long tradition of exhausted mechanical engineering and biotic personnel.

I surrendered to my newly found isolation, wondering

when I would be assumed to be a low risk of suicide enough to merit so much as a genuine, friendly hello. The warrant officer, Sergeant Jon Anderson, rated for space to surface flight, noncombat, inner-Oort, was in and out all year to the gas giants and their moons for water and carbon and other minerals and gases. When supplies were needed, he had to run to the surface to trade raw material with the monastery for fresh food and vitamins. He'd spend less than two weeks on the ground, before taking off again, to drop off and go back to the gas giants.

Sergeant Anderson's flight schedule was so tight, it was barely felt. A man came to shake my hand and check my progress. He was little more than a supply jockey, and he had no training on anything more complex than a remote control gas diver, but he towered over me, with burnt orange hair and a proud look like I was a raw recruit to his lofty experience. He left as soon as he arrived, time and again.

I accessed his ratings after he left for one of his supply runs, and I was shocked at how low he had scored. I had beaten him, even early on in my flight career. I was more than his match in a cockpit with all those complex variables, but you wouldn't know it from looking at his posture and attitude. Naturally, I immediately disliked him. Corporal Adebayo Anderson, Jon's beautiful, strong wife, was devoted to him. She held his hand while she sat with him in the cafeteria. There were four women on the Citadel Station, and the strongest and most beautiful was married to a man I found distasteful. Sergeant Jon Anderson's booming laugh echoed into the hall. I imagined, spitefully, that he was sent often on supply runs to preserve the peaceful engine hum on board. I was envious. I admit that it colored my impression of the man. Many of my juvenile fantasies revolved around his wife, at the time.

As the youngest officer, I stood at the end of the line, looking out upon the assembled enlisted. We stood at attention at morning mess, called out roll, read by the admiral, and listened to Obasanjo read out the daily reports in his thin baritone, barely audible even to me at the front of the room. Procedure mattered. Appearances mattered. Maintaining order among the fifty-nine enlisted, here, meant a clean, crisp facade of order, even as the station groaned around us in the stellar winds. Listen to the wind howling outside your monastery walls, do you hear it? We have wind on the station, too.

That mighty Citadel stellar wind blew upon our orbit from the powerful golden star of this system. It pushed against old solar plating and caused parts to slowly wear and strip and groan against their safety locks. Techs rated for Exterior Station Repair suited up before breakfast, if it was bad enough, repairing the groaning paneling where automated drones were too slow and repairs required more direct control than their limited AI circuits could muster. The drones were ancient models, refurbished and refurbished until they were simply unreliable. They often required human eyes to check their work.

Oh, that odd wind, it was much stronger than it probably should have been, and I know that it was a subject of scientific inquiry, related to the contents of the inner star itself. As an Astral Navigator, I was more interested in the outcome than the cause. It impacted every voyage calculation's escape velocities.

At night, I woke up with nightmares to the howls of bending steel, and the knowledge that the station was collapsing around us, ejecting us into the void. In the morning, when nothing of the sort occurred, we gathered for calisthenics, then breakfast in the cafeteria. The walls continued to groan and groan, and the echoing stomps of repair machinery filled the rooms and halls.

Calmly, we stood, and waited for the world to stop groaning long enough to permit the admiral to speak, and he shouted into the storm. Obasanjo finished and gestured to the cook staff that he was done. We formed a line, then, with officers in the back and enlisted in the front. It was important to the admiral to maintain this custom. We formed a line behind the enlisted, Wong cheerfully describing his plans for the next calisthenics session, and Nguyen cheerfully pretending to care. Obasanjo, annoyed, pushed through into the enlisted line, muttering about the stupidity of waiting. As he did so, with a shocking suddenness, the groan and clamor ceased. The enlisted all took a breath as one.

The admiral was uninterested in the sudden absence of the stellar wind and called out Obasanjo for cutting in line with the enlisted, instead of waiting for the officers. "Captain Obasanjo, have you forgotten your rank?"

"Your rule is stupid," said Obasanjo. "Write me up if you like."

"I order you to get back in line with the officers, at the end of the mess line," said the admiral.

"I have no desire to stand around while I'm due for mission-critical ansible transfers, so you can pretend we are a real military operation."

"Captain Oyede Obasanjo, if I have to come over there and . . . Wong, stop him."

Wong looked over, his unflappable smile unfazed. He stepped toward Obasanjo. Enlisted backed away. Obasanjo raised one eyebrow. "Wong, don't be an idiot."

"I have to obey orders."

"The rule is stupid and meaningless. Why can't we just all get in line together? We have no food shortage now, and I'm very busy today."

"Don't make this hard, Captain."

"I control the pipeline, Wong. I do, not the admiral. You want your letters home?"

That paused him. Obasanjo passed into the food line, through the line, and sat down at the officers' table unhindered. The admiral glared at Wong but said nothing. The enlisted were all staring, all concerned but staying out of these petty squabbles.

We stared at him.

"What?" he said. Huffing at us, he stood up and took his food out into the hall, presumably to his office where he would be hidden for the day, working and working.

The admiral looked around. "Any other *officers* feel like disobeying the admiral's standing orders and military protocol?"

I was shocked at the open disobedience. I couldn't believe Obasanjo, the executive officer and my secondary supervisor, would do such a thing in front of everyone. It was like watching a mutiny!

Obasanjo took all the demerits, and thought nothing of them. He got demerit after demerit every week, had his pay docked, and just waved his hand when asked, like we were wasting his time with nonsense. Obasanjo also knew that the admiral wouldn't take him away from the ExO desk. The admiral had no desire to take over the ansible negotiation duties, for even the few weeks until an emergency replacement could transfer in. The admiral did as little as possible—as much as he could push off onto Obasanjo, the better. The admiral's only joy, beyond his secret stash of forbidden alcohol, was flying patrol out into the black depths past the gravity well of the Citadel star.

Obasanjo knew this; I did not. He looked up at the officer muster after breakfast, in the cramped conference room that was once used as a weapons closet before the conversion of warship to station. Obasanjo pretended to be indifferent to the air of dissent hanging around him. He smirked at me. "You can hold your mouth open like that as long as you like, Ensign, but we don't have any flies to catch here."

The quartermaster rolled his eyes. "We are completely surrounded by foolish men, admiral."

Wong chimed in. "You should come and play poker and get out of your room. It's bad for you to spend so much time alone, Ensign. You'll end up a philosopher like the captain." We were waiting for Lieutenant Jim Nguyen, the network security officer. "Do you play poker, Ensign?"

"I have been known to play a little," I said. It was all video poker, during school, to practice math and odds. The lesson also encouraged students to believe that when gambling, the odds always won, never the gambler.

"Leave the new kid alone," said the admiral. "I don't want any of you influencing him while he's too green to know any better. That goes double for you, Oyede. I can shut down your little philosophy club if I want to. That is something I can control. Your enlisted friends won't cross me if I tell them not to go."

"You're welcome to join us for discussion, Admiral," said Obasanjo. "You too, Ensign. Poker's fun, if you prefer that."

"I never gamble," said the admiral. "Remember that, Oyede. Ensign, if you want to make anything of yourself, don't trust the snakes. They'll ruin you."

"Even Q plays poker, and he's a dedicated monastic!" said

Obasanjo. "Wong, too. You love your little pet positive attitude!"

"Snakes, all of you," the admiral grunted. "I've got better things to do, but Ensign Aldo is welcome to join you if he wants to throw his money away."

"I'll think about it," I said. I couldn't gamble until I got paid. It would be a while until I existed in the financial networks, and I had nothing to gamble with.

Jim Nguyen arrived late, as if nothing had happened in the room. He pushed his way past Wong, indifferent to the tension, and sat down. He pulled out his tablet, and put a cup of tea down beside it on the table, finally looking up. He looked around, then got uncomfortable. "Uh . . . I miss something, gentlemen? Sirs?"

"Just Oyede pissing me off again. Let's get this meeting over with. Captain Obasanjo can run it for the next few weeks. I'm going to be indisposed with other duties."

Obasanjo laughed. "Yes, sir!" he said. "Of course, sir!"

"Insubordinate ass," said the admiral. He stood up. "Why don't you just try running this damn station without me, you cocky bastard." He threw his tablet at Obasanjo, who barely caught it. The admiral left, and I didn't see him again for three days. When I did see him, at another bitter breakfast, he looked hungover.

Q was the one who clued me in to the special relationship between Obasanjo and the admiral. The admiral went through the motions, if he was sober. Obasanjo did everything, bemused at his own authority, which he viewed as some sort of alien punishment to endure. Wong suggested avoiding Obasanjo's philosophy club. They believed that we probably lost the war, if it was even real.

Lieutenant Wong was my favorite, at first. He was station security ops, and handled physical training as well as what amounted to a police force with the fifty-five to sixty-three station personnel. He had two corporals in his direct command. He was a tall, vigorous Chinese man, from Hong Kong, with an easy, constant smile. It was the kind of smile that couldn't be removed even if the admiral himself was scraping at it with a razor blade. Wong, no matter what, remained upbeat and dedicated to the mission. For a young officer, he was the sort of role model we had been told to seek out in our postings.

He invited me to join the poker games.

"I don't really know how to play poker," I said. "I've done video poker only."

"You'll learn quickly when you start running out of money," said Wong. "It is an easy game to learn, but hard to master." He had an inscrutable expression that I could only interpret to mean that he was an excellent gambler. We were in the garage, after the meeting, where I was recertifying with the emergency welding lens.

"I'll think about it," I said. "I will need to focus on all my re-certifications, first. I'm still not legal for Officer on Deck."

Wong pressed his hand on my shoulder in encouragement. It occurred to me that this was the first warm gesture I had received on board. This simple moment where Wong touched my shoulder and squeezed with a smile on his face made me well up with an emotion I could not explain. When I returned to my welding, there was a sudden lump in my throat, and I pretended to be checking the safety equipment while I pushed it down in the bustling garage.

Captain Obasanjo was the executive officer, the admiral's right hand. He was in charge of most station business, scheduling, contracts, and resource planning with projection models. He was also constantly negotiating with the monastery and the ansibles across the two galaxies for more food and supply. Interstellar negotiation and report was supposed to be the admiral's job, but Obasanjo did it all, and filed every report for Admiral Diego's official stamp. I believe Obasanjo was nominally my direct supervisor, but I flew no war missions and did most of my work under Q, where I was technically in charge of the flight crew that was too busy working with Q to do anything with me. Our colony, as old as it was, was still not self-sustaining. We did not have the water supply, the hydroponics, or the economy on the ground. The ansible was a lifeline, but we could not afford time on the ansible to get everything from there. We also had to trade with the colony for her limited supplies, and the colony could not survive without our supplementation for their seed stock and their capital equipment. It was an impossible scenario.

Captain Obasanjo was cynical about our colony, and about everything.

The earliest memory I had of him expressing kindness was in the cafeteria soon after my arrival, but before his open mutiny. Obasanjo was already getting up to get to his terminal before I was done picking at the bland, green and red porridge.

"You get used to it," he said, apologetically.

The NetSec—network security officer—spoke up with a snort. "Speak for yourself, Oyede."

Computer security was handled by Lieutenant Jim Nguyen. He, like Q, spent much of his time and energy cobbling together functionality out of the decaying and ancient station materials. He ate far too much, and was obviously out of regulation, but nobody said anything about it. I watched his weight bounce from one extreme to another my entire posting. He did not give off an aura of good health. He sat behind a desk, and occasionally sent his skeleton tech crew spelunking through ancient passageways after ports and connections that were slowly eaten by rust, damp, and various microbiotic and fungal pathogens.

Nguyen pushed his half-eaten food into his throat in one, giant gulp, and choked it down like medicine. Then, he sipped something that pretended to be a cross between a fruit drink and a tea. It was the closest thing we had to coffee. He grunted to himself, and spoke little.

"You're pretty political, aren't you, new kid?" said Nguyen.

"I don't know what you mean," I said.

"Exactly. See? A very political answer. You're going to try to be an admiral someday. Don't dream big. Dream small. Small dreams don't come true either, but they hurt less."

I shook my head, confused. I said nothing else, and continued to shovel the red and green gruel around the bowl.

I will say this for the cafeteria food: Gluttony, of all the deadly sins, was no longer part of my spiritual life. Without wine, without rare and precious vegetables and fruits, there was only gruel and vitamins and pushing them around a bowl until they were cool enough to consume.

I remember sweet champagne, and smoky whiskey. I remember the sweet sea smell of grilling fish. My past gluttony haunts me now.

———————

Where we were, on the edge of the galaxy, there was such a huge gap between stars because we were near the edge of the Sagittarius cluster, where it looked out to the Magellanic Cloud. Astral navigation was quite challenging, actually, with so few reliable demarcations in the celestial sphere. Each pinprick of light was so far away that one could easily miss targets and waypoints, without precise radio signals. The most minute, fractional variations in degrees possible in the long, dark void were just enough to make maneuvers challenging. The planets of the system were so few. The single, yellow Citadel star, so much like our own solar star, had only three planets, two gas giants and our little desert rock. We relied on their placement for nearly every maneuver in and out of the Oort cloud. And the admiral was the one who flew patrol beyond. He was the only one permitted to fly outside the Oort cloud, into the black depths, firing off probes and engaging in advanced maneuvers with the gravity and debris out there in the dark.

I was not permitted this flight. Recertification with perfection was just a ruse to gently slow down and remove such dreams from my head, and I would have to score perfectly just to earn a confession of the truth: I would never fly patrol under this admiral.

Admiral Antonio Diego brooded into his breakfast gruel. He ate slowly, hunched over, angrily observing his men. Wong took his gaze in stride, always positive, always smiling, in every gesture, a large or small smile that was the mask he wore against the world.

"Wong, don't you think you should go check the exterior paneling?" said the admiral. "Take your pick of scrubber techs and see what you find on the hull. I want an extensive report."

"A great idea, sir! We will check on the work of the most recent maintenance crew, and inspect for any new damage the drones are missing."

"Do you cry yourself to sleep at night, Lieutenant Wong?" said Obasanjo.

I felt alone, torn between obligations, waiting for someone to do something, confused and uncertain about the true path of my devotion. Call it idolatry, but at the time, I favored the admiral, because I saw, in him, my service oath and the path to other colonies.

Wong asked me if I wanted to join him on the hull, and take some air out there.

I agreed with gusto.

"Watch yourself, Ensign," said the quartermaster. "We don't need two chirpers kissing up."

Theories of reality clashed in the air, unknown to me. I saw things as I believed them to be. I believed that I was a clone of a man born on a boat in the Pacific Ocean, on Earth, across the galaxy. I did not believe I was placed in this colony to suffer, but to work hard and transcend. That is the life that was told to me: Work hard and transcend to other colonies.

Wong can explain his reality well enough. Catch him sometime on the town, in his retirement. He married well, and has children coming soon. Theories of reality are ways to negotiate the complex stimuli of misery. Ask him, and he will tell you that healthy bodies, good investments, and many strong children are the best things in life. Ask him about the way he came about his good investments, and he will pretend that he is just very lucky and very persistent.

In the chamber of the airlock, Wong looked over at the four of us. "Private Farshi, you're sick. Feel that cough coming on, don't you?"

"You're right, Lieutenant. I think I need to lie down," he said.

"I will stamp your sheet. Just send it to me. Get some rest, technician."

Private Kumal Farshi handed his equipment to me. It was a series of lights with laser tagging. Wong looked at the two of us remaining. "Keep your recording devices off when we suit up. Don't make me say it twice."

"Safety protocol . . ."

"Ensign," said the other tech, one of the four women on board, "recording off."

I nodded, confused. Wong handed me the helmet and the suit. I checked for any signs of damage. We sprayed ourselves with UV blockers, and suited up. We were not in heavy gravity. The airlock door, once opened, would lead to a long tube that ran straight to the central axis upon which we spun. We would fall down into weightlessness and then climb out with ladders to the surface of the station's outer shell. First, we checked each others' suits. Never assume a suit is sealed unless it is checked twice by two diligent people. Then, plug in the interface, and check the diagnostics for a seal. Recording begins, with the computer interface. It can be turned off manually at any time. In cases of imminent death, I am told, it is considered wise to say what needs to be said, then turn it off to protect others from dying screams. There are also situations where communication signals are possibly compromised in wartime, and individual units need to be able to unplug from the network. I did not understand why Wong would want recording off. Even on board the station, while on duty, everything was recorded. We were so accustomed to the microcameras and microphones, we didn't even see them. Who could bother watching all that footage, anyway, except a machine?

I had to choose between my rigorous training and my new

role model's odd command. Safety protocols trump chain of command. I only pretended to adjust my computer. I consider what I did sinful. Wong had his reasons, and only with the communication recorders off could he even dictate them aloud, but I didn't think about that, in the moment.

Suited up, the three of us checked the airlock doors in turn, securing the station with our redundant safety protocols.

With the door sealed, Wong checked internal com signals, and tested emergency backups in the remote suit systems. We could talk to each other without recording anything. Then, he turned the hard crank, and swung open the door. The silence came on so swiftly, it was misinterpreted in the ear as whooshing. Space is an instantaneous and overwhelming silence. The black sky was a surprise. We were so far out of the main galaxy cluster that whole swathes of sky had limited starlight in our range of vision. It was the black void that I had studied on charts and simulations, but seeing it through a pane of helmet shielding was different. It was like black ink had been spilled in spreading lines across the celestial sphere. Certainly, with telescopes and wider ranges of vision, galaxies and stars appear in the darkness, far out into the depths, but the distances were so great, and the competing lights and black holes and nebulae too great, that the minute pinpricks were shrouded in a black fog. The other half of the sky, toward the rest of the Sagittarius cluster, and the Milky Way, was a horizon line of swept marbles.

Wong chimed in. "Open com. Signals off. Focus on the mission. Sweep and clear, and check for anything we need to tag for drone repair. Walk carefully. She is an old hull, and we need to be gentle with our steps."

He took the first step over the edge.

Drones swept the hull, keyed in to the quartermaster's terminals. We were a redundancy check, able to put naked eyes on the hull, where drones just gave cameras and data readouts. It is the difference between studying the void in a simulator and seeing it firsthand. To pilot a ship, I need to feel the difference in my gut. To keep our station aloft and repaired, we would need to walk the hull and get a feel for what looks right. We were looking for things that intuition alone would know. Exosuit walkers were regular jobs, and were expected to know the hull as intimately as an old pair of boots. If something was wrong, they could just feel it in the close study of the stellar wind–battered, micro-meteorite-struck panels.

We had simple tools: a radioactive measuring device to check for unusual spikes, a biometric light sweeper to scan for biotic evolution leaking out onto the outer hull or into it, and a good, old-fashioned flashlight to sweep for obvious mechanical defects.

"We will take a long walk to get some calisthenics, out here. Check in every quarter click, and follow Tech Jensen. She knows the hull better than anyone and she can get us home in time for lunch. Remember, Ensign, only move one foot after the other is magnetized down."

"I have spacewalked before, Lieutenant. I am rated for hull repair, if need be, on moving vessels."

"That wasn't you," he said. His offhand comment revealed his theology. Wong was more in line with the legalists who are quick to divide living quantum errata.

Tech Corporal Jensen punched my suited boot from inside the tunnel, where she was waiting for me to move out of her way so she could climb up to the hull. "Ensign, I don't think you understand what is going down. I am checking the hull.

Wong is checking you. You walk in the middle. You follow me. I have been doing this for six years and I have had no accidents on my walks. Mistakes on a walk are very bad."

"Oh, okay, Corporal," I said, confused.

"I am sure you will do excellent," said Wong. "You arrived with all the necessary training."

Jensen stepped out next. Her boots pulled her hard to the hull. She checked the magnetic pull, and worked her switches. "My left boot button is sticky," she said.

"Want to go back and grab a new suit?"

"I think it will be fine. Sock lint has probably jammed it up. If it gets worse, I'll signal for a drone ride home. My signal line is working, even if it's off."

"I trust your judgment," said Wong.

The walk was going to fill my dreams with night for years afterward. The sky bent all around me where the suit pulled me over the edge. The smooth, clear hull was lined with solar panels that soaked up energy from the sun and stars. The panels were very small, and very efficient. We would never run out of energy here. Water, perhaps, and food, perhaps, but energy, never.

We walked a circuitous path along the edge of the hull, with our equipment. The ship was welded together out of extra parts and a ruined battleship from long ago. It was perfectly smooth and round along the sides, leading up to the two major points: the antennae array on one end and the warship dock on the other. The station was like a pointed, painted egg. Our little warship was so small where it docked below the spin.

Have you ever spacewalked, confessor? It's exhausting for toes more than anything. I lifted toes to release the magnet. I curled the toes to latch in. We set out single file. I felt the clamp in my boots, but I did not hear it. The deafening silence of space was all I heard, with the blood pumping in my ears, my breath in and out, my body cells burning and humming with energy—the black expanse above until we reached the starry side of the sky and saw the Milky Way in all her glory. The glistening solar paneling created a horizon so vivid and near to the eye that I was glad to have Corporal Jensen in the lead. Her walk was calm and straight. She swept the hull with her tools with precision built of repetition. Behind her, all I saw on the hull were the occasional remnants of her flashing light sinking into the sensitive cells.

"A beautiful day for a stroll," said Wong. "Perfect weather. No strong wind. No meteor dust."

"Low radiation today, too," said Jensen. "At least until we turn out toward the planet's albedo."

"Where is the Planet Citadel?" I said. I saw only the black strips of the gap between galaxies.

"It is behind us," said Wong. "It will be in front of us soon enough. Be patient, Ensign."

The suits were quite flexible, and I could turn around, but it would slow us down. I did not wish to slow us down. I had enough of a view.

At the dock of the station, I saw the tiny warship like a knife with wings. I had flown newer versions, and larger ones at the War College, before cloning here. This old scout was a survivor of the last battle, where so much was stripped for parts in the aftermath. It was a relic of a war I would never fight, despite all my training.

"How much farther, Lieutenant?" said Jensen.

"A little more. I still have a recording signal popping in and out, right now. We need to go a little more, where the hull is really thick."

"For what?" I said.

"Ensign, please. All in due time."

Scanning the hull, I saw the ghostly flicker of biotics where the scanner saw them, purple shining above the solar cells. It had already been flagged for scrubbing by Tech Jensen. I saw the red dot on the scanner. With my other hand, I moved the flashlight out and over the area. If I hadn't scanned it, I wouldn't have known there were rogue biotics there, eating into the organic matter on the hull.

"I don't see any obvious damage. Should we go closer and investigate?" I said.

"No," said Wong. "No, we will not. We know where it came from. It will take a little more scrubbing to clear it all out, for good. Biotic crew know about it and are always checking underneath."

"Have they already repaired the damage, then?"

"Something like that," said Wong. "I will explain it another time."

"That is where Edward, the last AstroNav . . . That is where he did it," said Jensen, with an inexplicable flatness to her voice, even through the com link. "I flagged it. It is all that's left of him. And it is getting radiation and mutating in open space. It's just a couple biotic lines. Almost everything couldn't survive. He certainly couldn't. We keep walking."

We were silent a while, then, walking the hull.

Before us, the planet rose like a huge, golden moon, pale yellow dunes and mountains without a single sign of human habitation from this distance. It was nearly the same size as Earth, and nearly as habitable, in the "Goldilocks zone" of extra-terran colonization, with an atmosphere that began quite nearly breathable upon initial settlement, with some native biotics living in the poles that proved noninvasive, though there are occasional headache infections and any open water must be boiled.

The naked rock of the Planet Citadel, beautiful and gold, loomed immense, a coin stamped with antique effigies of geologic time alone in the sky. The world floated in this immense black. Behind us, the central star—we always space-walk with our back to the planet's sun when we could—extended our shadows out over the horizon of the station hull, as if we were, the three of us, bound by our shadows to the yellow surface.

"We can stop here, Jensen," said Wong. "Check your recording devices again."

"Off," she said.

"What? Oh . . . Uh . . . Off," I said, lying. I felt it in my bones, my dishonesty. After my inauspicious beginning, I think I wanted to be by the book. I think I am rationalizing the past. My sin was dishonesty, and a mortal one. My sin was also obeying the sinful station's ridiculous rule of law instead of respecting Wong's human judgment.

"Talk to me, Jensen," said Wong.

"I want out. Get me out."

"Dishonorable discharge is no laughing matter. No pension, no support, just let go planetside, and that's it. My fee is very high. You would be starting over with nothing."

"It is better to start over than to open my helmet on the hull."

"I am sorry, but . . ."

"We couldn't even tell anyone about us, Edward and me.

We couldn't even say the words where cameras could see our lips moving. Do you understand? The officer corps were not permitted to mingle with enlisted. You might transcend. We never do."

"The rules of the Milky Way are not exactly the rules of the Citadel. How about a nice vacation, first. I can get you admitted with a rare illness and forge some documents and you get a month planetside with my friends at the hospital below. Give you time to consider."

"You got Gudachowski out for good, and he has a hydroponic farm now, and sells seeds across the colony, and he's even hired on a tank for a kid with his husband. Come on, help me out!"

"He was fifteen years in, and I could early retire him. Plus, Gudachowski was not so critical to the mission of keeping this hunk of junk in one piece. He was one of Nguyen's computer flunkies. If the computers break, the hull holds us together until the patch comes through. You are the hull. You are uniquely skilled at maintenance, Jensen. Without skilled hull walkers, we all die."

"I am replaceable. We are all replaceable."

"And someone else comes here, and experiences this posting? I'll think about it, Jensen. Here's what I can do, for the right price. I can investigate you for theft, and pull you into the prison system. You can relax, read, and take some time to consider your future."

"How much?"

"Three months' pay for three weeks off."

"Okay," she said. "Poker?"

"I will arrange the game." His black, glass mask revolved toward me. "Ensign, is there anything I can do for you?"

I was speechless. "I don't understand."

"I'm the law around here. I can help you get things done," he said. He pointed up to the Citadel planet hanging in the sky above our heads. "I can get you there for long stretches of time. I can get you a break. Everyone needs a break."

"For a fee," I said.

"Yes, of course," he said. "Is that a problem for you?"

"I'll think about it," I said. "I didn't really expect to be asked that question, honestly. I'm taken aback."

"I understand completely," said Wong.

Jensen snorted. "When I was a kid, I lived in a forest. They have only just planted a few groves over there, all jujube trees and moringa. Drought-tolerant stuff, high in nutrition but they taste like paste and grass. I hate jujubes, and I hate moringa. When I was a kid, my grandfather had a plum orchard behind his house." She stopped there, catching herself in her own bitter nostalgia for something remembered, but never had in the existence we shared here. Is there such a thing as an apple tree, at all? Obasanjo asks that. To him, everything here is a fabrication, and that includes our memories. We are a memorial to the civilization the enemy destroyed, nothing more, and everything that came to us from outside was invented by them to keep us satiated in our tiny shell.

Oh, and all was recorded, oh, I recorded everything. I had it all sitting in the files, waiting to be sifted by the algorithms that searched out keywords and erratic behaviors. With two records empty and missing, and one present, it would get flagged for HR review. Following the rules of an unjust system, and lying to my peers about them, Jensen would never forgive me, even if Wong pretended it never happened for a little while.

We swept the hull, my sin ringing in my ears. I realized that I needed to try and delete the recording, or leave it to permit the truth to come out, as would be my duty. In fact, I should have reported the conversation, with the recording, but Wong was the security officer, and the only person over him was Admiral Diego. How would the admiral receive this message? How would it be perceived? He sent Wong out, with Jensen, and with me, and he must know about Wong. How could he not know?

I cannot dispute my own moral failure. I did nothing but leave the recording there, as if I didn't realize what had just occurred. I did not alert Wong. I did not alert the admiral. I did not sneak back and attempt to wipe the data. I did not even reach out to Obasanjo for help and advice.

Inside, I slept unsound, tossing and turning, and dreaming of the black void overhead, the crushing presence of the planet growing in size, closer and closer.

That morning, I received the first letter from my original self, on Earth, and it mentioned something that I had not even considered at all: money.

*Dear Ronaldo Aldo II,*

*I am glad you arrived safely. I don't really know what I should call you. Brother? Son? Clone? I shall use the moniker you have chosen. You are number II.*

*I have been dead bored making transport flights from one space elevator to another. Much of the time, space is duller than a boat at calm sea. There isn't even any weather. Still, I have plenty of time to read. I envy you, with your warships and probe launches and patrols.*

*I have decided not to set up an account for you. Your*

*planet is simply too sparse to need one. Your salary should
more than meet your needs. When you promote out, we can
talk about a joint account for him, but, honestly, you will
be living on the top of your world with your current salary.
Whatever luxuries you need through the ansible, please let
me know and I will see what I can arrange. I understand
that later in your deployment, you will likely be asking for
seeds and nursery plants for a farm there. I will help you
with that, truly and gladly.*

*Serve with honor, II.*
*Ensign Ronaldo Aldo I*

———————

I have mentioned Obasanjo's theory, that we are all mere fab-
rications of people created by the enemy and alone in the universe. I have not mentioned the man very much. He was a
gloomy sort, and until I returned from the first expedition
upon the hull, I had no clue how to reconcile the existence of
the ever-smiling Wong, with the ever-frowning Obasanjo. Two
important orbital bodies rotating at opposites to each other,
these men did not get along. Playing poker with them both
was like observing a long and bitter feud, each attempting to
break the other's facade. Wong told dirty jokes in an effort
to get Obasanjo to smile. Obasanjo glared through them, and
shared bitter narratives of his conspiracy theory.

"We receive radio waves from all over the galaxy, and they
bounce and become corrupted. I have been attempting to figure out if they all actually come from Earth, to see if the
colonies are only an illusion."

"Not just looking for illegal pornography, are you?" said Wong. "Find anything good, do share."

The quartermaster ignored them both, and stared at his cards. "Call," he said. He tossed in his chits.

My turn, and my hand was terrible. "But I don't understand why anyone would go to all the trouble to fake an entire civilization like that," I said. "It seems like a strange thing to do just to study us."

"It would keep us sane, and in control by external forces. Powerful enough computers and AI machines could realistically mimic a colony; why not many colonies? Why not worlds? We are creatures in a bubble, always observed. We are a zoo of humanity, nothing more."

"Play your hand, and don't goad him on," said the quartermaster. "Are you here to play poker or go to his stupid meeting group."

I folded.

"It doesn't really matter does it," said Jensen. She was not next. Tech Corporal Umbago, Q's head of the pipe and water maintenance, was next, and he called his hand. He looked around the little table, adding nothing to the philosophical debate.

Jensen continued. "We are here whether we believe it is futile or not."

"I never said it was futile," said Obasanjo. "We are sworn to fight the enemy. When I can find the edges of their reality constructed for us, then I can begin to plan our attack. Mankind was never meant to be enslaved."

"You sound mighty foolish to me," said the quartermaster.

We only had the one deck of cards. It was heavily abused. Looking at the back of the ragged cards, we could easily see that Obasanjo had the jack of diamonds. It was possible that he had the strongest hand. It was also possible he was holding it so that we could see it as a bluff. When his turn came around again, he bid higher.

"Another thing," said Obasanjo. "The planet below us is a world of scarcity. We should never colonize such a place on purpose. We never would have if it hadn't been for the last battle of the war. Think about that awhile. The very last ship, on the farthest corner of the galaxy. We remember a great sacrifice and victory here in schoolbooks from before we were made. Our repairs have wiped away the evidence of war. The planet below us is eternally impoverished of water. Even when all the current planned ice comets are brought in, we will still be only at 36.8 percent water on the surface. No large colony will ever be supported there without more. It is ideal for the limitations of a species proven to be poor managers of resources. The scarcity teaches us better than oceans in their abundance. Wait, whose turn is it?"

"Are you quite finished?" said the quartermaster.

"So," said Wong. "I met this fellow the last time I was on the surface. He said he had a dildo so far up his ass that he had lost it up there, and it completely plugged his butt. He can't poo. When the dildo was discovered, they made him an abbot in the monastery immediately."

"That doesn't even make sense," said Jensen.

"He's full of shit," said Obasanjo. "I've heard that one before, told better. It isn't any funnier this time, Wong."

He was smiling. "I think I won," he said. He placed his cards out. He had three queens. "Anybody got me beat?"

"I do," said Jensen. She had four of a kind, straight six.

"I bet you didn't think I was paying attention," said

Obasanjo, who also had four of a kind, all jacks.

The quartermaster and tech corporal surrendered to curses and weak hands.

Gambling is not sinful, but it can lead to sin. Greed came over me when I watched Obasanjo pulling in all his chits. I had no extra share in anything at all.

"How about you, Q? What do you think is real?"

"I have spent the last seventeen years keeping this hunk of junk sealed and ventilating properly, with air and water flowing in their proper pipes. In the next life, I will be judged a saint for dealing with your ridiculous notions without slapping any of you."

Wong tapped the table. "Pardon us," he said, gesturing at Jensen. "Private hand, if you don't mind. Grudge match among friends."

Q snorted. "I'm leaving, then. Do whatever you want. We're going to hold a prayer meeting on Sunday in the cafeteria, and you should all attend. Every last one of you." He stepped up and walked toward the door, visibly disgusted with us.

"Thank you, Q," said Wong, eternally smiling.

The tech corporal, uncomfortable, stood up also. He slowly followed his commanding officer out the door, without a word.

"Anyone else?" said Wong, looking at Obasanjo and me.

"Deal," said Obasanjo. "I will be taking it all from you in the next hand, Lieutenant Wong. You know that, right?"

Jensen and Wong, then, played their cards, bidding up in hold 'em poker, each hand probably terrible. It took quite a while to get the amount high enough, and then Wong nodded. "Fold," she said.

Wong collected his chits. "Thank you," he said.

I watched Obasanjo. He was accepting of it, as if keeping a record of it in his own mind. "Ensign, would you like to sit in on one of our meetings? You should come if only to see what you are missing. There's very little to do, out here. Philosophy can pass the time faster than prayer and work."

"I don't know what I want," I said. "Should we go, Captain? Should we be seeing this?"

"It doesn't matter. Relax and play, if you like. Go if you prefer. Wong is in charge of criminal investigations into his own alleged corruption. The admiral doesn't care. I can tell you're flustered. Your cheeks are rosy, Ensign. It's adorable."

After two more hands, I could not bear to stay. The turmoil inside of me was too great. I had been witness to a crime, and other officers had witnessed it, or chosen not to witness it. I had made a recording on the hull, and I didn't tell anyone, and it would be investigated by HR in the Milky Way, and word would return to the admiral and come back to me.

Wong had been a bright, cheery, physical man, leading calisthenics exercises and security training. He was always positive, always upbeat. Obasanjo, until then, had been a brooding, subordinate presence. He was lost in conspiracy theories, and obviously did not like Wong. Yet, Captin Oyede Obsanajo chose to stay and witness.

I did not join his philosophy group for quite some time, and did not find it satisfying.

Obasanjo's investigations were interesting enough for discussion, but the very nature of deep space was distortion. Perspective mattered. Assuming givens as a starting point mattered in Euclidian geometries. I gazed off into the black void, during my day-to-day duties, mapping the unknown where probes revealed it, and trying to identify tiny hidden objects in space, mapping their movements. I wanted to prepare for the patrol voyages. I wanted to seek out the enemy hidden in the dark night of the sky while slicing across the black veil in an elegant warship at near lightspeed. I had no desire to discuss the confusions of space with a bunch of enlisted and Obasanjo. I apologized to him, and declined to attend. He offered to meet for dinner, then, alone. I declined that, as well.

The admiral had a staff meeting, all officers on deck, every two weeks. He was often surly. He glared at us with remarkable redness in his eyes. "Seeing as I am the only completely certified pilot on deck, I shall be flying the patrol, myself. Sergeant Hobarth will be my second, and he will choose the gunnery crew from among the junior ranks. In my absence, Q is the highest ranking. Obasanjo, you have too much to do to bother with staffing concerns and trivialities."

"Like I don't," said Q.

"You outrank him, anyway," said Lieutenant Nguyen, disgusted. "Can we skip the theatrics, Admiral? I have to debug a sewage line terminal today. My boys will be getting very dirty checking wires."

"Can I go along with you, Admiral?" I said.

"No, Ensign. We can't have both AstroNav-trained pilots on the same voyage."

"He should fly it to preserve you in command," said Wong. "After all, an ensign is more expendable, sir."

The admiral stopped, horrified that Wong had spoken up against him. He turned and glared at Wong. "You don't question my commands, Lieutenant." Then, he leaned over and snarled at me. "Ensign. New meat. Let me be plain. Your scores will never be good enough to fly my warship. Do you understand? When I am not the admiral, you can take it up with the next one. For now, the warship patrols are mine. You will always be lacking in some qualification that I require."

"Go easy on him. He's green as a frog," said Q. "Anyone else object to the admiral flying patrol?"

"I do," said Obasanjo. "I always do. The admiral has no business doing anything that dangerous. It is against protocol for a reason."

"Protocol that important to you, is it?" said the admiral.

"Some of the protocols are stupid. Some of them aren't."

The network security engineer, Lieutenant Nguyen, whom I rarely saw outside of staff meetings, shook his head and tsked. He was one of those computer engineers who saw uniforms as a suggestion. His shirt was always untucked, and his curled, black hair and beard were bushy and wild. "Let the admiral do what he wants. He is going to do it anyway, and we are better off without him. Sorry, sir, but we are. You just slow us down. I have a stack of reports waiting for approval."

"Your reports are terrible. Is everyone against me? Wong, even you are against me? I can't believe I'd ever see the day you spoke against me."

"I am sure we can find a solution where everyone wins, sir. There's also Sergeant Anderson's supply runs. The boy needs to fly a little. That's all I'm saying, sir. We can't let him get rusty if the war comes."

"Lieutenant Wong, you are correct. Ensign, you will alternate Anderson. If he gets his wife pregnant and she opts for early out, I will be blaming you."

"I understand completely, sir," said Wong.

"That is going to piss off Sergeant Anderson something fierce," said Q. "You won't be helping the ensign make any friends with the enlisted."

"Ensign. Do you want to fly?"

"Yes, sir!"

"Then it is settled. Anderson needs to spend some time in gravity anyway, or else he'll end up on early medical release. He's losing bone density, and everyone knows it. Hell, just look at him. I've been avoiding sending him to medical to keep the lines running. HR might just opt him out without any consideration for the mission."

Later on, I learned what Q did to make peace. Alternating voyages would mean one of us always flies to the gas giants, then the other usually flies to the monastery. I was going to be the miner, and he was going to be spending time on the colony. Wong alluded to being able to reverse the timing for the right price, in a private message, but I decided against it. The Planet Citadel could wait. I was going to fly, and that was going to have to be enough.

The quartermaster was not helpful, and I had to lean on Corporal Adebayo Anderson to ensure adequate preparations were made. The lumbering supply ship was en route back to us from the planet. Obasanjo's negotiations had him and his second grounded, waiting for a full tank of supplies—especially fresh amaranth grain—before flying home. I got a message from him.

*New Guy,*

*I heard I'm going to be sharing my flight duties with you. With all due respect, Ensign, don't do anything stupid with my ship. When I am sitting around doing nothing, you had better be quickstepping your way back. Aren't you supposed to be flying patrols and playing space warrior or*

something and leave the lowly resupply to the warrant officers?

    *With all due respect, sir, I object to this bullshit.*

*Master Sergeant Jon Anderson*
*Warrant Officer Citadel Station*
*Pilot 2nd Class*

I did not respond. Instead, I watched the quartermaster prepping the warship for a deep patrol, envious of deep space flight at near lightspeeds, expanding the signal pathways and early warning systems. He would be delivering free-floating spyware systems out into the gap, where whatever forces and gravities were present would pull and expand the network of listening stations organically. I was supposed to at least help place the devices where the network would be most likely to expand, but he was not interested in my input. I had been studying these empty zones, attempting to make sense of the unseen forces swirling there, where distant gravitational pulls slowly work upon the open artifacts floating, and investigating whatever tiny particles and quantum errata that have been cast away from other galaxies into the black abyss. These occasion-ally included larger objects, which I tried to identify regarding our unseen enemy, out beyond the black. At night, or what we called a night after our shifts and porridge suppers, I prepared for my own tedious supply run to the cloud of gases at the edge of the atmospheres of the two gas giants, in this system, and looked with sinful envy upon the satellites and probes being constructed for deployment along the patrol route.

This is my meditation upon sinful thoughts: They are a distraction that oftentimes lead to nothing, but it only takes one terrible mistake of distraction to lead to disastrous consequences, and such sinful distractions pull us all away from our true purpose. My preparations for the vessel were not adequate. My mind was consumed with dreams of deep space instead of the mission that I had.

When Sergeant Jon Anderson returned, the drones and enlisted men cleared out the tanks and quarantined everything against contamination. Then, the cleaners swept through. Afterward, as pilot, it was my job to go behind them with the maintenance crew and run the diagnostics on the vessel. I was ultimately responsible. My signature and stamp were on every clearance document. The quartermaster did not even look up from his monitor when I was done checking the vessel. It went straight through to the admiral, and into the official records.

When we flew, I was responsible.

———————

Confessor, forgive me.

I am not ready to discuss my disastrous voyage to the cloud and back.

I stall. I have little else to do in this prison cell but write my confession. If I stare at a blank page, I will feel the weight of what I am not writing. I must write something. Let me discuss the measure of a day. I believe it helps to explain the numbing effect on the mind that is widely reported among longtime service members upon a station like this one, and perhaps contributes to so many sins. It is little different from a monastery, as there is no spontaneous amorous congress of whatever sort among the uniformed staff without written consent, all prearranged—often matrimonial and contractual in nature.

There is a weekly card game, a prayer group led by Q, and a philosophy club led by Obasanjo, a volleyball team led for enlisted PT under Corporal "Red" Watkins, and for entertainment, we have religious media approved through the monastery only. What little pleasure we derive is circumscribed by the colonial laws that dictate official censors at the monastery.

As officers, we are supposed to be upholders of stricter moral weight as the arbiters of life and death aboard the station. As such, our days are as strict as a monk's. The lights and alarms go at five o'clock. By five-fifteen, we are expected to report for calisthenics in the main gymnasium facility. This is, of course, just the cafeteria with all the tables and chairs put away.

Captain Wong, then, will lead a hand-to-hand combat class. We are expected to be sweating and grunting for at least thirty minutes in an imitation of close combat. I have often wondered at the amount of preparation for combat, when the reality of space warfare against our unknown enemy was such that no hand-to-hand was ever likely. No boarding had ever been recorded, and the enemy ships, upon defeat, self-disintegrated into mysterious parts with no clear entity inside of them worthy of a punch. We don't even know what they look like, separated from their warships. Sifting through the ruins was beyond what even seasoned scientists could distinguish into meaningful parts. The objects discovered in the wreckage, and the other carbonaceous materials, were so distinctly alien, they were often just named by shape and color, and sorted as such. Last I heard, the general accepted theory was that our enemy was some sort of gaseous entity, in a high pressure environment completely unlike our own, that dissipated upon exposure to zero gravity conditions. What use to sidekick an enemy such as this? Where would we kick? What would we be kicking?

Ultimately, this training session ended with us pairing off against each other practicing different techniques with varying levels of pain and bruising. I did derive great pleasure in squaring off against Sergeant Anderson, and flipping him over my shoulder. He had spent too much time in lower gravity, spinning a treadmill bike for his calisthenics and taking bone supplements. He was a big man, with thick red hair, and the sort of jowly, dogged gestures that were awkward in close combat. Compared to his wife, the man was shockingly soft.

I confess the sin of pleasure in his defeat. He lumbered toward me with an open palm, and then attempted to swipe underneath with his other hand. I blocked the lower hand while grabbing the upper one and twisting his wrist around. I ducked underneath his huge frame, jamming my hip into his leg and unstanding him. I felt a genuine pleasure besting him, locking his arm until he gave in. Wong looked on and cheered me my early and quick victory. I smiled and did not let go. I looked around and Sergeant Anderson's beautiful wife looked at me and I realized that I was holding on too long. She looked at me, and I felt that I had been gloating over another man's humiliation, and even if I disliked him, he was loved by someone. I let go, ashamed.

Sergeant Anderson rubbed his arm. "Jesus, kid. What do they feed you at the academy these days?"

"Sorry. Let me help you up."

He smacked my hand away. "I'll be ready for you for when you get back."

After calisthenics, the enlisted showered in gender-separated facilities, where the handful of women would finish early and the men would struggle to finish in time. Two exhausted men ran the entire kitchen, both enlisted. They put the chairs and tables out for morning breakfast, and heated up premade nutritional gruel. Officers went back to our quarters where we had some privacy for at least thirty minutes, which was generally spent clearing paperwork. Before breakfast, the admiral often said a few words to the men, grandstanding mostly, and it was all relatively harmless. The most memorable prebreakfast rally was when he said, "Today is the twenty-first day of April, and that means you are all going to do a great job, because every twenty-first of April, your metrics show amazing outcomes. This is the most productive day of the year, so get your meal down your gullet and get to work, boys and girls!" The room cheered, confused and forcing enthusiasm, if only to open up the cafeteria line as soon as possible.

Of course, Obasanjo was rolling his eyes. He had his own daily ritual, and after the confrontation with the admiral, he continued to step into the chow line with the enlisted, gather his nutritional gruel, and duck off to the office where he maintained the entire command structure of the station in the absence of the admiral's efforts. The rest of us waited for the enlisted to get their gruel before going in line, ourselves, with the quartermaster second-to-last, and the admiral at the end.

Breakfast was often an amaranth gruel supplemented with dried red fruit paste, and various vitamins and minerals. It often tasted like something between oatmeal and limestone. After breakfast, our task lists for the day populated out to our tablets, with whatever changes were made by our commanding officers, and we were beholden of what was scheduled there.

As officers, we could create our own tasks, and schedule them, with weekly sign-offs from our direct commander. Enlisted were mostly unable to do so, outside of the biotechs, who seemed to have their own little kingdom inside the quartermaster's loosely held fiefdom. Regardless, we were primarily ruled by a calendar of actions that preceded all of us on the station by nearly ninety years. The maintenance routine was meticulously plotted. The schedule of the year was absolute. Only the rare expansion of duties merited any change. My day was mostly spent working with the quartermaster, preparing ships, testing myself for flying the ships, and—for a few brief, glorious moments—flying in open space. Beyond that, I explored near and distant navigation routes in the huge gap where our stellar system's Oort cloud ended, and the deep void began.

Lunch break was a brief respite from the various forms and figures that kept me occupied, reviewing safety data and double-checking the handful of space-worthy vessels. Lunch was often something resembling a burrito with protein paste and vitamin supplements mixed into a mixture of amaranth and leafy greens held together with a grainy, seedy flatbread of sprouted amaranth flattened and emulsified with gooey, gritty chia. The afternoons were devoted to paperwork, and such meaningless meetings, where the tiniest things were debated ad infinitum. I recall with some horror an entire afternoon with Wong and Obasanjo and Nguyen, and two sergeants, discussing how many bits of ansible data was permitted for the sending of personal letters back to the Terran solar system. The sergeants were negotiating enlisted ansible time, while Nguyen was angling for some kind of give in exchange and Obasanjo and Wong and I couldn't care less about Nguyen's

O/S updates or the enlisted letters. We just wanted to set fire to the room and walk out.

Commanding officers were expected to be walking around, patrolling the halls to observe the enlisted who efficiently and thoroughly maintained the station with or without our help. They did good work, and nobody was a shirker. Death was too close to allow for that. Nominally, I had the flight crew under my command, but the admiral monopolized them, and I was shunted off to a side. When I did my rounds, I was often looked at like a child getting in the way of the work, and would I please move along?

Sergeant Hobarth retired before I could fly with him. He was as old as the admiral, and as indifferent to me. His crewmen followed his lead, not mine.

After a few months, I felt like I was only an inconvenience to everyone, that my very presence slowed everything down. I was embarrassed to say anything to them. They were so industrious and I spent my days in meetings, checking ships that were still in excellent repair, and training for a flight into the darkness beyond the galaxy that never came. I hid behind star charts and astral projections, and collated reports from the probes, naming and predicting the pathways of all the strange stray bits of rock and debris that were big enough to get a readout. Much of what was there was ship debris, leftover from the battle and tumbling away into the night. I flagged some of it for drone salvage, if we ever had a drone capable of getting out and back in a timely fashion. Very few pieces were larger than a human hand, after all. What little chunks were of any size were nearly all human in origin, or else just bits of stray meteor lost and looking for an orbit.

I dreamed of stars, and the huge, black sky. What does the faith of the monastery teach about dreams? I know some mystic sects still interpret them, but I am uncertain what our order here teaches. I dreamed of stars and darkness, and objects floating in space, more than I dreamed of the faces of men.

At night, after a dinner of steamed vegetables and more amaranth gruel, officers retired to their rooms to file more forms and paperwork, writing up everything that happened in the day, and everything that would happen tomorrow or next week. From there, when we finished, we were free to engage in our own pursuits. There was usually a game of cards, unless there was a meeting. The officers only played once a week. The little decks of cards were so bruised and broken, handed around every night by some small group. There was very little else to do. Imagine knowing the day every day for twenty years, and feeling the cycle of it and the heft and weight of days, an alarm that rings exactly the same, and the people and days that are all the same. As an officer, I was expected to maintain morale. I was supposed to smile and salute and click my heels and shout and bellow my commands, if I had any commands, and I had not even the pleasure of pretending to be in charge of others. I was in charge of a skeleton fleet. Seventeen vessels had passed through these walls since the station was stabilized after the battle, but only six remained, constructed from the recycled parts of all the other vessels that had worn down and been replaced, and of these only three were kept spaceworthy at any one time to preserve resources. And there were certifications, simulations on holographic screens lacking the heft and haw of true flight, lacking the gravitational shifts in zero-g when thrusters burst to life and swirl.

Day after day, all this movement and activity and talking and preparation for a war that never came, and we didn't even believe it would ever come. No one talked about war or defending the station. No one spent their nights gazing into the AstroNav charts and planning assaults, except the admiral and me. Both of us did this, I think, because we didn't know what else to do. Stare out into the black ribbon darkness. Study the gap between galaxies, and wonder which direction hides the enemy's ships. Prepare, always searching, always wondering. If they come, the colony will fall as surely as stars burning out into singularities. We have no great battleships here. To call one up would take months of construction and staffing up. To call enough to turn the tide of war would take years, and what would they eat? Where would the water come from? We know, out here, that if they do truly come, when they come, all our human activity is for nothing. Our only true hope is to be the warning bell that rings alarm, and the enemy will slow long enough to let the other colonies rise to the alarm. Thinking about this alarm, I believe my plan was slowly sinking into my mind.

I saw the enemy ships at night in my dreams, their sleek silver obelisks and altered asteroids and reticulated hammerheads crushing into our hull, like metal fish, but without a reason or a soul.

Always death, somewhere in the gap. Always our death just beyond the darkness between the galaxies like a black star creeping toward us against the expanding tides of the cosmos. In the ansible, in transcendence upon promotion, a rebirth somewhere new, a hope against the dark that consumes us, and the only material salvation visible where all our descendants will be but a bump on the road to war. This vanguard at the edge of the galaxies lives under the cloud of the abyss beyond the gravity well. Stare into the dark at the Laika's edge. It is as black as blinking.

Oh, my confessor, I have sinned against my duty, truly, but I cannot bear to feel sorry for my sinfully born sons. I cannot bring myself to it. Imagine anything else for this world. I cannot. The quartermaster says we should believe the enemy will come, at last, and the colonies will have new warships, new ramming rail guns and atomic might, and ansible mines that convert hull matter itself into the bombs that destroy the ships, but the enemy has seen our weapons, and they, too, will be evolving at the edge of some distant galaxy, or perhaps they reside in the darkness itself, so alien to us we cannot even imagine the manner and scope of their way of life, at all.

Admiral Diego said, every day, that he prayed to be ready, to fight this war. It seems un-Christian, but he laughed to call the enemy's return a glory. Hear the beating drums of war? It is a kind of annihilation that grants a release of death without a loss of face or sinful suicide. I understand his chosen delusion. It kept him alive for a while.

———————

The planet called to me after my fateful journey to the gas giant and the nebulous clouds there. I hear it now, even in my cell, a calling to live in peace, as far from the miserable station and the sudden death of space as I can get—to be free of this weight of lost days, joyless, meaningless work and the vast chasm of routine yawning before me, so many wasted years. I confess that I truly felt alive only in my transgression in the end. To stand out, to achieve promotion to other colonies, I needed something to change. The only true change I ever saw was an abject failure, and so early in my career, it marked me forever. With no more changes, even after Admiral Diego died, what could I do, but manufacture my own? Oh, I get ahead of myself in my confession. Let me describe my flight to the gas giant, and the bad luck that has plagued me since that night in the restaurant where I offended my friends forever.

Flight came, at last, into the slip of darkness we called the void, for me and for a humble tech sergeant who lost the toss of a dice and was forced to ride along with the newly made pilot. It was the worst assignment, if only because the destination was a gas giant and a nebulous cloud of vapors that drones would harvest while we did nothing but float and feel our bones loosening, crawling on ladders around the hull to watch the gases separate and compress into storage, all automated and we only observers of the machine, repairing parts as needed.

I was not allowed to fly solo. My tech, Corporal Jamila Xavier, was one of the four women on the station, an experienced tech nearly old enough to be my mother. She was calm and bored, and uninterested in dealing with a brazen ensign. She spent much of the voyage out quietly running drones along the interior, scanning for any problems, and sweeping to keep the biotics clean in our shared chamber. It was a couple weeks out to the cloud, and we remained together in the can, about fifteen feet away from each other at all times. During shift, we had to keep the curtains open, but if one of us was scheduled for sleep cycle, we could pull a curtain shut, and tie down into a sleeping bag. We had separate bathrooms, which made no sense, but officers always had separate bathrooms, for some reason, even on this tiny vessel. I expressed my displeasure at the waste of resources over such a ceremonial luxury.

"You may think that sounds egalitarian, but it doesn't," she said. "I don't want to share a bathroom with you. It's the only privacy I have."

"I just mean that... Look, it's ceremonial, though. It wouldn't materially change your privacy because you could close the door, and my bathroom is larger than yours for no reason."

"You want to trade?"

"We can. Do you prefer the larger one?"

"It doesn't win you any points with me to pretend to be on my side."

"I'm not trying to win points, Corporal."

"Yeah."

"Is something wrong?"

"This assignment is stupid. This is just a supply run. Sergeant Anderson should have done this, by himself. I'm here to hold your little hand."

"I did not assign you to this mission, and I agree with you that your presence is likely unnecessary. I am not in command of staffing the mission. Do you have any complaints about my actual proficiency, Corporal?"

"No, but..."

"No, sir."

"No, sir."

"Okay, Corporal. I was only trying to make conversation. That was my mistake. Do you need something to do?"

"I've got plenty to do, Ensign. You were keeping me from my duties."

"I release you, then, with my apologies for the distraction."

I watched the dials, and their green hope, all things copacetic, within normal range. Truly, and this is no boast, but experienced pilots at HR pored over my records and found no wrongdoing on my part.

I seeded navigation beacon data, taking in all the data and passing it on to a simulation computer, even though I knew that likely nothing would come of it. I simulated basic evasion procedures of this vessel, in case of attack. No piracy out this far, I could only dream of war and police actions that were likely to never come. Corporal Xavier discouraged my barrel rolls and twists and loops. She said this wasn't a battleship.

"Every ship of the line is a battleship," I said. Gas storage vessels had been rigged into giant bombs, before, and hurtled at the enemy hull, full of drilling drones. Pilots ejected into space before impact and continued to fire sidearms during the battle until they were killed. The corporal was not really interested in war history from the academy. "Each ship has tactics and must be ready to fight." It was drilled into me in the academy.

"Ensign, a word of advice: Don't believe that crap. The war was invented to fund the colonies. There are no aliens in this galaxy to compete with us. Most of space is dead zone, with minerals and gases we can use. There's some single-celled life, but hardly anything more complex. We've never found an alien microbe large enough to see without a microscope. We are the only sentient life. If there are aliens, they aren't even in radio range."

"You sound like Captain Obasanjo."

"He's got some interesting theories," she said. "I don't make trouble, Ensign. I do my duty, but I understand it's mostly an act. If it wasn't, the enemy would have returned by now. Have you been to the planet surface?"

"Not yet," I said. "Flying is what I wanted. I am a pilot."

"We get leave once every three years. You should visit the monastery. You could use some perspective. There are descendants of the veterans, still, among the monks. Talk to them about the war. There are still survivors planetside. The last battle wasn't so long ago, way out here."

"Do they believe it was fake?"

"No, but their stories are ridiculous. Shooting militarized ansibles out and constructing warships on the other side of wormholes? I am an engineering physicist and it doesn't even make sense to do that when the supposed enemy could just fly past us to the next system, the next star. Look out there into the bottomless sky. Can you even imagine the kind of scarcity that drives a war? There is no scarcity. Once intergalactic travel opens, there is no scarcity for any civilization. Just fly on to the next star if there's resistance. The violence we face will be intersolar only. There's no reason to fight over territories when there's so much free space. Even Obasanjo will tell you that. So, what the hell were the aliens doing fighting? What was anyone doing fighting? We could just push the wormhole out, build another ansible ship on the other side, and keep pushing until we've got all the resources in the universe. They fought . . . something. I don't know what. It was probably just us, constructed simultaneous to the warships. We are the enemy; the enemy is us, giving humanity an excuse in the blood of clones to push into the sky."

I am glad that the last thing she said was meaningful to her. The black void of space all around us did not hear her. We were still a day away from the nebula. We ate in silence on either side of the screen, cleaned our mouths and did our ablutions to the little gods of flesh in our separated bathrooms. We did not even say goodnight to each other. I was sleeping first, while she watched the console. She would wake me in four hours and I would take my turn there while she slept. We would then repeat this four-hour shift again, and spend twelve hours awake, and call it the day. The computer console did all the work for us until morning, and I was responsible for checking flight systems while Corporal Xavier checked the inner hull.

I do not recall if she was beautiful or not. I know it is a trivial detail, and matters little for her or me, but I wish to recall whether she was beautiful. I remember her as a grumpy woman, undoubtedly exhausted from all the pressures of living and working in the station, and impatient with the new ensign who might have been flirting with her, but I know that I was not flirting with her. I was younger than her, and at night, when I dreamed of the fairer sex, it was Shui Mien with her long, black hair humming to herself while bent over her console in her work, or Corporal Adebayo Anderson arriving in darkness and smiling at me. When I woke up and took the console, Xavier was strapping hooks to her boots to do a manual check of the interior.

"Something doesn't look right in the drone cam," she said. "Be right back." She had her zero-g emergency kit on her waist; we both did. Space is tremendously dangerous. Microfractures in the pressurized hull can crackle and pop and take whole ships down. Broken shielding can flood our cockpit with stellar radiation we don't even notice, and we die weeks later with painful tumors all through our flesh. Microbiotic revolutions can become toxic plagues. We check. We double-check. We check and check. We clean and check. Disaster always comes for us, eventually.

I pushed the sleep from my eye, and I pulled awake, a bad feeling in my gut. "What is it?"

"Probably a broken drone. It banged into something. They're old. They break. I'll be back."

I nodded. "Check in check in, this is supply line zero zero one," I said, into the communicator. Obasanjo grunted at me through the com. "Good morning, sunshine," I said.

"What is it, Ensign?"

"Corporal Xavier has a broken drone. She is checking it out in the inner hull."

"What happened to it?"

"Will advise," I said.

She slammed open the supply tunnel that joined the cockpit with the tanks. "I said that it's probably a drone. I don't know what it is. Keep your hands on the wheel and an open line, Ensign. I will have to depressurize the tank if I need to make any repairs, so be ready on my mark."

"Probably a drone?" said Obasanjo. "Sergeant Anderson reported some caustics in the air, in the vicinity. You didn't fly through any gas, did you?"

"No, sir. We gave a wide berth to the caustics."

"I will stay in the line, but I have a lightspeed quickconnect conference call with Station Argo and Station Cypress in five. The drone's probably nothing serious. Anything strange on the dial?"

"Nothing," I said. On my readout we were just an object floating in the black, our engines humming and kicking out microwaves behind us. Everything was green on the dials. "Should I kill the engines?"

"It's your call, Ensign. You're the pilot."

I decided to flip them off. "Corporal, I am about to kill the engines. Do you hear me? We're in no rush, and I don't want to take chances."

"Yes, go ahead, Ensign, but I don't know if it's necessary yet."

"It is procedure, and . . . Done. Until we know what you see, I don't want to risk anything." Before I could finish my sentence, she was likely already aware of her imminent death. I heard her curse through the line, to herself, but did not know what it was about. I heard nothing else.

That was my fatal mistaken judgment. When I switched the engines off, as was a usual procedure when unknown damage was possible, energy stopped flowing along the outer shield, leaving only the hull alone in place. Generally, more energy on a broken hull only exacerbated damage. It should have been fine. There was no indication of a damaged hull on my dials, and troubleshooting always began with turning off the engine. We only had the radiation blockers up and if we needed larger repairs, we would suit up and turn those off, too. It was all standard procedure. It was normal.

The blowout, when it came, was so suddenly quiet that it was like a single, loud knock at the door, within moments of flipping the switch. All the dials went red. A drone had banged against the wall, while we were sleeping, having malfunctioned. It had a rogue biome impacting inside the silicates of its circuits. It caused a microfracture in the hull, that was not exacerbating because the shielding was up, and all wires were on, and the pressurization was supplemented by the engine line. Once turned off, only the radiation wall remained, and the microfracture lost the grip of the power lines. The structure of the old bird shattered from the contorting pressures of vacuum pulling on old metal.

Cursing my name, the corporal jumped for her safety gear, but lost her footing. The vacuum grabbed her. She slammed into the crack, headfirst, knocking her unconscious. That was the knock. The crack was large enough to pull hard, but not so large that a full body could pass through. The sliver in the hull cut into her, ripping out her soft flesh from her body, where she was unable to fight against the flood. Her body sealed the crack just long enough for me to turn the emergency hull re-inforcement system on, but this only made it worse, because what parts of her that were outside of the hull, parts of her head and some shoulder tissue, were sliced away, and blood poured out far beyond what little first aid could be rendered here. I did not know it was happening until I saw the nearby drones going all alert at the breach and the detection of blood. Then, I saw it on all the screens, from every angle, her body being pulled out into space in a sudden pressurization acci-dent, cut and broken in multiple places, blood glittering like lost rubies.

Her death was very quick, I am told.

It was an accident. I held still a moment in horror, watching her bleed out through the monitor screens.

"Obasanjo," I said. "Obasanjo. Jesus."

"What is it? I'm busy. Oh, shit. You're all red. There's a breach. Are you all right, Ensign?"

"No."

"Put your zero gravity gear on right now. Right now. Put it on. Do you have it on?"

"Okay." I held still, staring at the blood, frozen in terror and shock.

"Are you putting it on?"

"Yes," I said. Air was leaving the ship very quickly.

"You need to put your zero gravity gear on right away, Ensign. Snap out of it. You're losing pressure. I can see it from here. I'm getting drone readouts now, and . . . Okay. Get your gear on."

I closed my eyes. Air was leaving, and I was exposed to air, breathing it and running out of it. She was already dead. I needed to put my gear on to save myself.

The worst thing, beyond the guilt of flipping the switch that killed that poor woman, is the freeze afterward, the sudden and overwhelming feeling of incompetence that haunted my career. In the face of such horror, I did not move fast enough. I took no lead. I froze in fear. I got my gear on because Obasanjo was shouting at me, and I opened my eyes.

"Now switch the drones into recovery mode. You need to check the ship. The corporal is already dead. You need to make the ship safe, and preserve your oxygen tanks and get the equipment home. Ensign, focus."

"Yes, sir," I said. There is no nakedness more than knowing one is losing oxygen days away from the station, alone in a broken vessel. It is like being naked in a blizzard, and holding a single sheet still against the wind to stay warm. I threw up before I did anything to save myself. I couldn't think straight. Obasanjo had to talk me through the damn pilot's manual, himself.

We sealed off the tanks, and shut down the airflow into the chamber. I sent the drones after her body as soon as it was safe to pull them off emergency repair, and saw the corrupted one struggling with navigation. That one, I turned off quickly, before it could do any more damage.

Forbidden from doing anything else until the investigation, I handed the controls over to the computer that flew us home on emergency navigation. I didn't even have a way to seal her body against the stink. The tanks were off limits, all connected and re-welded over the broken places in the hull. I placed her in the enlisted bathroom, and sealed the door. The separate bathrooms made sense to me in a flash. They were each perfect for a coffin, with water pipes and cleaning supplies ready to peel away the biota that would result afterward, and I could seal the door so I would not have to experience the smell.

Returning, then, in shame and infamy, and all the station would hold against me my foolish pride. Abashed, I waited for Admiral Diego to come down from his office to lambast me in the airlock.

I was surprised to note upon my arrival that Corporal Watkins was the ranking man present, with the biotic sweepers, to claim the body. He did not say anything to me about a judgment against me. He was calm and professional. He didn't touch my arm, even, to comfort me. He was putting on these huge rubber gloves, and asked me where the body was.

"I put it in the enlisted bathroom," I said. "I have washed since. I should be clean."

"Doesn't matter. Keep your gear on tight. Tell me when you're ready."

I held my arms out and let the bleaching mist pour over me in a cloud. "You need to keep your gear on and go to medical for clearance, Ensign. We can take it from here, okay?"

A biotic infestation in the circuits of a drone, a small microfracture in an ancient hull that quickly escalated into full breach, and death. I didn't even know what had happened. All I knew was that someone had died, and I was flying when it happened.

Humans were not made for space. We are made for oxygen

and nitrogen biomes, carbon landscapes with trees and long grasses, never space. Our guts don't work right, our bones elongate and become brittle, and our blood thickens inside. Then, when the slightest error occurs, it kills so suddenly it is as if we were never meant to be alive. I had a thought in my head while I followed my tablet to medical. The rank of corporal comes from the Greek just as does "corporeal." She had been promoted to the rank of body. There are enlisted men who aren't even worthy of being considered bodies yet. These people in space, clones all, are just a bunch of bodies.

Her body was taken to a storage room in a sealed bag for processing. Her religious preference was listed as Wiccan, and on the next transport to the surface, she would be taken down and placed in the grounds of an unaffiliated garden, and a tree or large shrub would be planted above her. Her faith suggested roses and oaks, but we have none of those here. A light-speed quickconnect exchange was arranged between Brother Goodluck, the head groundskeeper, and a Wiccan representative from a neighboring colony, with Captain Obasanjo's intermediation. They negotiated for a long while, waiting out the weeks for light to travel there and back, and settled on a jujube tree. They are gruesome, gangly, and spindly with copious thorns, but they are large enough and they produce flowers and the fruit is a staple of our diet here. They do not need much water, either, to grow and live a long time.

In medical, I expected the quartermaster to come howling at me, for killing his experienced flight tech. He did not come. Instead, the medical tech was checking my biome, and the medical computer was checking my physical health, and I was slowly allowed to peel away my emergency kit one piece at a time. The medical machinery found nothing wrong with me, and the tech gave me a high-fiber supplement to help my digestive tract recover from the influence of weightlessness. And the tech said nothing about the loss of a crewmember. Wong came for me just as I was leaving medical. He was smiling like any other day.

"Welcome back, Ensign. Good to see you survived the incident."

I didn't really know what to say. I looked up at him, and thought about responding, but all I could think of was how my very first flight ended up in the death of a crewmember.

"The officers want to meet with you in the conference room to go over what happened. Obasanjo has already shown us all the tapes. We still need to debrief you for the records, okay?"

"I'll see you there, Lieutenant. I want to take a shower in my own quarters, if I have ten minutes."

"I'll have to be with you when you do, Ensign. I don't want to see that," he said. He leaned back against the wall and smiled at the medical technician, who became uncomfortable.

"Is everything all right?" I said.

"No," said Wong. "It will be fine, though. This is all just procedure. I'm sure everything will be fine."

"A crewmember died under my command," I said.

"Exactly," said Wong. He patted my shoulder. "So, there's going to be an inquest, and it's happening in just a few minutes, and you are going to tell the truth about what happened and it will line up with the camera records and audio files. Then, everything will be fine."

"It was an accident," I said.

"The officers will decide what to tell HR in the Terran system," he said. "But, yes, it was probably an accident. If we say it is, then HR will say it is. Until they say it is, it could be anything. We would like to resolve this quickly. Understand?"

"Yes," I said.

The medical tech put down his equipment. "Do I need to leave the room, sir?"

"Of course not," said Wong. "Nothing confidential will be said here. This is all just normal procedure, and it's officer stuff. It shouldn't have anything to do with the enlisted. Everyone knows what happens when someone dies unexpectedly. We've all been there, Corporal. The number of suicides and accidental deaths on this station, we've all seen inquests. This is just like those. There will always be an inquest, even if the person who died suddenly jumps out an airlock after a bad breakup. It's a normal procedure."

"The suicide problem," said the tech. "We need more time planetside. We need more uncensored data access."

"We have addressed our concerns to the monastery, Private, and we have to abide by the governing body of the Citadel planet. Obasanjo's ansible restrictions are what keep us alive and floating. We are working toward a solution. In the meantime, don't kill yourself. It is a real hassle for your commander because we have to do an inquest. Then, some other fortunate soul arrives to this posting to reap all the rewards you have failed to acquire."

The med tech looked down at his hands. "Corporal Xavier was my friend," said the med tech. "I'm going to miss her." Then, he started to cry.

"I am so sorry for your loss," I said. I grabbed him by the shoulders. I tried to hug him. He pushed me away. "I'm sorry," I said, to his back. He pushed the door hard and locked it behind him.

In the hallway, Wong, ever smiling, asked me if I had been

trained on interrogation techniques.

"Pilots generally aren't."

"I can tell," he said. "In the future, never let yourself be seen apologizing until after the inquest. I say this as your friend. I will have to take note of that, as an officer, during the inquest. It looks bad to apologize if it isn't your fault."

"She was my responsibility, even if it wasn't anyone's fault. I will be writing a letter to her family and her original about her death. I know that. It is the least I can do."

"It is, but never apologize until the inquest is complete. If you like, I can guide you through the whole process. I can minimize everything I possibly can."

"You can?"

"Yes. It is not a hard thing to do, when the head of security believes a man innocent, and there is simply a procedural task to fulfill for an unfortunate accident. It will be good to have you back at the poker table. We could play a special hand, just you and me."

I felt very cold. "No poker for me, Lieutenant." I walked past him, and kept my back to him, then. I went straight for the meeting.

The inquest was in the conference room, which was on a floor with slightly lighter gravity, where the weight of the body felt lighter. It increased my nausea. Admiral Diego, Captain Quiswanathaa, and Captain Nguyen sat in triumvirate on one end in what was probably their best approximation of formal dress uniforms, while Wong took a seat on the other side of the table and encouraged me to join him. Admiral Diego's uniform was a crumpled mess, full of creases and a few mysterious stains. Q was missing half the formal uniform, and was wearing regular pants and no gloves. Captain Nguyen had managed most of his uniform fine, but he barely fit in it. I don't know how anyone manages to gain weight on the food we have.

"Has Lieutenant Wong explained procedure?" said the quartermaster. The admiral was stone-faced. Nguyen was uncomfortable, staring at his hands and fidgeting.

"No, sir."

"Whenever a crewmember dies outside of combat, the death is investigated to ascertain not only what happened, but if anyone is responsible. The tapes are reviewed, and senior officers come together to send our recommendation to HR," he gestured toward the three of them, on their side. "Obasanjo recused himself as he was present on the tapes. So, Captain Nguyen is standing in. Wong will ask questions; we will listen. Answer truthfully and it will be over soon."

Wong asked me everything, then sought clarification, and would come back to every point again long after it seemed done. Three times I answered every question in that fashion. The tape was played back, and I heard myself in my worst moment. I felt such shame, such incompetence. When it was done, the admiral finally spoke. "We're done here. It is getting close to dinner. Shut down the tapes of the official record and save."

The officers stood up, and held their hands out to me for a handshake. I went in order, left to right, from Q to Nguyen. Wong patted me on the shoulder and left, without another word.

Alone, I sat in the room while the others filed past me. Captain Nguyen paused at the door and turned back. "Cheer up, Ensign," he said. "The worst is over."

"Is it?" I was still at the Citadel Station, where the previous pilot had killed himself.

"Yeah," he said. "Q will go over the physical material and once we have the forensics, we'll write up a formal report. The next ice comet will arrive soon. You are still alive. Cheer up. We're going to send our recommendation to HR, along with the tapes. It's a big fucking waste of everyone's time. They aren't going to want to send anyone to replace you. Okay? No matter what happens, you're going to be fine because HR will not want to send anyone if they don't absolutely have to. Your career is procedurally inviolate as long as this posting is such a piece of shit. So, cheer up. Or, kill yourself. If you're going to kill yourself, don't make a mess on my computer networks. The last AstroNav was kind enough to go outside."

"Thanks," I said. "Between you and me, Captain Nguyen, I wasn't planning on doing anything drastic, but if I do, it will be a giant clusterfuck all over your most critical terminal, just for you."

He thought I was joking and laughed.

In my mind, I considered what would happen if I was found at fault, but retained my commission. I decided that the honorable thing was to offer my resignation. I questioned whether I had the courage to do it, then and now.

The corporal's funeral service was held the next day. We gathered in leg braces down by the tanks where her body was in cold storage until she could go down on Anderson's next supply run, and Brother Goodluck was video-conferenced in on a twelve-minute delay from the monastery to try and fulfill the requisites of a Wiccan ceremony. He was old, even then, and weather-beaten, and bald as a rock. He stumbled through a Wiccan ceremony, then stopped and looked up at all of us. He said he would pray for us, the human vanguard, and the repose of the soul to any god that would care to listen. He sang a little hymn in a bright tenor that seemed to come from nowhere at all, not those cracked, hard lips. It was a beautiful hymn, beautifully sung, whatever it was. It shook me deep.

Two days after the funeral, I got a message from the admiral.

*Ensign Ronaldo Aldo,*

> *HR accepted our unanimous recommendation.*
> *A malfunctioning drone caused a microfracture at a bad spot on the inner hull. The quartermaster is in charge of maintaining the drones, and he has taken full responsibility for the corporal's death. You are commended for following procedure under difficult circumstances, and getting your vessel back for repair with the body.*
> *You are cleared for duty, in full.*

*Regards,*
*Admiral Antonio Diego*

------------

Released from the bondage of fear, of a blemish on my record, I did not intuit the temptation of sin, and my own responsibility at the time, taking instead the judgment of the official reports as a kind of truth. In time, and upon reflection, it was my pride that pushed the whole situation. An experienced space pilot, like Sergeant Anderson, might not have touched the controls at all, if he didn't know what was happening and all the dials were green. The very odd, rare instance of damage from the interior opposed to the exterior, and the very specific place where that damage occurred on the old, refurbished hull, made procedure foolish. Perhaps he would have intuited that.

A new tech was ordered from the network of ansibles; a new recruit from Earth would be called to this miserable station.

Sergeant Anderson's wife, the beautiful Corporal Adebayo Anderson, sat with me at dinner, after the funeral service.

"Piloting is dangerous," she said. "My husband tells me all the time that every voyage could turn so quickly into disaster. Bad luck happened to you, and poor Corporal Xavier, and that is all."

"I appreciate your faith, Corporal," I said. I didn't believe my own words.

She didn't let me get away from them. "If you hadn't swallowed this bad luck, my husband would have been there, and maybe he wouldn't have come home from it. I am grateful to you for swallowing his bad luck. Thank you."

I had no way to escape the conversation, then. "I don't like to think about what might have happened," I said. "I only know what happened, and it was bad enough. Did you know Corporal Xavier well?"

"We were very good friends. I miss her already very much. She did not like you one bit, I am sorry to say."

"She and I barely knew each other. She seemed diligent in her duties. Beyond this, I cannot say anything else about her. I am putting a letter together for her people, to let them know about her. If you can tell me anything good to say, I'd love to hear it."

She patted my hands. "We shall pray for her together. We will be faithful to some mysterious God for just this moment, regardless of what may come in others. Death is a time for faith, not philosophy. Philosophy is for living, not dying. Give me your hand, Ensign."

At the time, I had little faith to pray, but it seemed wrong to deny Mrs. Anderson this. We bowed our heads together, and I felt the pressure of her strength, the depth of feeling carried in her hard hands.

When she finished, she took a deep breath and held back the darkness inside of her. I saw the tears welling up. She made a smile, like a thin veil over her face, and left.

Oh, time creeped along. I waited, dreading what would happen next. The admiral left on his patrol, at last. I watched the passage from the top floor of the station, up at the upper observation deck, along the axis of the spin, and on the side opposite the passage to the warship's dock. There was a bubble of see-through materials, wrapped one on top of another, and the ribbons of stars and darkness enveloped the slowly winding engines of the sleek machine. It cut through the darkness with a deadly beauty. I still wish to fly one, even now. I imagined being alone on the station, in charge while the enemy came in their terrible ships. I could ride an emergency signal, then, if the station was doomed to fall. I could push the emergency button and leave this whole world behind to die, my second self with it, and clone out to deliver intel on the fatal attack.

I was not alone. Obasanjo arrived soon after I did. He brought the sticky red jujube dates that passed as dessert, and something that quite nearly resembled a flat, herbal root beer. We drank it from bags with straws while floating weightless, tied to the floor with long ropes that we could climb when we were ready to return to the station.

"The air itself, is different when the admiral is on patrol," said Obasanjo. "As if a hundred voices sigh and a knot leaves all our backs at once."

"I didn't expect to be alone up here," I said. "Considering

how well the back of him is liked, I am surprised it's only you and me."

"One can watch from the monitors, if so inclined, but there is work and there is sleep and there is the time between. Believe it or not, my little circle of atheists is going to be meeting here, soon, and I only came a little early to watch the bastard go. If I didn't have the meeting, I'd have never come. I have to get the schedule ready for tri-annual performance reviews."

"Will you be handling tri-annuals instead of him?"

"No. The admiral hoards that power like a black hole craves starlight."

"I don't expect to get a good tri-annual. A crewmember died under my command."

He did not let me sit with that attitude for very long. "It's kind of awful to frame someone's death with how it relates to your performance review, though."

"Don't do that," I said. "For a moment, I thought we were friends. I should stay for your group, shouldn't I? I should learn to be more philosophical?"

"Yes. And I can be a good friend. Ask me for something realistic, and I'll see what I can do before the admiral returns. Since the admiral came to power, no one has merited transcendence. It's been a long time. I think he was the last one, in fact. It's not common out here, as it is at other colonies. I don't know why. At least, I have my suspicions."

I chewed the red date. It was thick, like a kind of dry, semi-sweet taffy. I watched the engines gently fading into the darkness. Once momentum was built, the engines would be shut off, and the gravities of space itself would carry the momentum to the correct destinations. It was all so carefully planned. As the different probes drifted off, the mass of the ship would change, and the pilot would have to adjust power output of the engines, and restabilize the mission trajectory each time, resetting and checking computer models against the known and unknown gravitational influences, pushing up momentum to near lightspeed.

Obsanjo gazed up and kept sipping his sweetened drink. "So, do you know what Wong does when the admiral's away?"

"Trains for war?"

"Nothing. All his stupid training stops. He cancels everything, even daily calisthenics. He calls in sick. He spends the whole time trying to convince me to sign reports that I know are bullshit with the admiral's rubber stamp. He hides out in his room."

"No way."

"The only thing he cares about is leverage with the enlisted. He has that, and he has them by the balls, and he takes their money for it."

"Do you take their money? You have leverage."

"Sometimes I do. It depends. Money doesn't seem worth the trouble when we're going to the same damn rock with the same damn food."

"The admiral will not recommend anyone for transcendence if they are caught taking bribes. Maybe if we did a better job, and we were better leaders . . ."

Obasanjo laughed. "As if he would recommend me if I didn't. Good luck in your review. Maybe you're right. Fortunately you have until he gets back. He can't review you if he's not here. Make good numbers with your work and your assignments and you might see some real positive outcomes. Or not. I've noticed that it doesn't seem to make any real difference, either way. Tomorrow would be a good day for it. Nobody does anything tomorrow if they don't have to. You'd really stand out on the daily sheets."

"The biotic techs must hate us all."

"Q doesn't care for us either. He is still trying to repair the transport you broke. Anderson comes back tomorrow, and that vessel will need to be checked, also."

"I would like to fly again," I said. "Is that a realistic request?"

"I cannot make that happen for you in any official capacity without the admiral's approval. His orders. Sorry, Ensign. I do have an idea. Do you prefer men or women?"

"Women."

"Ah. Too bad," he said, quickly, then: "Well, there aren't many women here or there. Strict population controls are in place. Most women on the surface have more than one husband, or some other interesting arrangement. The monastery does not approve, but . . . It does mean that upon the surface, beyond the monastery, customs are a little more relaxed. I will put you in touch with someone who is always looking for a handsome-enough young man. You aren't as pretty as Wong, and you certainly aren't as pretty as me, but you'll not be charged very much, regardless."

"I have never been interested in prostitution, Captain."

"You are not a moralist like Q, I hope? Look, desperate times, as they say. I will give you the contact. What you do with it is up to you. This is a very long, dull posting. You may need it someday."

Confessor, I received the contact, for a middle-aged woman with very sad eyes who lived with three husbands in an underground bunker that was far from the monastery, but not far enough to be an inconvenient flyer ride. I never indulged. Paying for it seemed, somehow, more pathetic than going without. So, regarding this indulgence, I have nothing further to confess.

"I wish I could fly out into that darkness, Captain. I wish I could go beyond the known particulate pathways, in the warship that flies into the black of the Greater Laika, toward the Magellanic or Andromeda."

"The admiral is supposed to cede that duty to you, and remain here. After performance reviews, we are all to be scheduled for a planetary vacation. We're on a three-year cycle, and you'll be last in line, I'm afraid, but I can pull some procedural strings as a personal favor. You can be last in line for this cycle, which means you are due for your vacation now. It is critical for everyone to go down planetside, get some fresh air, and feel the heat on our backs. My advice is to focus on that. Honestly, this was the admiral's idea. He thinks you should see the surface before he does your tri-annual. He thinks you need some perspective. It's not even a favor. It's almost the admiral's orders."

"I appreciate it," I said. "You don't think I'll ever fly again?"

"No. The next admiral, perhaps, might indulge you, but not this one."

"It wasn't my fault."

"No, none of us believe it was, not even the admiral. He insists that it was your bad luck, though, even if it wasn't your fault. He bent the rules for you once, and that's enough for him. He is kind enough to downcycle you, and that's the limit of his mercy. Take it, with my blessing, as well. Sergeant Anderson's next voyage down will have you on board."

Outside, in the darkness, the warship was a speck in the black, a tiny, dwindling star. I thought, for just a moment, I might have seen the first of the deep probes launched, but I wasn't sure if it was that or a side thruster adjusting the angle of flight. I squinted and used my tablet to zoom in on the darkness, but the probes were not lit, and the reflection of the starlights on the solar hull of the warship were so slight, I could not be certain I was seeing anything at all, or just willing it upon the void.

Scouting missions did not go deep. They extended with haste beyond the Oort cloud and out a few light years, moving at blistering speeds. The people on board the ship experience only a week or two, but it is a month or more when they return.

I was thinking about the thrill of near lightspeed, and how it would quicken my assignment. I would gain days and weeks upon my posting, and be even younger when I reached the end of my assignment. It was no wonder that the admiral reserved that duty for himself, alone.

Obasanjo's philosophy group arrived one at a time. I greeted them each, and was pleased to see Corporal Adebayo Anderson. She pulled herself up into the observation deck and smiled.

"You will be joining us tonight, Ensign?"

I opened my mouth. "Uh, sure. I cannot promise I will have time to return, but I have time tonight."

"Very good, Ensign. Very, very good. You are a clever man, and an AstroNav. You can help us by investigating the data that comes in from the probes, and the maps."

"Investigate them for what?" I said.

"Inconsistencies," said Obasanjo. "Convenient coincidences. Things like that. My thesis, if you will, and our course of investigation, is that the universe is not real. We are shadows, nothing more. We are some grand experiment in the dark. We investigate this possibility."

"My thesis is that, with respect, Captain Obasanjo is wrong," said Corporal Anderson, "*but* we are still not allowed full access to what is happening in the universe. The god men tell us to pray and focus on our duties, but I prefer to question at the devils what is happening."

Private Farhouk, a grumpy-looking network tech, pointed up at the glass. "Did you see the bastard go?"

"Only for a moment," said Obasanjo.

"I have been reading some old Margalit texts, and I wonder what relationship our little hobby has to our duties. Does undermining our duties with doubt impact them? Do we do as well as if we had no doubts? I want you to check the statistics of completion, Captain. I want to see how the quartermaster's prayer group does in their daily tasks compared to us."

"What is your theory?"

He grunted. "I'll wait to see numbers before I have a theory."

"Everyone is equally bad," said Obasanjo. "I assure you that much. We are such a disappointment in our leaky hull. How did your insight into the genetic history of our oldest O/S bugs go? Any interesting discoveries?"

"I'm still developing the virus lines," he said. "Maybe next week I'll have something for you. What is the ethics of what we do compared to our little group? Are we undermining our duties?"

My head began to spin while they discussed the question. It seemed circular, honestly. Those who believed that we were, as Obasanjo believed, some distant experiment for the mysterious enemy, felt there was no problem going through the motions of our duties compared to true believers. The whole mission was a farce, so why feel pressure to perform for a farce?

The others believed that the only way to prove the mission was a farce, if it was, was to engage with it as if it weren't. Another faction—if I can call Corporal Anderson, by herself, a faction—was a rejection of both camps in the pointlessness of questioning reality in this angle, when so many other more fruitful lines of inquiry were available. At the end of the meeting, I was bored and confused and I tried to escape without promising to attend another meeting. I believe I said something like, "That was a lot to take in. I'm going to have to sit on that, awhile, and think on it."

In the morning, transfer procedure began for replacement enlisted, and Obasanjo asked me to sit in as officer on deck during the procedure, to monitor station protocols and signals and paperwork, while he took over the transfer from the ansible. Officer on deck sounded prestigious, but it was just a procedural safety-valve job, where I was ready to push a button and get someone else to do something outside of normal task protocols in an emergency. I sat at Obasanjo's desk, and stared at his monitors, and if anything came over the transom, I rubber stamped it for the system computer in his absence. I was approving shift changes and work reports from the different sectors of biotic clearance, watching the computer's steady stream of data about oxygen levels, station energy, and water supply. I felt the role of rubber stamp could be played by an algorithm, not an officer, but the procedure was sacrosanct, and the absence of the admiral meant that everything he hadn't bothered to approve could finally get done. It was not long before I stopped even reading what I was stamping in any depth. I skimmed it, and as long as the header matched the paragraphs, I approved.

During this time, my first concrete idea of actual sedition arrived. I could request anything, now, that was in my power to request. As officer on deck in the admiral's absence, I was sole arbiter of the approval chain for anything that did not cross the quartermaster's devastatingly solid queue. I could not approve any new warships, for materials go through the supply chain and the quartermaster. But I could approve time off, medical leave, and any number of personnel shifts that could happen so invisibly. I put in a request, as a joke, to move Mrs. Anderson to flight crew, where she would aid in ship maintenance. I did not approve it. But the realization struck me that this is why Obasanjo was so happy. Whatever was in his power, he could approve. He was as corrupt as Wong, in his way. He would not demand money, but I knew that there would be a price to pay for his sponsorship, someday. I could sense it about him. Everyone demanded something in exchange, even if it was only favors for friendship in this miserable post. I began to think of ways I could use this power to transcend the post. All the scheming seemed so small, to me. Favors for better pieces of a semi-inhabitable rock, and what else? I began to try to mentally connect the dots between the emergency data signal procedure, and this thoughtless rubber stamp.

I also listened into the transfer protocols with the distant ansibles, and the arrival of our new crewmember, replacing the one we lost, and heard a bright, warm woman's voice announcing herself to Obasanjo.

The guilt that I felt, already, was so high. Here was this beautiful voice and she was here because someone died in my command, and I was glad it would be someone beautiful, but not at this price.

I imagine the better she looked, the kinder she was, the nicer and the more dutiful she was to me, the worse I would feel about Corporal Xavier's death. The worse I should feel, at least. As time passed, I did not feel worse about anything. I just felt numb.

Tech Private Chet Detkarn was very beautiful, with a body like a slender willow bending in the breeze, and long black hair that she maintained long contrary to regulation for some cultural reason I never had explained to me. I saw her from across the cafeteria when she completed quarantine, and I forced myself not to stare. She was uncomfortable with all the stares, or uncomfortable just being present in this posting on the far edge of time itself, a beautiful woman with only a handful of other women, and all those leering, bored, horny men.

Despite her quarantine, a sickness overwhelmed us all from the new biotic vector. Diarrhea spread out of the women's enlisted area with fevers and chills as soon as Detkarn moved in. I was one of the last to catch the illness. I watched as others spent the day in medical, waiting out the infection with fluid lines in their arms. I hoped that I would be strong enough to avoid infection. When I was hit, it was worse than the early victims' illness. I spent a week laid up in medical, reading approved media, and writing letters home to Earth that would be queued into the ansible for some far future delivery. The admiral returned while I was laid up, and came in to medical with the same infection just after I was starting to feel better. He lost consciousness for a little while. He was pale and sweating bullets, shivering cold for days. The med tech put him on an IV, and he came out of his fever enough to lean over and scowl at me.

"Ensign," he said. "If you don't stop staring at me, I will put you on latrine pipe cleaning duty for a month."

I looked away. I had not thought I was staring.

Private Detkarn was assigned to my nominal supervision, along with two other techs, Sergeant Germaine Hobarth and Private Andre Khan. Our new job was to construct a new shipping vessel from the parts we had, to replace what had been badly damaged.

My trio and I were assigned one corner of the quartermaster's chamber, presumably so I could be watched with my minor hint of meaningful command.

I made a checklist of things we needed to accomplish. I assigned duties. I gave myself the most technical ones. Private Detkarn was assigned to work with Hobarth, an older and experienced crewman, on the skeletal frame that held the whole shell together from the inside. I observed their work from the cockpit area, assignating wires to wires like lovers twisting. Khan was to work on propulsion lines and engines, which I was made to understand was his specialty. I trusted him to work fairly unsupervised with his personnel records. I observed aging, balding Sergeant Hobarth attempting to seduce Detkarn repeatedly with his long smiles, his gentle, too-friendly mannerisms. I observed her cold to such advances, focused on her work, as if he did not exist, at all.

After Hobarth pushed her for something she would not give, I called her over.

"Sir? Is anything wrong?"

"I am asking you that. Is anything wrong?"

"No, sir."

"Hobarth giving you any trouble?"

"I can handle dirty old men, Ensign."

"You shouldn't have to handle them. Go see if Private Khan can teach you any of his tricks with engines."

Hobarth was watching us, pretending to tighten a bolt.

I looked over at him. "You're distracted. You can get some-one killed."

"You would know, sir."

"What was that, Sergeant?"

"Sorry, sir. Nevermind. I spoke out of turn."

"You sure did. Why don't you go see if the quartermaster has any latrine pipes that need cleaning. I hear there's always buildup in the damn latrines. Be back here tomorrow ready to work quietly and respectfully."

The old soldier went pale and turned toward me.

"You heard me, Sergeant," I said. I realized that I was much smaller than this man. "Latrine duty. Now. I was not at fault. It was an accident. I will not have you insinuate anything else to my face or behind it."

His bald head reddened with his anger, but he saluted at attention and left for the quartermaster, who was elbow deep in broken drones on another side of the facility, and did not appear to be in the mood to take anyone's side in a personnel matter. He looked up, and heard the sergeant request latrine duty. He looked over at me, with an eyebrow raised. I dragged a thumb across my neck. Kill him, I was saying. Put him to work on the nastiest pipe. Q shrugged and took Hobarth over to the supply closet for a face mask and some scrubbers.

I still had to keep our ship on the timeline, and Hobarth's work was critical to the next layer of the hull. I realized I was going to have to get his job done without him, but I trusted the young man to be more appropriate to the new girl, considering that I had just made an example of Sergeant Hobarth. Khan was, apparently, worse than the dirty old man. Detkarn came around the side of the engine shaking, near tears, within the hour.

She asked to speak with me in private.

I took her to the quartermaster's desk and heard what happened, with recording devices on, and the quartermaster sitting and listening in while he was observing his own crews at the side of his attention from his desktop terminal.

She spoke quickly and precisely.

"Wait here," I said, after I heard it.

I walked over to where Khan was working, like nothing has happened.

"Private Khan," I said. "What did you do?"

"Nothing, sir. She say I did anything?"

"Yes. Put down your tools and go stand in the corner. I need to review the tapes."

The quartermaster was watching me closely now. He looked over from the drones he was repairing. He huffed at me, exasperated. I gestured to him to speak in private.

"Can't you keep control of your people?" he said. "I won't have you sending them all to me when you have a personnel issue."

"Detkarn is accusing Khan of groping her sexually," I said, quietly.

"That's all?"

"What do you mean, 'That's all? We need to review the tapes."

"What is the severity here? Are we to pull Khan into Wong's holding tank over a passing gesture? Or, should I just get your crew ready for latrine duty instead of building a damn ship."

"Until I review the tapes, we don't know what we're talking about. We might need Wong. You can't be telling me to let it go, sir."

He rubbed his temples. "I am telling you that there are . . .

what is it now? Four women here, and something like thirty, thirty-five men, depending on accidents and suicides. It happens. Ask any of them. Maybe have one of them speak with Private Detkarn. Coporal Jensen is just back from repairing. I could call Corporal Anderson, if you want the one with the most seniority. She's going to be a full sergeant as soon as my recommendation clears HR, but Jensen's closer and mostly done for the day."

"First, the tapes. Isn't that the procedure?"

"Procedure demands a woman be present. I don't need to be there. Khan is not in my command line. Have Jensen with you when you review," he said. He picked up a tablet and flipped it over to the camera eye on his crewman. She was doing a double-check on her exosuit after her repair walk. "Jensen! Put down the scanner and come to my office with Ensign Aldo. We need a woman's eye."

In the quartermaster's office, I asked Detkarn to show me the tapes. It took a few minutes. Jensen saw her fellow soldier trembling and crying, trying to get the system to work.

"Take your time," I said. "Come on, Private Detkarn. We need to see the evidence against Khan before we can decide to pursue."

"I don't know which camera is which."

Jensen took over the controls, switching from one view of the hangar bay to another until she had the angle for that side of the hull. I saw the quartermaster chatting with both Hobarth and Khan, and I resisted the urge to turn the sound on.

We rewound until we found the incident. Khan was showing her how to weld two gas lines together with a hand clamp and small lathe. He placed the tools in her hands, then wrapped around her to place his hands on hers, to guide her movements. She started to panic. He leaned in and licked her neck. "We could do it right here, and no one would notice as long as we were quiet," he whispered.

Horrified, she began to protest, but Khan planted his mouth over her mouth, in a grotesque mockery of kissing. He slowly ran his other hand over her uniform, touching her stomach. He chuckled and let her go where she stood horrified and trembling with rage.

"It's not the worst I've experienced," said Jensen, to my great horror. She turned to me. "Ensign, this is all on you. Never send a woman off by herself with a man where others can't see them. Never leave a woman alone with just one man. In your command, maybe you will find there are men who can't be trusted no matter who is around, and maybe two or three of them together are worse for the woman. Do a better job, god-damnit."

"He should never do that!" shouted Detkarn. "I did nothing to provoke him."

Jensen looked sadly upon Detkarn, barely twenty and so newly made, so innocent looking, and Jensen nearly thirty, looking for her early out. "Let it go," she said, to both of us.

"I cannot," I said.

"No one will care," said Jensen. "The rules and regulation are very clear. It isn't sexual abuse unless there is evidence of contact with a sexual organ. He was careful not to do that."

"It was sexual abuse!" shouted Detkarn.

"It was," I said. "Absolutely, it was. That is without question. And Khan will be punished. He must be. But, Jensen, you don't think the other officers will support my verdict?"

"The quartermaster did worse to Mrs. Anderson before she started fighting back. She did a month in the brig for breaking his nose, and Sergeant Anderson gets to fly his way to an early out because of it. Tech Private Detkarn, I understand completely what you feel right now. I've been there. Khan must be punished. Ensign, let the women take care of the women."

"You can't be serious," I said.

She placed a hand on my shoulder. "I appreciate your concern, Ensign. Mrs. Anderson and I will take care of this."

"What do you have planned?"

"Ultraviolence is a very effective deterrent to men like Khan. She is in charge of maintaining and replacing cameras. Stay out of the way."

I turned over to Detkarn. "I see you have developed quite a fever, over there. You are on medical leave for the next two days. If you aren't ready for duty, check with med tech and let me know, and I'll see what I can do. No rush to head back to the dormitories."

Jensen looked over at me. "Bad idea. Thanks, but it's a bad idea. Private Detkarn, compose yourself, and strengthen your resolve. If they think you are weak, they will do it again. You have to be strong. Fight back. Give as good as you get."

"Goddamnit, there's nothing I can do? What's the point of being an officer if I can't handle the personnel? Who does it?" I asked. "I want you to give me a list of the men that have done things. I want to know who does it. I can help with a more permanent solution, eventually."

"It's kind of a long list, and there's two officers on it."

"I can't help you with anyone who outranks me. Leave the officers off the list." The quartermaster was one. The admiral was the other.

"What could you possibly do?"

"Have faith in me, Corporal Jensen. I can't make any

promises, but I can pull some strings. Our posting is very long, and there are no transfers. I will do what I can when I can."

Private Detkarn cried awhile, then straightened her uniform. She set her jaw like a boxer, and wiped away all her pains. Then, she returned to duty, with Jensen, like nothing had ever happened.

The quartermaster came in and consulted with me, privately. He watched the tape. He sat back in his chair and crossed his arms. "Of course it's assault, and we can prosecute him for that. But it is not clearly, legally sexual. She's new. She's going to be hazed, Ensign."

"I wasn't hazed."

"You're an officer. Your recertification was your hazing. And losing poker."

"Are men hazed differently than women?"

He smirked. "You're not thinking of getting involved in justice, are you? This is a military ship, and the chain of command is the only justice you need."

"I'm only asking questions," I said. "I agree with your assessment that no criminal proceedings should be brought against the man in question. Khan's a good tech. We shouldn't ruin his career over some stupid stunt. The real question is one of consequences. Actions should have consequences. Bad actions should have bad consequences. What do you and I do to send the message that hazing is unacceptable, Commander?"

"Is it unacceptable?" he said. He was surprised at me, and confused. "There's not a lot to do up here, Ensign. No one was hurt. The mission wasn't impacted. The new private is going to need thicker skin to make a go of her life here. That's all."

"I see," I said. I did not see. Part of the code of conduct was clearly designed to discourage the kind of behavior I just saw. I left the meeting and called Khan over.

"I didn't do anything," he said.

"You did do something. You absolutely did. I saw it on the tapes."

"It was just a joke," he said.

"Some joke, Private. Nobody was laughing. Nobody."

"Am I in trouble?"

"Are you? Build me an engine. Build it fast and build it now. You want me to cover your ass against Wong, you had better build the best damn engine in the known universe."

"Yes, sir."

"And, Private Khan, you will never, ever touch a woman again. For the rest of your military career, you are a monk. Do you understand?"

He mumbled assent, but he looked at me with daggers in his eyes. My relationship with the enlisted was not something I thought much about until right then.

I did not observe Khan's punishment, personally, but he was bruised badly the next day, and walked with a limp. He had a black eye, and bruises along his arms. He was quiet about it. "What happened to you, Private Khan?"

"Volleyball practice, sir," he said. "My team lost."

"I see that. How's my engine?"

"Getting there," he said. He scratched what seemed to be a solid lump in his skull. "I know what I'm doing."

I had an idea when I got the list of troublesome enlisted men. I reached out to Obasanjo, whom I thought might be sympathetic to the plight of the female enlisted, considering his suggested preferences. I asked if it was possible to cycle out all of these men for some reason or another, as quickly as possible. We could flag them for anything, declare them unfit, and cycle them off to the planet.

*Let me see if I understand your logic. The only thing anyone wants is a free early retirement, and you want to make it as easy as possible for someone to escape upon the molested bodies of our female enlisted? Is that what you want?*
—Captain Obasanjo

*Okay, I understand, but is there any way we can isolate the offenders? Can we shuffle them off to some special work crew that throws them off-cycle?*
—Ensign Aldo

*No. I'm sending you on your vacation, though. The plague threw you off schedule, but there's plenty of time for your performance review when you get back. You're trying to do the right thing, and I respect that, and I also happen to know doing the right thing is a huge mistake. You've had a rough year. You lost a crewmember. Don't let it get to your head. You need to see what we're fighting for, and get your head a new perspective. I gave you the person to contact, didn't I?*
—Captain Obasanjo

The question I ask of you, my confessor, is this: I took the side of justice and righteousness, with the oppressed women, and this was another step in the diminishment of my career. This should have been rewarded by God. Instead, the men looked upon me as if I were not worthy of my uniform, as if the guilt I felt for one woman's death was enough to make me lose sight of the accepted gender-imbalanced realities of our posting. Why was I diminished for trying to be just? Unless my ultimate reward was my crime against the universe, and it was no sin, then what else could it mean?

At least the women on the station had some respect for me. Jensen and I ended up on the same cycle down to the planet, and she was kinder to me than before, when she should have been furious. At the time, I interpreted it to my foolish sense of justice.

———————

Sergeant Anderson, at least, was kind enough to let me take the controls for part of the journey down. He didn't go far from the controls, and there was very little to do with them on simple planetary runs. Until the troposphere, nothing even rattles in the hull, and there is no question about our destination trajectory with the huge, golden planet right there before us. "You all right, Sergeant?"

"Everything is fine, sir. I just get anxious if I am not close to the controls."

"That sounds like a personal problem, Sergeant."

"Yes, sir."

I gently coaxed the ship out of dock and turned toward the planet surface, where an autopilot would take us most of the way on such a simple trajectory.

"You should be the last one of the officers, and you're down even before Nguyen. He's not going to like that. How did you get a downcycle early?"

"Captain Obasanjo likes me," I said.

"Huh," he said.

"What?"

"Nothing. Nice takeoff, Ensign. Very smooth."

Takeoff is easy. The ship decouples from magnetic lock, and starts to float. Air jets push away from the station over our heads at the same rotation as the station. I had gone through the whole checklist before taking the controls, even after Sergeant Anderson went through it all. I checked the drones in hold. I double-checked them. I ran a biotic sweep, myself, early this morning. Takeoff was a seamless drift. My instructors would be pleased to see how smooth and clean my spiral was. Sergeant Anderson was not pleased. He was gruff and polite, but I could sense his discomfort like a storm on my radar screen.

We had a short flight to the ground, only twelve hours. The station was set to orbit the planet, but there were changes to the distances based on orbital variations, and the precise placement of the station on the ground.

The Planet Citadel was golden sand in the black, like a false oasis in the bleak void of darkness and space. The oxygen in the atmosphere and the thin shell of ozone that shielded the planet surface was partially artificially generated by repurposed wreckage turned into algae tanks. Before it was stable, no one was able to walk outside safely without a helmet and a personal tank. When it became stable, the algae tanks were dumped into one of the few bodies of water that had been cultivated from the first ice comet. This first lake became water recycling facilities, and no one could travel too far upon the dry desert plain away from the lake. The monastery built up out of the native granite rock, like a medieval fortress on a desert plain, with the lake walled off on the other side of the mountain from the town. The worship hall was modeled after the Great Mosque of Kairouan in ancient Tunisia. The huge minaret holds the bell that rings the hours, where the call to prayer sings out across the courtyard. Food is sold at a market inside the courtyard daily, brought in from across the planet, wherever enough water accumulated to permit the growth of crops of some sort, often in underground hydroponic systems. It is a sparse world. There are groves of jujube trees where pumps and sand shields keep them alive, in vast thickets of thorns and flowers, slurping water and producing the annual crop of red dates. Desert amaranth grows in fields shielded on all sides by jujubes, pollinated by the winds that tear through the groves. Vegetable patches are often kept in underground tubs, fertilized through fish tanks that house the only livestock on the planet surface: tilapia. Tiny drones handle pollination. Many of our best repairmen retire to build and maintain the fertilization drones.

Anderson wouldn't let me land. He put us down directly in the courtyard of the monastery, right in the middle of the four beautiful walls. No one greeted us there. Sergeant Anderson led us straight to the cafeteria, where food was ready for us in covered pots.

"Do you remember rabbit stew?" said Jensen, with tilapia on her fork and a look of boredom slowing her down despite our hunger.

"I lived on a boat, mostly. We didn't eat a lot of rabbit."

"Oh," she said. "Well, we ate a lot of rabbit stew, when I was a kid. I think about it a lot. Like, am I remembering it better than it actually was? Some of the atheists are all about conspiracy theories. Like, we're all just implanted with memories by the aliens that keep us as some sort of experiment or test case or something. Captin Obasanjo's the worst."

"I don't believe in nonsense," I said. "Memory is good enough to build a life here, and I never thought I would ever be defending the fabric of reality itself with an experienced soldier of humanity. The fish is good. We should see about getting some set up on the station, instead of just trading in powdered, dried flakes. I understand they aren't hard to cultivate once the tanks are adjusted and there's food for them."

We tired quickly. The weight of the planet's gravity, which was heavier than Earth enough to be uncomfortable to us, was exacerbated by our week in zero-gravity on the way down. Sergeant Anderson fell asleep at the table, with his head resting next to his soup. He snored a little.

"You should hear yourself," said Jensen. "We're lucky our sewage pipes work, at all, and you want to bring fish into the system."

Jensen was talking to me as if I were her equal, and for a moment it occurred to me that this is probably the first time an enlisted had done that. I should have realized it was a sign of a problem. Instead, I interpreted that to mean that I was finally establishing myself as an officer.

"Nobody likes the food, Corporal," I said. "Not even the monks who make it like it. I grew up with fresh fish. I wouldn't mind more of it."

"When is the next ice comet scheduled for the terraforming?"

Sergeant Anderson woke up with a start and went back to eating like nothing had happened.

"What was that?" he said. "Did you say something, Corporal?"

Jensen leaned over. "I was asking about the next ice comet, sir."

Sergeant Anderson struggled with his spoon. I watched his hands shaking under the weight of soup in his weakened state and exhaustion. "Not too long," he said.

"Are you all right, Sergeant?"

"I need some more bone supplements, but I'll be fine in a week, sir."

Jensen and I exchanged a look. We both knew he was lying. She wasn't going to say anything, and neither was I. She looked out over the cramped little cafeteria built into the ground below the monastery. "Someday this will be a museum, and kids will visit it and shudder at the conditions we keep. We might as well be on a space station if we're living without windows."

Our rooms were on the second floor. These would have tiny windows, with the best view possible. The windows swept over the orchard, what there was of an orchard. A man in a brown smock and mask strolled across the scene, arms folded, and sweltering hot, measuring air temperature and moisture under the leaves. I assumed, correctly, that it was one of the monks.

Sergeant Anderson stood up and stretched just before our little quarantine ended.

"Ready to go on a tour, Ensign? Our hosts should be back from vespers shortly."

"I can't wait," I said. "What are we touring?"

A knock on the door, and a smiling monk opened it for us without waiting to hear if we were ready for him. Brother Pleo was lean and tan, with scars along his hands and arms. His plain brown monk's habit was woven from strips of reeds and old fish leather. It didn't look comfortable. "Everybody well?"

"The fish was good," said Jensen. "Thanks."

He nodded and paused at me. "I don't believe we've met before," he said. "Brother Pleo. Welcome to our humble planet."

We shook hands, briefly. "Ensign Ronaldo Aldo," I said. "I am in my third year. This is my first time on the surface."

"Welcome, brother, and may you find peace in our humble colony." He led us into a changing area, where we put on masks and gloves over our uniforms. We were encouraged to stay completely covered, day and night, and follow the seminocturnal life of the colony. The days were too hot to work and live. Everyone lived in twilight hours if they could. Outside, around midmorning, it was very warm and getting warmer, with little shade to mitigate the oppressive weight of the star in the sky, blazing down on us. The wind blew sand up from the vast dunes that would cut tiny abrasions into exposed skin. The orchard had an artificial windbreak that helped to provide shelter from sun and sand, but even the trees looked defeated, battered, scraped down.

"The courtyard is the only place we can really keep sand clear long enough to get you down on the ground, but that will change in another few years. Our modeling tools indicate the next ice comet will give us a reasonable-sized lake nearby, not quite an ocean. Once the water's in the system, there's going to be a lot of changes here . . ."

I stopped listening, honestly, because the changes were years away, and modeling software of water systems postintroduction were always so incredibly unreliable. On other colonies, predicted lakes ended up being completely dry, while mountains that looked stable fell over from the sudden collapse of sensitive mineral deposits in the new groundwater. No one truly knows what happens when water comes and sloshes around, evaporates, rains, sinks in. On Mars, it took a century to resolve the air pressure issue, where water would simply evaporate exposed to air, and the natural magnetosphere had to be reinforced against the strong solar winds here, which makes everything stranger. Atmospherics was one of the greatest challenges to terraforming. By comparison, building up a healthy biome of single- and multicellular life was easy.

Instead of listening, I looked over at Sergeant Anderson, who looked terribly sick.

"Are you sure you want the tour, Sergeant?" I whispered. "You've seen it all before, right?"

"I'll be fine," he said. "I just need to sit down for a while and get some more iron and B vitamins."

"You shouldn't spend so much time in flight," I whispered. "Seriously, Sergeant. It's foolish."

"I don't really have a choice," he said. "The admiral has it out for me."

"The admiral has it out for everyone. That's no excuse."

He shrugged. He pointed at the tour guide, Brother Pleo, who had pretended not to notice us ignoring him.

The tour, of course. We were turning the corner to an underground hydroponic farm where all the amaranth we ate was grown in isolation from the world, seed pods fat and hanging off large, spindly plants bred for productivity and self-fertility, not vigor or flavor.

"We hope to develop corn and rye farms on a small scale in the next four years," said Brother Pleo. He reached out and touched the green leaves. "After the amaranth seed is harvested, we will plant our first, experimental seed crop of both, with many different strains to see which is best for our conditions."

Past the hydroponic room, which seemed to break the symmetry of the building and lean out off the side like a clumsy addition, we reached a common area with storage along the walls where two brothers were sorting and folding cloth. I understand they were also engaged in the great debate of the Baha'i heresy. Brothers Mohamed and Dimwu continue to engage in this eternal theological debate. They stopped long enough to shake my hand, and ask after the sergeant's health.

"I'm fine," he said. "Probably get early release soon, at the rate they're flying me in zero-g. Hell, look at me, right?"

Brother Dimwu raised an eyebrow at Jensen. "Where are they putting you, young lady?"

"Wherever you put me. I promise not to seduce the Brotherhood with my womanly wiles."

Brother Mohamed smacked his dour companion. "Pardon my brother. He is a tactless fool and stubborn. You are most welcome, soldier."

"Sara Jensen," she said. "I get called soldier enough."

"There are seventeen brothers in the monastery," said Dimwu. "I need all seventeen. We do not attract as many new members to our life of celibacy and contemplation. It is not your gender that concerns me, Sara Jensen, but your atheism. You have had heated discussions with Brother Pleo in the past. You are just as bad as that annoying officer . . . What is his name, Pleo?"

"Obasanjo, Brother Dimwu. Oyede Obasanjo."

"Yes, the foolish philosopher. Yes. Jensen, you agree with his foolish nihilism. I call you to repent, but I know you will not. At least, please don't start confusing the children of the village with your impossible theories during your stay, and don't bother the brothers during their duties."

"I will say what I like, where I like, Brother. I will say none of it to you."

"Can we cut the tour short, Brother Pleo?" I said. "Just show us beds and food. We have been in low-g for a while and we need to get our strength back slowly before we go on a grand tour of the whole monastery."

"Of course," said Pleo. "It is a grand monastery. The mosque alone is a careful reproduction of a World Heritage Site, and the trees are a thrill on the dunes. I had hardly imagined I'd ever see a tree when I was a boy, and here they are."

Sergeant Anderson looked like he was going to fall over, and Jensen looked like she wanted to hit something. We were tired, and Pleo was not. I suspect he was wearing us out on purpose to keep us out of trouble, later, when the trap sprung.

"I don't care if they don't like me," said Jensen, out of nowhere. "I don't care if you two don't, either."

"We like you just fine," said Sergeant Anderson. "They're a bunch of crusty old fools. They don't even let us download what we like."

"I'm a woman. There are so few of us. Someone will take me in, even if I am hated."

"No one hates you," said Sergeant Anderson. "Ensign Aldo, here? Everyone hates this asshole. Nobody hates you, Sara."

"Hey," I said. "Who hates me?"

She looked up at me with surprise. "You didn't notice? How could you not notice? They hate us all. There is nothing but hate and disgust and shouting and protocol. Everyone hates everything, and nobody is happy, and that's why we average two suicides a year."

"We are colonists on the edge of a galaxy so far from the center of humanity that time itself has slowed down around us," I said. "The future will be green and our grandchildren will plant forests here, and everything is going to be fine. We're tired. We're all tired. We need to rest in a bed for a very long time. We are on vacation, downcycle, and we don't have to do anything but show up when Sergeant Anderson calls us. Obasanjo says he knows where we can get some booze."

"The ensign is right. Calm the fuck down, Corporal. So one monk wants to shut you up, so what? All they do is argue with each other over pointless shit. They're afraid you'll say something sensible. You needed a vacation. Wong was right." He winced. "God, I hate saying that."

She laughed. "Wong is the worst. He will rob you blind and smile, like it's a favor. What did he do to let you downcycle early, Ensign?"

"He never really hit me up for anything," I said. "I don't know what I did to get down here early. Obasanjo thought I needed a break."

"Obasanjo likes you. You haven't slept with him, have you?"

"Of course not. It's against regulations." Also, I prefer women. Beautiful, strong women, with dark hair and dark eyes, sometimes married to someone else, but I would never tell him that.

"Right. Wait until your pay increases, Ensign, and see what Wong says about regulations. He's the admiral's lapdog. When is the next review?"

"The plague slowed it down. As soon as the admiral is cleared for duty, the reviews will start. They'll be going while we're down here, I'm sure."

We reached the first bedroom. "Hell," said Jensen. "I am going to bed." She didn't ask whose room it was. She just took it.

The next one was Sergeant Anderson's, and at the last,

Brother Pleo took my hand. "Morale is very low," he said. "Suicide is a great sin."

"Brother Pleo, I'm not suicidal. No one here is."

"Do you have the power to do anything to make it better?"

"No," I said. I shook my head. "I have no power, Brother Pleo. I have no authority at all."

He assented, sadly, and wished me a good night.

When we woke up, it was evening twilight, and we were still running late from the monk's strict schedule. Food was left for us on the table—three plates with three blobs of nutritional gruel.

Jensen pushed it around with her fork. "I swear to God it wouldn't be so bad if the food wasn't so awful all the time. It's some kind of torture to remember apple pie and chocolate cake and rabbit stew and eat this bland, nutritional goo all the time."

Sergeant Anderson chuckled. "Our wedding cake was awful. Just awful. Remember the cake? Nobody could even eat it. Corporal Miswa was so embarrassed. He just kept pretending it was fine."

Jensen started laughing, then. She laughed and Anderson laughed with her and I sat, apart from them. I kept eating, and remembering Shui Mien and my best friend, and the world they shared just under my nose. People remain a mystery to me, oh confessor. I simply do not understand how people connect and disconnect and see transparently on the surface what is happening in human hearts.

After dinner, I sought out Brother Pleo. He was in one of the daily masses, with all the brothers, chanting and praying. It reminded me of whale songs. I sat in the back, listening and observing. After service, the muzzein climbed the tower to sing the city to evening prayers.

The brothers walked past in their contemplation. I did not know why so few spoke to me, but I am sure I will learn more of the traditions in the years to come. Many did not even look up, so lost in meditation.

Brother Pleo did look up, and I gestured to him politely to speak in private. He sat down next to me, in the back pew.

"I am concerned for Sergeant Anderson's health. Is there a medical technician or emergency medical terminal available to examine him?"

"We have a technician available in the village. It is probably better to wait until you return to the station. Your facilities are much better than ours. Your technicians have the latest training. Our tech is just a retired soldier, with training forty years out of date and challenges with his equipment. With difficult cases, in the recent past, we sent our sick man up to the station for medical care."

"I have my reasons not to desire that at this time, Brother," I said. "A second opinion is never a bad idea in traditional medicine."

"I can arrange an appointment," said Brother Pleo. "Is he amenable to seeing the doctor?"

"Probably not. I outrank him, though. I will tell him. Can the doctor come here?"

"He is not a full doctor, only a technician nurse, like your man up above. Yes, he can come up here."

"Thank you," I said.

"Does he need anything right away?"

"I don't know. I don't believe so. Thank you for your consideration, Brother Pleo."

"We do not lock the doors after dark. It is much more enjoyable to walk the orchard at night. There are flashlights and GPS devices charging near the door, if you would like to see the jujube and acacia fields, where we will be cultivating honey bees soon . . . ?"

"Perhaps another time," I said. "I am not on the proper diurnal schedule for my stay. I need to force it a little bit. How long is the day, the night? I recall a twenty-nine- hour cycle?"

"Twenty-nine point seven three hours. We are negotiating with the city elders to create our own time system. They don't like our muzzein, Brother Mohamed. Or the bells."

"How long until daybreak?"

"About seven hours, give or take. This is summer. The days are very long, and can get very hot. You've woken up to the hottest part of the day. Don't overexert yourself until you are accustomed to it, Ensign. Make yourself at home here, and wait until nightfall."

"Thank you, Brother," I said.

He shook my hand to tell me that the conversation was over. He had other duties, and I was keeping him from them, of course. Officers are always an inconvenience to the people who actually do the work.

The rooms were small and narrow novice chambers, but they all had windows out over to the city built into the rock itself. Bits of red and green cloth were really all that truly distinguished the carved stones of the village from the stone ground and blowing dunes. I sat in the room, feeling the strange weight of dry, warm air in that enclosed space, which lacked the familiar damp and dank of algae recycling tanks and recycled air over the very tanks that processed our bodily wastes. The station always had that smell, just below the threshold of our active noses, of algae and sewage and cleaning supplies that tried to mask it all. It was like living in a meticulously clean bathroom, in a hospital somewhere. I did not realize it until I sat in that room that smelled of dust and dry, hot wind. I remember the way oceans smelled just after a rainstorm. Memory is the story we tell ourselves, and it is a story of loss that feeds our suffering in the absence of all the great comforts of the Terran system.

I did walk the orchard that night. Restless, I went back on my word to Brother Pleo and found the lamps and flashlights and GPS trackers. There were many empty hooks. I was not alone in the orchard. Irrigation lines ran dripping all night to slowly soak into the root zones. Field workers walked the lines, clearing out blown sand among the living ground covers with huge brooms. I did not recognize any of the plants, except the ones Pleo had identified. I was born at sea, and I knew only the sea and what vegetables and fruits could be found in cans and frozen bags. The brothers waved to me. Out at the edge of the fields, I ran my hands gently across the windbreaks that kept the worst of the dunes of sand from swelling over the trees and swallowing everything. The vast plains beyond rose and fell, empty and desolate. There were mountains, somewhere, and earthquakes and groundwater sinking in, destabilizing everything. People lived out there, in the far dune seas of this world, as isolated as I had been as a child on my parents' boat. Out past the windbreaks, a single light shone in the windy dunes. I stared at it awhile, imagining what could bring someone to go walking out there in the shifting sands. The light flipped off by itself. If the person was in trouble, they could just push an alarm button on their GPS or their flashlight, or even just call on to the mainframe on any handheld or wearable, if they had one. In this wind, they could even shout. There were enough workers ready to hear and help. I was weak and tired and feeling all my days in zero-g before landing. I thought nothing of the light in the dunes.

It was probably Jensen.

I never spoke of it before. My career was clouded enough without this tiny revelation, and I guess it was my duty to report what I saw, and I omitted it. Not my greatest sin, but still, I am here to confess them all.

By daylight, I was asleep, and woke up when Brother Pleo knocked on my door. "The medical technician is here, Ensign. Sergeant Anderson is not amused. Did you talk to him?"

"On my way," I said. Dragging myself from bed, exhausted and thirsty, I splashed cold water in my face, drank cold water, and got dressed quickly.

Sergeant Anderson was already awake, sitting in the common room drinking red jujube tea. He was stiff and pale and furious. A man in plain denim stood apart from him, nervously tapping his foot.

"Sergeant Anderson, are you amenable to a quick medical exam?"

"I'm fine, Ensign."

"I'm sure you are . . ."

"Then why call the damn technician? I don't need a nurse. I'm fine."

"Sergeant Anderson, as a pilot talking to a pilot, I am concerned. You are displaying what appear to be symptoms, and I want a med tech that doesn't answer to the admiral to check you out, okay? If I'm wrong, I'm wrong. We are still waiting for the contract negotiations to clear, and our shipment to load up. You will lose a few hours, nothing more, and it could keep you on track if you are cleared."

"Can we talk in private, Ensign?"

"My room," I said.

He stood up slowly, and walked gingerly to the room. He winced when he sat down on the edge of my bed.

I closed the door.

"Of course, I have zero-g issues. Of course I do."

"You will get time planetside, possibly early release. Isn't that what you want?"

"No," he said. "It's what the admiral wants. I pissed him off once and he never forgave me. I got married. I brought her down to the planet and did it behind everyone's back. I created paperwork and the need for a separate quarters for us both when I was in station, causing new cycling issues for the biotic crew. I did it without clearing it. We would not have been granted permission, Ensign. The military frowns on families until after retirement. I'll retire. She'll be up there. It's his goddamn revenge."

"With early release, you will have to wait until the end of her assignment to see her, at all. That's it. That makes sense."

He folded his hands. "Don't let the bastards win, Ensign. Please, don't."

"Your health could be in serious danger. Without treatment, you may not be any use to your wife at all when you retire to your homestead. No digging. No shoveling. No lifting or walking."

"Ensign, whose side are you on?"

"I'm not on anyone's side, Sergeant. I am not political. I am just concerned for your health. We can arrange some time down here to recover, and I can pick you up on the next supply line. I am in command, and can talk to the monastery. We do not have to force early release unless it is absolutely necessary. I don't want you to experience a medical disaster when the station relies upon you. Think of your duty, Sergeant. If you lose blood pressure and pass out on a supply run, what happens, then? AI aren't permitted to develop enough intelligence to navigate independently. You would be floating until someone comes to get you—me—and you might not even survive. You'd throw the supply chain out for months. I am concerned about the crew on that station, up there, all of them. I am not political, and I am not scheming. You had trouble holding your fork at dinner, Sergeant."

He didn't say anything.

"This is off the records, okay? You will be examined in private. No one needs to know but you and me and the tech if there's something wrong, and we will find a solution that is best for the whole Citadel, Sergeant. Nobody 'wins' in my command. We aren't playing a game, out here. I don't play games with people's lives. I don't do that. Not me."

"If nobody wins, everyone loses. Especially you, Ensign. Send the goddamn tech in here, and let's get this over with. Goddamn. Good goddamn you're stubborn. Goddamn."

The tech was tired. He had huge circles under his eyes, and dust on his clothes. "He don't like me none, do he?"

"He doesn't like anyone, but he will see you. Go on."

"Anything in particular you want me took for, Ensign?"

"Just do an examination. Discretion is critical. He is a proud man, and there are, apparently, political complications. Let's keep this by the book, okay?"

"You got it, Captain."

"Ensign," I said. "I'm still pretty new."

"Want me to check you out, too?"

"I don't fly much. Maybe in a few years."

I waited in the cafeteria. Monks passed through, some chatting on obscure things, others silent and nodding. I did not see Jensen anywhere, but her recreation was her business. Likely she had left the monastery for some place nearby where she could be free of their derision for her heretical ideas. She probably knew some of the retired personnel on the ground, and was filling them all in about the latest gossip from the station. Undoubtedly, word had gotten around that Xavier died on my first flight.

The tech returned with a grim look. He said he was sending his findings to the military tech to confirm the diagnosis.

I nodded at him. "Am I correct in thinking he has spent too much time in zero-gravity?"

"His bone density is fine. He has been exercising and taking supplements. But his tendons are really loose, and he could blow a knee out just walking too fast. More than that, he has Yakusaki syndrome. His involuntary muscles are too weak. He is having trouble keeping his blood pressure up and swallowing food. We need to keep him in bed for a while until he can recover his vascular strength. His heart is really weak. Ensign, I don't think he should go back with you to the station. Every minute for him in zero-gravity is potentially going to push him into cardiovascular collapse."

"I will support whatever decision the station medical tech makes regarding the sergeant's treatment. I wish my suspicion wasn't accurate."

"Anyone could see it. Was someone trying to kill him with all that flying? He told me his schedule . . ."

"The admiral always has good reasons for his decisions. There are more concerns in space than a single soldier's health.

We are not here on the ground, where a whole atmosphere protects us."

"Still, he could have died if he had kept flying."

"He knew that," I said. "He knew better than anyone. He is not going to die, though, is he?"

"No," said the tech. "The syndrome was caught in time. I've already got my cardio machine coming up from the house to get his veins going stronger."

"Thank you for coming. I appreciate your time."

I knocked on the sergeant's door. He called me in.

"Bullshit," he said.

"It isn't up to me what happens, next. Not even the admiral and HR in concert can overrule a medical diagnosis like this one. It goes up the ansible and back, and everyone takes what it says, period."

"You think I didn't know?"

"Suicide will not help you start a family with your beautiful wife."

"Do me a favor. I am not supposed to move. Get out of here before I get up and kick your ass."

"Of course, Sergeant."

I left for the town. What was I supposed to do, while I waited for the contracts to clear through Obasanjo? I went for a walk in the sun, and it was very, very hot and I had to stop and rest and peel my uniform off my back, lean into shade, and observe the empty village. Sunset was coming, and people were dusting off the solar panels and watering scrubby acacia trees and vegetable gardens with irrigation pulled from the monastery tanks. People saw me, and I saw them, but no one came over. A man was hanging cloth out to dry on a line. I felt a hum of insects: wild miner bees, black flies, and sweat beetles. They were brought with the trees to aid in decomposition of organic matter and pollination, but they weren't enough. Buzzing with them were the pollination drones. They all came for me in the shade, where my back was wet with salt and sweat. The man waved me over when he saw me swatting.

"Hi," he said. "You military?"

"I am. Are you?"

"Retired," he said. He was an older man, with a hard, muscular frame. He was hanging wet blankets up to dry. He reached into his basket and held out a bottle for me. "Put some block on, or you'll cook like red meat, kid."

"Thanks." It was hard to get it on with the sweat, but he invited me inside to cool off, too. "Corporal Garcia, retired," he said, with one hand out. "Call me Jack. My daughter is boiling water for tea on the roof. She'll be down. Her name is Amanda."

I shook his hand, and he was much stronger than me, and I felt like a kid in his grip, without any real knowledge about the lay of the land, the customs of the place. "I am Ensign Ronaldo Aldo. I am the new AstroNav."

"Not a lot of need for war pilots out here. Not much to steal and nowhere to take it. No sign of the enemy in a hundred years. Mostly jujube trees, and some cucurbits and peppers and buffalo grass. Acacias for the nitrogen and wood pulp. Amaranth in every garden. Lots of sand. Lots and lots of sand. We won't be green enough for a real colony for two hundred years."

I made a noise of noncommittal in my throat, neither agree nor disagree. I changed the subject. "How do they keep the windbreaks from getting swallowed by a dune?"

"We dig them out every couple days with tractors. Come

on, I'll get you some water. You need to drink more water, Ensign."

I accepted his invitation because I didn't know what else to do with my time, and I was thirsty. He led me in deeper, away from the heat of the front wall, and it took me a few minutes for my eyes to adjust to the darkness. It smelled earthy, not dusty, and there was a damp in the air. A fish tank was pumping water through a hydroponic rack in the corner, and it filled the room with the smell of life. Everything was stone and recycled plastic, gray and dusty brown and worn from years of use and repair. He pulled a chair out for me. "Windbreaks," he said. "I spend every night at the windbreaks. We dig it out in teams with heavy machinery if it gets bad. The monastery has a few backhoes in storage. I have to go through and clean out the joints afterward, get all the sand out of them. That's what I do, these days. I used to be under Q."

"I haven't seen a high level of technology here. It's like something out of climate crisis history, all these desert huts and so few trees . . ."

He pulled water from a tank in the wall. He handed me a mug of it. "Terraforming takes time, unless you want to risk getting a lot of people killed. We do fine, Ensign. Don't say dumb shit. We work hard for this ball of dirt, and we don't want some smarmy officer talking shit about our home."

"Sorry," I said. I took a sip of the water. It was clean and warm. "I'm sorry. Honestly, all anyone talks about on the station is how difficult it is down here. It isn't exactly easy up there, either. It's our home, of course. But I admit that it is a challenging post for everyone."

"My wife used to say that anything worth doing is going to be hard work."

"She sounds like a smart woman. I will remember that when I meet her."

"She's been dead a long time."

I opened my mouth, looking for something to say. I took a long drink of water instead.

My eyes came around, and I considered the man in the dark hut. Jack Garcia was a lean, hard man, with a deep tan. He had thick black hair that fell down his back in ropy braids. He was looking at me with a sad smile.

"I'm sorry about your wife," I said.

"It was a long time ago. It's fine. Down here, everybody knows everybody's business. It's a small community. You can't change your underpants, people don't hear about it. It's always nice to meet new people."

His daughter came in from a door that led to a stairwell with a hot, heavy pot. She was wrapped head to toe in cloth with nothing but her eyes showing. She placed the pot down and looked at me, pausing and confused. She peeled back the sun-bleached cloth, a face beneath long and smooth, and surprised. "Uh . . . Hello? I don't know you. We haven't met. New clone?"

She began peeling back more layers. First her gloves, then her mask. She was dark and beautiful, with pale blue eyes. Her hair was a dirty blond cotton puff with red streaks. She held out her hand. "Amanda," she said. "You're down from the station. You're new."

I took it, gently. "I am. Ensign Ronaldo Aldo. A pleasure."

"I'm Amanda Garcia. Tea?" She rummaged in cupboards for cups. "Usually don't see visitors during the day. You really should stay out of the sun. High UV here. You can get really burned. You look red around the edges."

The tea was made from a mash of jujube and some green

herbs. It was sweet and medicinal and disgusting.

"Thank you," I said. "It is very good."

"I can tell you're lying," said Jack. "You remember real coffee, right?"

"I do, and spiced chai with real coconut cream. The tea is still as good as can be expected until the next ice comet comes and we can expand our agricultural base. I am grateful for it."

"That is a good attitude to have, Ensign Aldo," said Amanda. "I heard about you from Q, you know."

"Did you?"

Amanda sat down beside her father. She blew on the hot beverage to cool it, then put it down beside her. She had been up in the heat just now, covered in cloth. She had no desire to drink her tea until it cooled. Even I was sipping to be polite. I was still sweating.

"Do you want to know what Q told me?"

"I prefer not to play gossip games, Ms. Garcia. It hurts the mission. Keep it to yourself, if you like. I don't mind not knowing."

Honestly, I didn't care what Q thought of me. He hadn't minded the molestation of a new crewmember. To me, anyone who didn't care about that was welcome to their own opinion about everyone.

Jack Garcia took over. "He's my old boss. He told us you were very green, and probably had no idea how to establish yourself on the planet, for your retirement."

"I think retirement is fairly distant, and I have responsibilities on the station, first."

"Do you think you will be promoted to transcend?" said Amanda. "Dad says sometimes officers get to be cloned again across the ansible."

"It isn't up to me what happens." It occurred to me, quite suddenly, that if Corporal Garcia was in touch with Q, this could be a far more important meeting than I expected. Without a war to fight, we turned our eyes and mouths inward, jockeying among ourselves for pride and position. I did not understand the politics of the station, but I did realize, even then, that politics could make or break my ability to transcend. My gut reaction was to avoid it all. I did not realize that this was being interpreted politically, not as what it was: a willful ignorance and an attempt to avoid all politics. Every noncommittal expression sealed my fate as a very politically motivated officer, and all I wanted was not to offend anyone.

"Good luck with your review, Ensign," he said. "I hear you're gonna need it. Amanda, you think you can take the ensign on a tour of the planet? I think he could use some sightseeing."

"Do I have time to babysit him? I have actual work to do, Dad. I've got seeds to start in the basement, and I'm working on the sewing for the windbreak."

"I can do that, Amanda. Why can't I do that?"

She rolled her eyes. "You kill plants, Dad."

"I can do the sewing, at least. Ensign Aldo, if you want a taste of the future, you can go plant some seeds with us. Have you ever planted any seeds?"

"The kitchen grows a little watercress, but I've never seen it. I grew up on a boat in the Pacific gyre, Corporal. I have seen fish, but no seaweed."

Amanda looked at me with a squint. "Seaweed?"

"Plants that live in the sea, underwater."

"Oh," she said. "Like coral, right?"

"No," I said. "Like spinach, but saltier. Thank you for the water, Corporal. I have little else to do, today. I appreciate your hospitality."

"We like to see new people," said Corporal Garcia. "Always nice to see new people. Plus, you can earn your keep."

Amanda stood up and held out her hand. "That's right," she said. "Are you going to help me plant or not?" Her hands were so long. She had such rough, long, powerful hands, and I was afraid to take her hand. I looked at it, and thought that taking it would only make my smooth, space station palms, sweaty and limp, like a dead fish to her vigorous heat.

I got up without taking her hand. I handed her the tea mug instead. It was such an awkward moment. She looked down at the mug, confused for just a moment that I had handed it to her. Then, she turned away suddenly and placed it in a tub near the drinking tank. She was taller than me, but not much taller. Her hair and skin smelled like sand, even from where I stood. Her sand-colored skin, her sand-blasted hair, and her brown eyes made me wonder what her mother was like. She was much lighter than her father.

She led me downstairs to a large basement, an underground farm. Most of the things she grew were destined for the compost pile. They composted 75 percent of everything. Ten percent of the rest went to the fish. Soil was a precious commodity, in a desert. They were growing soil. We talked a little while we worked, mostly her explaining how to do it right, and what it was for. We didn't talk about anything personal. Afterward, her father was sewing, and we went to him.

———

"Which one do I take?" she asked him. "I don't want the Osprey."

"Fine. Take the Hemi. Have a good time. He's a pilot. He can handle a few bumps." He reached into his pocket and tossed keys to her. She caught them.

I couldn't, for the life of me, imagine a vehicle here that required something as archaic as keys. When I followed her downstairs, into the basement, she threw a tarp off a huge pile of lumps of metal and revealed a monstrosity. "My grandmother built it out of dead tractor parts, then Dad reconfigured it when he was betrothed into the family. It's the best way to travel over the dunes. The Ospreys struggle with the winds and drafts."

It was a beast of cobbled pieces, to be sure, but it was a polished beast, with shining chrome plates and reflective paint cooling off the joints from the beating of the sunlight. She paused before opening the door for me.

"There are currently thirteen unmarried women on the whole colony. They have all fielded numerous marriage propositions. My father has advised me to be very strategic and consider the future."

I did not say anything. What could I say? I had never lain with a woman, and I knew nothing of the mystery of their hearts.

"Don't propose over a ride in a Hemi, Ensign Aldo. Don't misinterpret this."

"I honestly confess to confusion in the whole affair. It is very hot. Do we have water to take with us?"

"We have some leftover tea. It will get stale quickly, but we must not waste it. I hope you are eliminating in the approved receptacles. Let me give you the tour of the beast." She popped open the hood and the inner workings exposed to air. Compressed air forced through joints and axels to push out any hidden grit. It was a cool, dry blast across my face. "The bathroom is in back. There is a sheet you can pull across for privacy. Dad will empty it into the septic, later. Water is precious. Do not waste water."

"I understand," I said. "I sweated so much, I cannot imagine anything happening soon. Must we discuss this?"

"Do not waste water. The ice comets aren't here yet. Let me show you the finger mountain. Strap in."

The seat was a modified pilot seat. The straps were probably older than everyone I knew, but they would work well enough. The engine was an ancient, biodiesel hack job, put together from spare parts. It was supplemented with solar, an electric battery, and even some tiny wind turbines generating energy out of resistance. It was an odd vehicle, and ugly, but Amanda was clearly excited to be driving. She revved the engine and cheered. A panel opened in the wall large enough to fit a spaceship through, and she pushed out away from the settlement and the buildings hunkered in against it.

We rambled downhill, bumping and grinding over the sand at high speed, dodging rocks. It was fun. I wanted to drive. Next time, I'd ask to be the driver. The dunes stretched out as far as the eye could see, once we got down to the valley floor.

She slowed the Hemi and gestured with her hand at the grand vistas of sand. "Doesn't look like much yet, does it? But the multimineral sand is excellent raw material once terraforming really warms up with more water. This will all be underwater, someday. Projections suggest forming a coral reef here, if we can get some coral polyps off the ansible."

"Terraforming projections are notoriously fickle," I said. "Onast was supposed to be an ocean world, but the water actually sank straight down into tiny holes in the crust where they became superheated. Now it is dangerous to walk the surface with all the erupting hot springs. Once water enters the system on a large scale, every projection is a rough guess at best."

"We have to plan land management and ownership around the projections. Most of the projections are right most of the time. Otherwise, why even place the monastery anywhere on the surface?"

"Perhaps you are right," I said. "We cannot hold our breath forever, waiting for stability. The station needs the colony for food and raw materials. The colony needs the station for colonists, advanced equipment, and ansible access."

"Do you like it on the station?"

I hesitated too long before answering. "It is an excellent posting. We are the vanguard against the enemy's return."

"Dad says it's a nightmare posting and ceremonial, mostly, but once you're out, you get in early on the real estate down here. Once the planet has the water for it, fortunes will grow for anyone who gets in early on the best land."

"How much land do you own?"

"I don't own anything yet. I have to save more, but the monastery doesn't pay that well beyond just food and water. My dad owns as much as he can afford, and we try to get more but there are regulations about how much any one person can own. We are almost at the finger mountain. Hang on." She turned toward something, but I didn't see anything mountainous. I waited for an explanation. We came over a dune and stopped, suddenly. The sand leveled out, and became rocks. Ahead, the ground dropped suddenly.

"Come on," she said. She hopped out and flipped up her hood and mask. She pulled a sack out of the side and threw it at me. It was a cool suit, an ice pack inside a full cover overcoat with a hood like hers. I pulled it over my uniform and flipped up the hood. "Borrow eye protection from the monastery, next time. You need goggles."

She bounded over to the edge and pointed over the side of the cliff.

"Check it out! The mountain is right there!"

I walked over carefully. The wind was strong. Gusts swept up from the cliff and pushed against my face. At least the wind pushed me back from the edge, not toward it. At the edge of the cliff, over the edge, a steep drop for miles and miles like an undersea trench. It was a fault line. The other side of the trench was far lower than this cliff side. Down below, a piece of our own cliff had snapped off and leaned over a little, becoming a thin mountain just below and apart from the cliff face, a huge edifice of golden sandstone upon a black, igneous plain. The fault continued on in both directions as far as I could see.

The wind gusted. Vertigo set in.

"When the next comet comes, this will become a river, flowing around the mountain. The one after that will be big enough to make this a vast lake. Then, we will probably not be around to see the third, but our great-grandchildren will fish in boats and waders in the marshland just above this cliff through the water that will come up to their waists, here, on this long plain. They will gaze down through the clear blue to the mountain, there. It will be so beautiful and blue. I have never seen an ocean. I hope I live long enough to see an ocean."

I did not want to explain that an ocean of dunes was, in many ways, the same. I pointed at the base of the pillar. A tent was set up. The reflecting lights of solar catchment revealed it to me, a mile below my eyes.

"What is that?" I said.

"I don't know," said Amanda. "Come on. Let's find out. They might need help. It looks like an emergency kit."

"How do we get down there?" I said.

"We call the Osprey. It's got an automatic pilot. See if you can find a network band to reach a signal down there."

Amanda got on the horn to the monastery and her father. I thought I recognized something about the equipment. On a hunch, I called Jensen.

There was no answer.

I left a message.

"I am at something called the finger mountain, on a tour with a local. There's a tent. Is it yours? Call me back immediately."

Instead of calling me right back, Jensen climbed out of the tent and searched the cliffs for us. She found us. She waved. I could barely see her, but the uniform was distinctive, as was the long hair.

Then, she called me back.

"What are you doing out here?"

"Checking on you. Are you all right? What is your water situation?"

"I am camping. I am fine. Please leave me alone."

Amanda grabbed my tablet like she owned it and went private line. "You are not authorized out here. You are way out of the safe zone. A dust storm could blow you away. You need to relocate. Don't be stubborn about this."

A pause.

"This is Amanda Garcia, not Jeremy. My dad is coming in an Osprey. We will help you relocate your campsite to unaffiliated land—*safe* land." She slammed the phone down.

"Did she say anything?"

"She says she isn't going anywhere. She wants us to go. When are you going back up to the station?"

"Captain Obasanjo should complete his supply negotiations shortly, and then we will oversee our pack and stack and calculate the lift."

"They have weeks to have negotiated until the orbital slow-down. Why does it take so long?" She had ropes in hand from a container on the side. She was bolting them to the vehicle for ballast.

"I am led to believe much of it is for show. It is the closest thing to a vacation most of us get, and it gives the monastery an opportunity to charge for our room and board and attempt to convert us."

"The fools. Dad goes to service, but a few of the monks don't even want me in the pews."

"Why?"

"I might tell you someday," she said. "Come on, and let's go down and talk some sense into your corporal. She could get swallowed into the sand down there if there's one bad night."

I placed my hand on Amanda's. "Hold up. Is she in mortal peril right now?"

"No," she said.

"How long until your dad gets here?"

"Soon. Less than an hour."

I scanned the horizon. "We will wait here for your father. No need to risk our necks climbing down there when we can just as easily wait an hour. Okay? Relax, Amanda. I will call her and talk to her. Hand me my tablet back, please."

The signal reached out to the computer down below, and it rang.

"What?" said Jensen.

"Corporal, I have been told that your campsite is dangerous. Why are you camping in a dangerous location?"

"Ensign Aldo?"

"Yes," I said.

"The Garcia boy got his claws on you, did he?"

"I don't know what you mean by claws. We were out for a drive to see the planet a little. It seemed more interesting than sitting in a monastic cell. Tell me, Jensen, why aren't you sitting in a monastic cell? What are you doing out here?"

"Camping," she said. "We aren't due back yet, are we? I haven't heard anything from anyone."

"Corporal, this is not a safe activity."

"Yeah, well, so what? I am safe so far. The whole planet is dangerous. It's one dust storm away from burying everyone. It is why the monastery keeps military-grade shielding in good repair. I have pickup soon. I just needed some time to myself to think."

"Corporal, the Osprey is coming. When it gets here, I want you to get on it and go with Corporal Garcia. Pack up your campsite. Prepare for pickup."

"Ensign, call Wong, okay? Just call him."

"Are we even in perigee to the station right now? I only have the tablet."

"Please, Ensign. It's your fault. You said you weren't recording, but you were. So call Wong and call off the Osprey. My pickup is coming soon enough."

I hung up. I gestured to Amanda. "Right," I said. "Let's get the ropes. We may need to bind her when we get there. Have you ever had any basic combat training from your dad? He's ex-military."

Amanda got a wicked grin of shock on her face and started setting up the ropes. "I've never punched anyone. I can get you down there, though." She was excited. She was a kid on her first military assignment, experiencing an excitement she never knew among the seedlings.

I checked my handheld to see if we were in reasonable perigee with the station to get a signal up without crossing the monastery's lines. I sent a message to Obasanjo that I thought Jensen was going AWOL and Wong was helping her. It would take about fifteen minutes to get up to his desk, and he might not be watching his messages.

Amanda got the ropes set up and helped me tie into a harness. She had a small machine that would do most of the work. All I had to do was keep my legs out and push off. It was a long and windy way down. We strapped on helmets, goggles, and masks. She checked me twice, and then gave me a thumbs up. She jumped over the edge with a whoop. I took my time easing over, and the device grabbed my weight. The rock face was hot and jagged. My boots had no easy purchase. Beside me, Amanda was already nearly at the bottom, and I was gently easing down.

At the bottom, I heard shouting. My handheld rang with a very weak signal, and it was Wong.

I let it go. Near the bottom, a message came through from Wong:

*Retrieve the corporal, if you can. I do not know what she thinks she is doing, but we cannot allow her to go AWOL in the dunes. She'll die out there.*

I sent it along to Jensen. Nearly at the bottom, I turned and saw Amanda on the ground, bolting her long rope line to the wall to keep it in place for the ascent.

"The two things that matter most on this world are water and sand," said Amanda. She pointed at the little camp. There was a huge tank of water, as big as the tent beside it. There was a small shield device, as well, to discourage sand buildup, with an emergency fan on a generator blowing sand away from the campsite, but this would be useless against a sandstorm. Wedged as she was between the base of the finger mountain and the cliff, she had some protection from the elements, but the precariousness of her campsite was driven home by the unstable sand beneath my own boots. It was hard to walk here, like a beach with the water pulling sand always away underfoot. But it wasn't water underneath, just sand and more sand with bits of black igneous rock jutting out in crags, and some footsteps didn't sink and others did. The ground itself was political, negotiating weights and alliances, shifting underfoot. I considered carefully what Wong was telling me. Officially, of course, he had to say that. If you can, if I can, if . . .

*What if I can't catch her?*

I did not wait for a response. I called out to Corporal Jensen. I released the rope device from my hip and walked around the perimeter of the encampment.

"Be careful," said Amanda. She went around the other way, holding on to a bolt gun like it could be used as a weapon, but it was a safety-locked tool not permitted to fire at a person. It was little better than a club.

"Goddamnit, Jeremy," said Jensen, from inside. "Ensign Aldo, please. Please just leave me alone." She came out of the tent dressed like a nomad, covered head to toe against the sand. She wasn't armed.

"Stop calling me Jeremy," said Amanda.

"Who are you if you aren't Jeremy?"

"Amanda. I'm not Jeremy anymore."

She snorted. "Well, that's nice. 'A man, duh.' I get it. Ensign, did you contact Wong?"

"Where did all this stuff come from? This is not casual camping gear. The monastery doesn't just have this much water sitting around."

"They don't. I told you to contact Wong and ask him what he says. He outranks you."

"I did. You are coming with me. That's what he said."

"I will not go back, Corporal. I will not."

She turned back into her tent. I followed in after her, wary of any surprises. It was just her, sitting on a bench and looking up at me. She was crying.

"Wong got paid, either way," she said. "That's right, isn't it? And if you get me back, it's your fault, not his. If you don't, it's your fault, too. He really fucked you, Ensign."

"Corporal Jensen, this is not a safe campsite. When Mr. Garcia gets here, we will relocate you back to the monastery. We will discuss your situation from there with the admiral. Am I being clear?"

I heard the sound of an Osprey getting closer.

She looked up toward it, though we could see nothing through the thick tent.

"The Garcias are notorious. Watch yourself."

"Notorious for what, exactly?"

"They want land. They can only buy so much, legally. They are always looking for ways to get more. Amanda used to be Jeremy. I don't know what that's about, or how far into the surgery she went. Watch yourself."

"Are you coming with us?"

"I am getting on that Osprey," she said. "Let me just get my kit together in private. Where would I run? Without water, I wouldn't last half a day."

We stood there, staring at each other.

"The Osprey is here," she said.

"Corporal, if Wong has done something against the martial code, there are ways to handle that. Speak with his commander. Go to the quartermaster, your own commander. There is chain of command."

She laughed at that. She smacked her knee. She looked up at the sound of the flying vehicle, and grabbed a small sack of personal items from under a couch. "That's my ride," she said. She moved fast, then, jumping out the back of the tent, where I didn't even know there was a door.

Amanda grabbed at her, but Jensen threw her off into the sand. The Osprey landed, but it wasn't Garcia flying it. It was Brother Pleo. He waved at me and winked, and in a moment, Jensen was on the cargo bay and off the ground.

I cocked my head, curious at what had just transpired.

Amanda pointed up. "That's not my father's Osprey. That's the monastery's!"

"Did he send them instead?"

She didn't know.

I checked my messages. While I was looking, I got a response from Wong:

*That would be too bad. I hope she comes back on her own.*

Of course, he hopes no such thing.

This was the moment I truly hated Wong. He had his revenge on me, by conspiring with Obasanjo to send me to the surface. I would be in command of the loss of Corporal Jensen.

I called the monastery, and Brother Phong answered.

"Where is Brother Pleo?" I said. "I was told this was his number."

"He is not at his desk, at present. May I help you?"

"Where is he right now?"

"I don't have that information, Ensign. I can leave a message for him."

"Do monks have handhelds?"

"Oh, no. That is against our vows of poverty and contemplation. No. We do not."

"Does the Osprey he was flying a second ago . . ." I took a long, deep breath, trying to remain calm. "Does that have a protocol I can reach?

"I am not aware of any Osprey flying. Are you suffering from heat stroke, Ensign? Do you need us to arrange a pickup?"

Garcia arrived, then, and Amanda waved him down. He surveyed the scene while Amanda filled him in. He thought it was hilarious. His big belly laugh annoyed me.

"I'm fine," I said, when he asked.

I sent a note to Obasanjo.

*I believe Corporal Jensen is deserting with the aid of the monastery. We need to file a complaint. She was just evacuated from where I found her by Brother Pleo in an Osprey owned by the monastery. I am being stonewalled by Wong. He knows. Please advise.*

Mr. Garcia waved me over. "Exciting day," he said. "I thought you'd be interested in visiting the mountain." He tapped the water tank. "Something funny was going on."

"If you knew, you should have told me from the beginning."

He shrugged. "Politics, man. I avoid it. The monastery is always pushing the military around. The military is pushing the monastery. Both are trying to be the kings of this hole. It's a waste of time. There's so much land out here. Come on, help me load up. We can sell this crap back to the monastery and keep the water in our own tanks. I'll split you in on a quarter if you help with the lifting."

Amanda was already loading up.

While her dad was folding a tent, and we were working on the hose for the water line, she stopped suddenly and walked over to me and put her hand next to mine on the hose.

"Hey," she said. "About me. I want you to know something, okay?"

"I am busy trying to figure out how to get my AWOL soldier back to space, Amanda. I just want to get back to the monastery and find my missing soldier. That is the only thing my brain is thinking about right now, okay? Can you help me with that?"

"I don't know. Okay, but, listen. Amanda was my mother's name. I wasn't born with it. I've had a lot of surgery. A lot of people in the monastery don't accept me, but I always knew what I was, and it cost us both a lot to get the ansible time for surgical tools, and I hoped meeting someone who didn't know me before . . ."

I turned to her. To me, it wasn't important. Is it sinful to say that I found her attractive? I admit that I did. She was beautiful in her desolated way, with her long limbs and long nose and red-sand cotton hair and all windswept.

"Amanda, I don't care about any of that. You are who you are, and it's not important to worry about it. This isn't the time to talk about it, either."

Obasanjo sent me back a message.

*They are definitely stalling me, too. They'd love nothing more than to convert the whole station into a peaceful ansible for their ministry. They don't think we even need a military presence here. Do you have evidence against them? Against Brother Pleo?*

*Brother Pleo was flying the Osprey that picked her up. I didn't get a picture of him. The campsite is well provisioned.*

*No pictures, though? Next time, get a picture. Look for serial numbers on the stuff. Get pictures of them. Send to me, not the admiral and not Wong. Me me me. I am the only one who can stop their reckless shenanigans. The war effort must not be compromised by self-indulgent pacifist assholes!*

I snapped pictures of serial numbers from the campsite, as I was able, and sent them all up the network line to Obasanjo. Nothing would come of it, of course, but it felt like I was doing something to help the investigation.

If anything, I was fueling leverage for negotiations with the monastery. I was securing more shriveled red jujubes, and more frozen vegetables, more amaranth grain, and more boarding space for soldiers seeking vacation from the difficult conditions in space.

As night finally fell, Amanda and I were following the rope

line up from the bottom of the mountain, to the top, where the Hemi waited for us, patiently, holding our ropes. Amanda smiled at the slow sunset over the vast plains. She was born here, to this desert and this way of life. Her mother was dead and buried here. Her father longed for an empire of water and trees. It was hard not to see the lines on her face where the starlight pushed through to skin and tanned her natural brown to something deeper. It was hard not to think that there might be a future down here, after all, and maybe Jensen wasn't so crazy to just walk away from the void above.

Amanda turned to me and smiled a siren's smile. She was tough and athletic and young and there was a ghost of the boy in her movements, if I knew to look. I never bothered to think about it, I must confess. She was what she said she was, and there are plenty of ways to procure children that humanity long ago stopped concerning with the traditional concept outside of lingering religious strictures. Even those seemed to ebb and flow with the ministers. If this ministry, here, spurns Amanda as she has spurned me, then this will hold my heart apart from the community of brothers.

I saw a future in that sunlight, with Amanda, on that day where I knew my career in space was damaged badly, again. I don't know what I would have done without that hope on the ground. I needed time for my plan to form.

I flew back alone, with a full hold. Jensen was missing, and the monastery was stonewalling us. Sergeant Anderson was on medical leave on the ground and could not enter zero-gravity for at least ninety days, possibly more.

The admiral told me he needed me to come in to meet with him when I returned.

The stars in the sky, the huge black veil of void between

galaxies, and the gorgeous golden star at the heart of this system all soothed my pit of dread with their eternity. I felt so small in that little ship, alone. I felt like I was not even remotely aware of the vastness of everything, and it was all so vast. Floating through the dark, observing my ascent past the gravity well of the planet, at escape velocity, I cut a clean delta vee toward rendezvous with the docking bay and coasted the rest of the way, with only minor correctives. It was the best flight I had ever accomplished, using the least resources, and I swooped in straight to the docking bay connection in a direct line. The thrusting microwave engines pushed against my flight, gently slowing me to a precise connect, not even a bump or a twinge. I wanted this to be on record, my perfect flight.

The quartermaster met me at the door. "I have been sent to relieve you of duty pending an investigation. Hand over your tablet, please."

I cocked my head. I handed over my device.

"Corporal Jensen is not aboard. Sergeant Anderson is not aboard. Just you. Is that correct?"

"Yes," I said.

"The admiral is furious. You understand?"

"No, I don't. I tried to stop Jensen. And Anderson was so sick he could barely walk."

"Excuses won't help you now, Ensign. Come on."

I wasn't led to the admiral's office. I was led to the brig. Wong was there, just promoted after his performance review, smiling and preparing a cell for me. Everyone had been promoted but me. "An interesting voyage, I take it?"

"What did you do, Wong?" I said. "You set me up."

"You were the ranking officer during the voyage. I told you to take her in. That you failed at it is cause for concern. An investigation is only natural. If you had nothing to do with it, you will be out of here in no time."

"Don't give him false hope, Wong. The admiral is pissed. You're under Article 32 now."

The quartermaster looked in at me. "Obasanjo has volunteered to be your advocate. Do you object?"

"No offense to Obasanjo, but I will decline. If the admiral is pissed at me, I would prefer an advocate that doesn't cause any more friction. Who else you got?"

"NetSec says he could do it, in a pinch. He doesn't like you, though."

"Well, at least the admiral likes him, right? This is actually not a criminal proceeding or a court martial. This is just an Article 32 trial—a big show because the admiral is pissed. I did my duty. Sergeant Anderson was very sick. He will be back. Corporal Jensen deserted on her own, likely with help from Wong. Let's try and make the old man happy, okay? What is his goal here? Am I an example to others to maintain order, or am I actually under investigation? I have nothing to hide. My reports are honest. I did the right thing with Anderson, and I failed to capture Jensen, who was in collusion with Wong and the monastery. I am a pilot, not a security officer. I have limited hand-to-hand, no investigation training."

Q put his hand on my shoulder. "The admiral hates you. The best thing to do is take whatever he gives you and preparing for the next phase, after service. I will alert Lieutenant Commander Obasanjo and Captain Nguyen."

I said nothing else. What was there to say?

I sat in my cell, and wondered immediately what was so different from quarantine, from the monastery monks in their cells, from my duties day to day, my meaningless, make-work duties.

This is where I first learned how pointless it was to concern one-self with prison cells when so much of our life is indistinguishable from prison out in the far colonies. Without that indifference to punishment, I could not achieve my greatest feat.

I waited for a day before anyone came to see me.

Nguyen came to me, early in the morning and exhausted like he had been sitting at his terminal all night, and he woke me up. "Hey, moron," he said. He was rail thin, sickly looking, and wore a scowl like others might wear a jaunty cap. "Wake up and talk to your advocate."

"Give me a minute," I said. I sat up and stretched and tried to shake the cobwebs loose. I had no data access. I had been sitting in a cell, staring off into the void and wondering what horrible food I would be served next under the terms of my confinement, and if anything could be worse than what we were already fed. "Okay, when am I out?"

"No such luck. You didn't do anything wrong, per se. Obasanjo and the quartermaster both think you're just un-lucky. Doesn't matter to the old man, does it?"

"Would you like my version of events?"

"Nope. You aren't guilty of anything but pissing off the ad-miral. You think Jensen's the first deserter? The monks have it down to an art. They want to shut this station down as a mili-tary installation, make it just another supply line for their mis-sion. They want to embarrass us with desertion figures. They want people to think of deserting before they think of sui-cide. They poke and prod our network, and we poke and prod theirs. We are not enemies, but we are adversaries. Did anyone explain this to you?"

"I'm afraid not. There ought to be a manual or training mod-ule."

"Everyone else sort of figures it out right away. You are dumber than you look, and you don't look smart. So you didn't do it. So what? The admiral comes back from the plague and immediately two crewmen are stranded on the planet, and we're paying the monastery for room and board on one of them, and here you are, the officer in charge of this disaster. Right after Ximenez, too."

"I messed up, but it wasn't my fault."

"It was your responsibility, Ronaldo. Just like when you lost a crewman the first time you flew. Man, you have got wicked luck. Right. Right. Your written statement is accurate?"

"It is. You can consult with Amanda Garcia if you like."

"No, we can't. Not without running over monastic wires, and why would we do that? You're telling the truth. So what is your goal here. What do you want?"

I wanted to fly on patrol, to hunt the enemy out in the long night between galaxies. I wanted to have a brilliant career and transcend to other colonies, and expand with humanity, where my descendants became as numerous as the stars.

"I will accept whatever the admiral decides," I said. "I respect his judgment and his authority. I do not feel I have the right to any assessment of my fate if I am such an incompetent officer."

"The admiral likes obedience. It might be a shrewd play with that angle. Okay, but beyond that, what do you want?"

"I am going back to sleep, okay? I appreciate your advocacy on my behalf."

"Do you want out, is what I am asking. Should I ask for your early release to the planet?"

"No," I said. "No, I don't want that at all. No. If it is suggested as a solution, I would prefer a vigorous defense against it. I came to serve in the war with honor, not slink away to some miserable rock. I do not want out at all." I was startled by his suggestion, by how similar it sounded to a prisoners' sentence. I wanted to transcend. I didn't want to die on a desert plain, disgraced and dishonored, living in a hole that stank of sweat and algae, waiting for ice comets and talking about ice comets.

"Good to know."

He left me just as suddenly as he arrived. He didn't see people much, and he was rumored to have a strange fetish, but I don't even presume to know what it might be. His weight changed quickly, and dramatically, and if he had been on planet with me, I might have wanted the medical technician to check him out.

When I woke up again in the morning, Wong knocked on my bars with breakfast, and Nguyen was right behind him. "After breakfast, you go to the admiral alone," said Wong. He opened the bars for me, and put a bowl of gruel in my hand. He left the bars open.

"I don't even get to speak for myself?"

"Nope," said Nguyen, "I did all the talking for you. It was better that way. He really doesn't like you."

"Okay," I said. "Thanks for your advocacy. I owe you one."

"You definitely do," he said. "Don't ever ask me to do this again, moron."

Wong stood waiting for me beside the open door. I ate quickly, just what I needed to keep the butterflies down, and not too much. When I stood up, I shoved the bowl straight into Wong's uniform, splattering the gruel. He laughed at me. "Jump out an airlock, Wong," I said.

I tried to push past him, but he was much stronger than me. He stood in my way, smiling like a cat with a mouse in its teeth. It was menacing. I pushed again, against the wall of him, smearing myself with the damn gruel on his chest, and I was outmatched and I knew it. "Get out of the way, Captain!"

He chuckled and stood aside. "I'd watch your tone, Ensign," he said. "You are being recorded." He pointed up to the cameras everywhere, in every pinhole and crevice and nook of the station. Everything here is recorded. We all knew that.

I stormed through to the stairwell, and up to the admiral's office from the brig. I saw no one in the halls, and I imagine they were keeping clear. Only the admiral truly knew what my fate would be. He would horde his decision like a miser, dripping only snippets of truth out to watch others dance upon the thread.

Obasanjo was also sitting outside the door. He waved at me and winked. "He's waiting for you, Aldo."

"You all right?"

"I'm fine, as always. You look a fright." He pointed to the uniform. He had a handkerchief in his pocket and helped me clean up the worst of it. He patted my cheek. He looked like he wanted me to kiss him, but I didn't want to kiss him. Even if he transitioned, I wouldn't be attracted to him. It isn't fair to him, but nothing is ever fair in the military.

The admiral bellowed my name. I stood in the doorway at attention and saluted my commanding officer.

"Sit down, Ensign. It's past time for your performance review. Let's see if you are going to be recommended for promotion up the ansible, or if you are going to be stuck here at this miserable post for your entire career for nothing."

I sat down. I thought of telling him to go ahead and tell me what he really wanted to say, sarcastically. Silence seemed wiser.

"To make this all official, I'm going to make it clear that this is your performance review. Officers are held to a higher standard than mere enlisted. We are leaders. We are the ones who stay for decades, sometimes long past retirement, to serve the mission. We are not just measured for tardiness and demerits. We are expected to build the future for humanity in the stars, to find the enemy where it hides, and to defeat the enemy wherever it appears. For this reason, our evaluations are different. If you excel as an officer, you may be recommended by me for a transfer along the ansible to available positions in the hundreds of colonies that need good officers."

"With respect, sir, let's stop pretending you might recommend me up the ansible today."

"This is an official proceeding, and interrupting your commanding officer will be noted in the official report of the file."

"Sir . . . ," I said.

"As far as leadership goes, Ensign, I don't see any. You lost a crewmember on your first mission. It wasn't your fault, technically, but plenty of officers manage to have a first mission without losing their crewmembers. On your second major assignment, you attempted to levy charges of sexual assault against my best engine man over playful hazing. Now his performance is down, and the other crewmember involved is angling for an early release. Hardly inspiring leadership, Ensign. Now, as to your recent descent to the surface of the Planet Citadel, you somehow managed to lose everyone who went with you. Sergeant Anderson, our mission-critical pilot, is stuck on medical leave and costing us a fortune in rental fees for his room and board during his recovery. Corporal Jensen deserted right under your nose. Right under it. You did not inspire any leadership in her, at all. I can't think of a single act of leadership you've gotten right. Correct me if I'm wrong, Corporal."

"Sergeant Anderson was very sick, and it was critical to the mission to get one of the only two rated pilots operational with safety, sir."

"Three pilots, Ensign. You, the sergeant, and me. Three rated pilots, Ensign. I will admit that you made the right call just at the wrong time. You should have alerted the medical staff here on board the station, and he should be convalescing here on board the station. He is costing me money that can't be used to buy supplies now. I will give you half a point in leadership, out of ten. Honestly, that's a gift. Nobody respects you, Ensign. Nobody."

"Thank you for that, sir."

"Now, as to your attitude problem. You are insubordinate. Never enough to get you in actual trouble, but you have been dishonest with me and with crewmembers, and I cannot in good faith recommend your moral character. So, you get no points there."

"Any other categories, sir?"

"Technically, you are proficient at your work, and other than the major, catastrophic error that led to the death of a crewman, you have not had any major issues. On a scale of one to ten, I rate you a six in technical skill and proficiency at your work. This is barely adequate, but you keep losing crewmen. Your physical fitness is also adequate. I will also rate you a six. With a 12.5, total, out of 40, you are absolutely not qualified to transcend up the ansible, much less promote. In fact, strictly speaking, a performance evaluation this low is usually met with early termination of our contract. You should be kicked to the colony with all the costs of your training and transfer strapped to your neck in debt like a dead fish. Ensign,

I have decided that as excremental as your performance has been, to date, it is far better to keep you on here until such time as Sergeant Anderson returns to health for exactly one reason: I do not like to fly supply runs. I would rather send a total failure, like you, to monitor the autopilot and handle launch than spend even one minute in one of those hulking tractors piddling around after supply. This will be your job. And, if you do not do it well, I will throw you out of the military so fast you won't even receive another performance review. You will never transfer up the ansible on my watch, Ensign. I promise you that. You will begin your flight preparations for an immediate departure. Your rank and pay will remain as they are, if only because I cannot demote you below the bottom of the scale. Get out of my sight. You're the quartermaster's problem now, not mine."

It was not as bad as I thought it might be, but I was shaking. I stood up and placed my hand on the chair to steady myself, my face a mask of a smile and a salute. I turned and left with some solidity. Outside, the quartermaster was there, at ease, with Obasanjo.

"Come on," said Q. "Let's go debrief."

Obasanjo patted me on the back and chuckled. "I can't offer you a stiff drink. The admiral has all the booze."

"I'm fine," I said. "I'm flying. I'm serving humanity. Everything's fine."

They led me up to the observation deck. We floated under the stars.

"Everyone gets slammed the first time," said Obasanjo. "It's the budget." He handed me a sipping bag of jujube tea. "We have to stay within the boundaries of the local economy. It's not just the budget, though. The admiral is a horrible person.

And, short of mutiny, which no one even remotely thinks is a good idea, we just let him play God."

"The new lieutenant commander is a bit hyperbolic," said Q. "Let me try to rephrase. We do what we can with what we have. The admiral earned his place at the top, and we respect that. We also do our best to ensure a smooth operation. I agree that you made some bad calls, Ensign. But I don't want the admiral's performance review style to influence your morale while you are working for me. The reality is that he will not be admiral forever, and you will still be here. Work hard, take guidance from your fellow officers, and you will soon be in a place to actually rise through the ranks. I want your next review to be a stellar one."

Obasanjo scoffed and laughed. "Q, you are hilarious."

Q was mercurial, sipping his tea. We had sweet amaranth bars to chew on, and the stars overhead, and the veil of darkness, there, beyond it.

"I am a little too busy keeping this old can flying to worry about promotions," he said. "An attitude that I have been instructed to impart upon our burgeoning Wong here."

"Do not accuse me of being anything like him," I said, with real vitriol in my trembling voice.

The two men said nothing. They were shocked by it, perhaps impressed. "I apologize if I offended," said Q. "Everyone's first performance review is a disaster. The highest first score anyone got was Wong at 18. This has been true ever since our current admiral came into power. There has been a stagnation in the ranks, but he has never thrown any of us from uniform. I do not understand it, nor do I pretend to, but we have our duty, and we do what we can."

Outside, a drone passed by, on a cleaning job. It scraped

against the glass with some sort of antibiotic cleansing agent.

"Explain to me," I said, looking up at the machine out there, "how do we produce our ubiquitous cleaning agents? On the surface, they are quite busy growing food to produce chemicals for cleansing."

Q smirked. "It's ammonia, mostly. Where do you think it comes from?"

"Urine," I said.

"It is quite processed before it becomes ammonia, and a cleaning agent, but it is mostly urine."

"We literally cover ourselves in our own urine all day long, don't we?"

"Welcome to military service," said Obasanjo. "It is one of many reasons I suspect we were put here by the enemy as an elaborate joke."

"Hey, they always said that war in space was going to be hell," said Q.

We ate more and drank more and talked about my new place in the heirarchy, which is to say that I had actual command duties over personnel now, and I would be in charge of the flight crew.

"If you mess up," said Q, "it's you alone out there imploding. You fly alone until the admiral says otherwise. The ships can do a lot on autopilot, and he can always go get you if you die in the can. Mostly, you're there in case something goes wrong, anyway. You don't get to pick your team, of course."

"Of course," I said. "How much of what we do is a show we put on for procedure, and how much is actually necessary?"

"Don't worry about it," said Obasanjo. "It is a deep philosophical debate. If you wish to avoid the seeking of truth in the matter, it is best not to question the surface appearances."

"My colleague says that for my sake," said Q. "We have conflicting notions of reality and truth. I will retire to the monastery someday, and work toward my immortal soul, while he will likely end up insane."

"It is not insane to doubt what we see. Quantum scientists do no less. Ansibles were built on no less."

The darkness above us, the universe full of swirling galaxies, an abundance of matter so profound that the mind cannot wrap around either the amount of everything that is or the stark emptiness of what we had on the station. I sipped my tea and imagined a future of abundance here. I could not seriously consider it for long. Most of the universe is a black void of competing gravity wells and quantum information fusing and interpolating and expurgating and moving. In the darkness between galaxies, that great void, there are still such wonders: floating debris of failed worlds, asteroids shimmering away chasing fragments of gravity and bent by other fragments, lost matter hiding to consume all ships and probes in the night sky, and the debris of warships from the last battle, both ours and theirs. I was still in charge of the maps, and I could use that for something, couldn't I?

"Captain Obasanjo, have you ever considered seeking out any of the debris of the enemy ships and studying them? There simply must be something out there big enough to study first-hand."

He smiled, sadly. "I'm sure the admiral would approve of that ridiculous waste of resources. By the time the enemy returns, who knows what weapons they will have prepared, just as we have great technological improvements of our own. No more rail guns, for instance. No more archaic bullets."

"I know, but . . . It would be interesting for you, wouldn't it?"

"Yes, it would. I would love to see the handiwork of our hidden overlords. Firstly, though, as a scientist, I would doubt it because they are powerful enough to drop a misleading crumb upon my lap. I would really need to study it closely, and compare to the records of the debris, and seek anything that is missing from the record. Anyway, it would be a diversion, nothing more. Our hidden masters prefer to keep us boxed up here, and why not? We can't do anything to stop them. The universe looks so huge, and it is huge, but it is not infinite. The amount of resources out there is absolutely staggering, but someday, far in the future, the limits will be reached and there would be no more matter to exploit and transform. Any species intelligent enough to play the long game would know that, right? There are always limits to resources, even these seemingly limitless ones. They can hold us here on the worthless rock until such a time as they need it. They can study us. They can manipulate us, even, and make us believe in things that help the cause of the enemy. Ultimately, we are locked in a nightmare from which our best and easiest path is the one with as little pain as possible: Obedience to the mission."

"My cynical compatriot. Someday you will abandon your nihilism for something. I pray for you."

"I weep for all of us," he said, "and humanity. Also, if you think there's a pussy shortage, consider how few interesting and likely young men are sent along. I swear it is a conspiracy against me by the enemy for attempting to discover their plot. The only one on the surface I know about transitioned."

"Amanda is very beautiful now," I said. "Have you seen her since the transition?"

"I have," said Obasanjo. "I remember before it, and she was

still so young. She was a beautiful boy, but too young for me, then."

I sipped a bit of my tea, and felt full and empty at the same time. Of all my sins, I regret my failures of lust the most, even though my pride is probably the worst of the bunch.

Now, oh confessor, this was my early life on the station. Please, if I may be forgiven for skipping ahead a little. The actual details of my life from there were mostly a long series of busy tasks, and all the supply flights Sergeant Anderson could no longer fly. Actually, his healing went so slowly, he was discharged in the second month, to spare the military the expense of his room and board, and he was left to his own devices on the planet surface while his wife remained alone in the stars. The thing that hurt me the most, during this phase of my life, where I was slowly coming into my own as an officer, was the specter of Sergeant Adebayo Anderson, proud and strong, and miserably lonely in the dining hall, or on duty, or anywhere else. I often tried to sit with her, just to keep her company, when I could. I, too, was very lonely. I felt a terrible weight around her, and when she gave me her familiar smile, with such sadness in it, I wished I could do something for her. She was a reminder, in case I ever tried to forget, that my decisions had consequences and doing the right thing would often still cause suffering in others. She was very grateful to me for his healing on the surface below. That made it worse.

I flew down to the surface, and I waited in the monastery, and Amanda often came to me there, and we shared lunch and I helped her with her jobs. We wind surfed together, leaning into the sails that powered simple skiffs over the dunes, wind lashing against our safety gear, and huge speeds in such strong winds. She taught me how to climb along the cliffs after salt rocks, with a rope and an anchored line. We kissed, occasionally. Of course we did. We leaned into each other and felt a closeness that I had never before felt. She was younger than me, and she was afraid I would not accept her body, I knew. I was afraid that I didn't know what to do with my own, much less hers. Oh, confessor, I would admit if during my brief respites on the surface, during negotiations and loading and unloading, if anything happened then. We were good friends. We smiled warmly for each other. We wrote letters all the time to each other. It was little more than this for a long time.

Permit me to skip ahead, then, to the death of my first nemesis: Admiral Diego.

Only barely promoted up to lieutenant, but four years older with one more terrible performance review behind me that seemed to have no connection to my actual on-the-mission performance and promotion, the spiteful old man drank himself into a stupor and shot himself in the head with an antique weapon. We don't even know where he came up with the flintlock pistol.

The day of his death, he shouted at Obasanjo for hours through the wall. His spew of invectives seemed to cease about four hours into his tirade. By then, he was into the depths of his third bottle. He stared at it for a while, slowly drinking it down. After the third bottle, he reached into his desk and removed the replica of a thousand-year-old weapon, an astonishing artifact to find out in the middle of space. He smuggled materials in with every transport. He had a massive seed bank hidden in his room, but no one has found any more whiskey. He had baubles, books, and priceless treasures passed along from the ansible, somehow. One of these things was a flintlock pistol. Understand the ferocity of the old style, the black powder and ball. Round things passing through flesh do far more damage than puncturing things. The shape of bullets for hundreds of years was more of an arrow than a ball, because the arrow was considered more humane. This ancient weapon would shatter everything in a cascading wave of pain, like stabbing oneself through the chest and bone with the handle of the knife instead of the point. It was a horrifying, disastrous mess of blood and tissue. His head was blown apart. He slumped over the desk, while Obasanjo—curious at the sudden boom—poked his head into the office assuming a bottle had been dropped or thrown and might need cleanup. Obasanjo closed the door quickly and locked it from the outside. He called for Wong and Q and the rest of the officer corps.

Between performance reviews, I saw Admiral Diego only in the cafeteria at breakfast, and he did not speak to me and I did not speak to him. When he died, I was horrified by the tapes, but I was more horrified by the ranting and the drunkenness and the stain on his honor that his end entailed.

Our staff meeting the day afterward was very grim and quiet.

Wong broke the silence. "My investigation is complete, by the way. I know when the weird little device was passed through the ansible. It was with Tech Private Chet Detkarn. I haven't told her what was in the briefcase she was ordered to carry through. I think we can all agree that she didn't know anything. Antiques like that are far above her pay grade. He had no will and testament. Everything goes into a storage room, even the antique. Legal decisions will be sent to us. We cannot dismantle anything until decisions come from HR on Earth."

"The monastery can't have any interest in an antique pistol used to commit suicide."

Wong shrugged. "I don't think they're interested in anything. No one is. That's the conundrum. Except the seeds, there's a whole bunch of contraband he copied over, that is priceless among collectors on Earth, but this is the Citadel. Now nobody knows who owns it, and nobody wants it. It's junk. Anybody want his toy collection? I can report it stolen and refuse to investigate and leave it at that."

Q grunted. "Can you at least forward me an inventory. Some of it might be useful for spare parts and raw materials."

"I can do that," said Wong. He bent over his tablet and started pushing the keys to make it so. We sat in silence, waiting for him to finish.

Eventually, Captain Nguyen, the NetSec, stood up and kicked the wall. "Who's the boss now? Q? Wong? Obasanjo? Me? Who's running the show until the new guy gets here? I'm a moron computer tech. I don't know how to run a damn station. I'll retire before I'm put in charge. Obasanjo, don't you run most of it?"

Obasanjo looked over at the quartermaster, with a wicked grin. "Q, you outrank me, don't you?"

"Oh, no. Don't even set me up for that."

"Sorry, Commander," said Obasanjo. "It's true, though. You outrank us all, right? You haven't been here as long as Nguyen, but you outrank him, and you've been here longer than Wong and me."

"Lord, have mercy on my soul. I'm so close to retirement. Fine, I'm the acting admiral. Who's going to be the new Q in the meantime? I can't do both. I can't manage personnel work crews and ship maintenance while simultaneously coordinating with HR and writing all the reports."

"Not it," said Obasanjo. "I'm the supply line to the monastery, and I'm local HR. I don't have the tech certifications, either."

"Don't even look at me," said Nguyen. "I'm software, not hardware."

Everyone suddenly looked over at me.

I took a deep breath, and then exhaled. "I just wanted to fly. That's all."

"You've flown. Pilots can build things, and understand how to build things. You have technical training Obasanjo and Wong lack."

"I've never flown the warship. Who will run patrols for the enemy? And what about Wong? What does he do all day?"

Wong laughed. "You think anyone would put me in charge where I'd have more power?" He flexed his muscles. "I volunteer. Quartermastering is mine."

"No," said Q.

Obasanjo snorted. "Wong, shut up. You know we don't trust you with that. You don't have the certificates in all that mechanical engineering like a pilot does. It has to be Aldo."

"Let Wong do it," I said. "He'll be fine."

Q placed his hand on the table and tapped to get everyone's attention. We all looked over at our new acting admiral. "Aldo is the new Q. No one will be flying the warship for a while, and we haven't seen anything for two hundred years. Survival first, then scouting. You're the new Q, Lieutenant Aldo," said the old Q. "Sergeant Adebayo Anderson will keep you moving in the right direction until you find your sea legs. Don't blow up the damn station."

For some reason, no one ever stopped calling him Q. No

one ever called me Q. I was just the person who came in after him to the job no one wanted. It was long and dull and full of personnel charts and supply charts and by then, we had a master sergeant qualified to fly supply ships when I was off-cycle and needed time in zero-g to get my bones and guts in shape. He would need a pilot, though, to pace him, eventually, and even this wouldn't be me. A new pilot would come, fresh from the War College, eventually.

And I was going to sit behind a desk and stare at reports all day, and run the calendar, and look for damage in the hull, in the wires, in the whole station, and hear the groaning of the hull, the plumbing sputter and break, the rot of biotics rising up from broken pipes.

I wrote Amanda immediately and told her of my imminent promotion to acting quartermaster. I would not be able to fly down on supply runs. I would not be able to lean in close to her, and smell the sand in her hair. I admit that when I imagined my time in retirement, what I thought about most was Amanda, and the cost in medical materials and procedures to make children with her. I wanted to build a future on the planet, because I felt more and more like I had no future in the service. It was a distraction from the scheme that was building in the dark places of my mind, where I was cataloging different space objects in a mental file for possible use, and trying to figure out the precise procedure that would put all the pieces in place.

As the new quartermaster, I met with the staff of grumpy enlisted that lined up under Sergeant Anderson's command. She introduced each one to me, from senior staff to junior. I had mostly corporals, with the one sergeant, and four privates. All four of the privates were going to be dead from a group suicide by the time I finished my first month in their command. They were going to be repairing and cleaning out the biota near an empty airlock where the transport ship was going to be flying. All together, they'd climb inside and shut the door and depressurize into open space so suddenly no one even realized it happened until repair drones started screaming outside the hull.

We were all depressed. We walked around from duty to duty in a daze. There was nothing to do but work hard at tasks that repeated weekly, and monthly, and felt as tedious and meaningless as the war effort itself.

Sergeant Anderson and I were alone in my office, discussing the sudden suicide.

"You'd tell me if you were feeling that bad, I hope," I said.

"I would never, sir."

I had been compiling all the video records together into the report, and paused at my recommendation for future action.

"What do you think we should do, Sergeant? What's the answer to the suicides?"

"Hope, Lieutenant. I will be done in four years. I will go to the planet to reunite with my husband. We will have a life there."

"It's a long, hard life," I said. "The colony is still desperately underprovisioned. Terraforming takes decades, centuries. Our grandchildren still will not know what it means to walk barefoot in green grass on a bright, sunny day, or to fish in deep water."

She said nothing, and crossed her arms. She looked up at the ceiling and spoke. "We have some pleasures, still. There is enough food, medicine, and housing to live well enough. More than enough. There is rock climbing. There is windsurfing. These are worthy distractions. The world will be built. We will build it slowly."

"I applaud your hope, Sergeant. How is your husband?"

"He has been deputized by the monastery to fly surveying missions in the atmosphere to aid terraforming projections. He says it is quite dull, and the food is just as bad there as here. He says Ospreys are not well suited to the winds."

"At least he's flying something," I said. "Is it wrong that I am jealous of him?" I looked over at the report, with the video showing our drones and crawlers grasping futilely at the frozen corpses of the four privates who had each been here less than seven months. "This is what I am doing today. The inquest is tomorrow. I won't be flying again for a long time."

She squinted at me. "You have your own little hope on the planet, as well, I am to believe?"

I blushed. "Hope is such a strong word," I said. "I have a friend. I hope she will be a good friend."

"There aren't enough good friends to go around. We are all so afraid of pregnancy until retirement, when we are afraid to fail at it."

"The supply line is not robust," I said. "Two or three broken pieces in the chain, and we could all starve."

She shrugged. "Or, your team could fail to seal an airlock correctly, or more micro-meteors chip away at us, or our radiation shielding is not working correctly, or we accidentally develop a terrible plague in our little biotic island. Does anyone even smile? Is there a reason to smile? Volleyball is a great distraction. You should come join us. Everyone should. Games and sports can really help us all."

"Poker night," I said. "When did you abandon Obasanjo's philosophy club?"

"It circles around the same conundrums, without release." She rolled her eyes. "No, there's no physical release here. There's just gambling. Action, and competition, are best. Physical release."

"Philosophical release is far preferred on the station, and poker."

"And that leads to suicide."

"Athletes have killed themselves here, Sergeant. My own AstroNav predecessor ran laps on the lower floors until he developed arthritis in a knee."

"Would you accept a suggestion on the way we run the crew here?"

"Of course, Sergeant. If I had any choice in the matter, I'd have put you in charge of the whole quartermastering operation the moment the admiral died."

She nodded her gratitude stiffly and politely. "Lieutenant, can we make our work here competitive? Can we reward those who do the best job with something tangible, like a trophy?"

"I may be able to offer antique soap packets. They are as old as the station. I have an idea, actually. Can we rig anything to make lots of soap bubbles? Lots and lots of them?"

"Of course, but . . . Why."

"We need more parties. More fun. We need joy, Lieutenant. I dream of flying, and it is the thing that brings me joy, and I dream of riding deep into the space between the Sagitarrius cluster and the Magellanic Cloud, out to the next leap into the Laika. I want to go farther than any man in history into those black depths, Sergeant. And I never will. This is the farthest I will travel. I try to reconcile that in my mind. I have told no one these things, you understand, and I trust you not to tell anyone. But I feel the darkness descend upon me. I feel the darkness, and I need to fill myself with energy and noise so I do not fall prey to it. We will have a biweekly party, to celebrate a long cycle. We will fill a long, empty hallway with soap bubbles and put a plastic liner on the floor and walls and we will hold a contest to see who can slide themselves upon the liner the farthest."

She chuckled. "Sir, that is ridiculous."

"It will be fun. It will be a new tradition until the other officers shut us down. They will, Sergeant. In the meantime, there is a lot of useless soap lying around and plenty of plastic insulation lining. Call a biweekly meeting on the schedule and find a nice, long, empty hallway. When I first arrived, the room I was in under quarantine had packages of soap. Where are these oldest, most useless soaps in the entire universe? That is what we will use to make the hallway slippery."

She was critical, but smiling. I was very pleased that I had the capacity to make her smile. "I will make it so, Lieutenant. Anything else?"

The tapes were still playing. I turned them off. "I don't think so. If you ever reach the point, come to me, okay? I need you. I will help you in any way I can."

She didn't say anything to that. She saluted and she left.

Pleased with myself, and my whimsical command, I turned, then, to the duties of the quartermaster. I spent hours just flagging and approving work orders on my tablet. Then, I had to inspect work—much of it I knew nothing about, but Sergeant Anderson did. We walked the halls together, where she taught me what it took to keep the hull and pipes intact.

In what little time I had, after work, I played poker, always poker, with the other officers and any enlisted who merited an invitation to the table. At some point, it occurred to me that over half the time, the enlisted was involved in a bribe with one of the other officers. Obasanjo and Wong were both commonly involved, and occasionally Q or Nguyen, but only occasionally. That the admiral was receiving a bribe, in the person of Q, was disappointing to me, but I had long ago accepted that the whole situation was corrupt. And to what purpose all the extra credit in the bank? The planet economy was sparse. Being king of a desert dune seemed to me such a trivial thing. I accepted no bribes, but I am not proud to say it. I was often approached when I became quartermaster about possible favors and reassignments, always mentioning a poker game in passing. I pretended not to understand what the private or corporal was saying. The enlisted corps seemed to realize I was in that, at least, beyond reproach and left me to my own devices. A signal would pass between the betters, and the money would appear on the table in the form of chips, and at the end of the hand, the money would pass over to the officer who was being paid off. It was perfectly legal to do so, and no camera or recording device would flag anything untoward in a poor poker hand, and under the Q's admiralcy, there was a dramatic uptick in Obasanjo's wealth and status, while Wong smiled and cheerfully played his hand as if no one was busy trying to have a private bet, as if only to annoy Obasanjo.

Over poker, with a private sweating his hand against men who had little else to do but gamble at cards in the evenings, Q turned to me and casually mentioned my scheme to turn a hallway into an amusement park for a night.

"I do not approve of wasting supplies, Lieutenant Aldo. Have you considered the cost in water alone?"

"The water will be recycled quickly back into the system. The soap is ancient."

"But it is still useful." He threw two chips down. "I see you, Private. And you are in over your head. Get out while you can."

"With respect, sir. I call." He was a biotic scrubber, and one of mine, and I didn't want to appear foolish in front of my own man.

"My unit has low morale. The mission is impacted. Not every soldier is content to train and pray, sir. They are not men like you."

"And women," said the admiral.

Wong surprised me by taking my side. "Sir, if I may offer a suggestion from history, when naval ships crossed the equator in the age of the British Empire, there was always a party of sorts, and an initiation. It was quite ribald, but it probably helped maintain order. Blew off some steam."

"A festival, of sorts?"

"Yes, sir. And a ritual," said Wong.

"Spacers have their rituals, Wong. I have never been interested in superstition."

"I have no ritual in mind," I said. "I am just trying to give my soldiers something to look forward to that wasn't approved by the monastery first. We will clean up afterward. Nothing will be wasted."

"You had better be sure. I want it all recycled in the tanks. No water loss. Even the soap goes back into the system. Faith and prayer are excellent rituals. I recommend them to anyone. We live on a monastic world, under monastic law for towns and villages. There are religious festivals we could share. Feast of the Resurrection, the Passover, and the holy fast at Ramadan. We could bring up a monk to serve as a counselor on a permanent basis."

"No, thanks," said Obasanjo. "I will take a soap slide over religion any day of the year. HR would never approve without all the officers on board, and I'm against it. Can I come to your soap party, Aldo?"

I shook my head. "The hallway will be crowded. Let us try it first. We can expand if it is successful."

Q looked over at the private at the table. "Are you quite finished, Private?"

"Yes, sir," he said. He folded his hand and stood up at stiff attention.

"I'm sitting right here. It isn't like I don't know. Who are you hiding it from, anyway?" The admiral threw his cards down face up. "Three aces. Anybody beat that?"

Nobody could. He gathered all the chits. "This is the last time," he said, to the officers at the table. "After this, if I see it on the tapes, I take action. My station. My rules. No more of this. No more gambling of any kind. I have nothing against it, personally, but the way things happen here? No more." He pocketed them. "I'm putting all of this money toward a fundraiser to bring more entertainment items here for the enlisted. I'm not keeping this money." He pushed his way past us, and looked back into the room. "No more gambling. That's an order."

In the room afterward, everyone was silent for a time in the admiral's absence.

Eventually, the private said, "We can keep playing. We just can't bet anything, right?"

I laughed like a maniac. The men stared at me.

Wong stood up and placed his cards face up. He had four of a kind, all queens. That set off Obasanjo, and the rest of the room.

Another round, and another hand, but the chips meant

nothing. We played without real money. It was all sport and pointless for personal gain. For a time, we continued to meet for poker. Without real money involved, it lost its luster. Bored, I stopped and Wong stopped and Obasanjo kept it going with some of the enlisted. Then, even that dwindled.

Lecture night began. A com link was set up to the monastery for weekly sermons with the theologians who argued over obscure heresies in the monastery. They took turns presenting on different topics of interest to only themselves. Officers were expected to attend to set an example for the enlisted. I confess that I paid little attention and preferred to sneak out the back with Sergeant Adebayo Anderson to catch up on work details that didn't get done with our staffing shortage.

We clambered over the hull together, looking up into the darkness and stars, where the panels groaned and trembled. We bolted them down and soldered them in place with emergency stickies to last until the next certified hull jockey could get to it on the list. We did biotic sweeps together, blasting empty hallways with hot bleach and squirting the walls and corners with samples from our station's approved biotic colonies. We climbed into the pipes and wires in the walls while our crewmen slept through lectures, picking up the coverage rate. It was hard work, but I actually enjoyed it. Her calm strength gave me calm strength. I learned the station's secret chambers. We gained the kind of camaraderie that can only come from working together late into the evening.

Soon, in conversation with Sergeant Anderson, she made a joke I did not understand about the possibilities of shadowed closets while we were in one. I don't recall what it was, but she pointed out that two young men often lost a few minutes in their duties in the very dark closet we were sweeping while the rest of the crew were at a lecture or eating or resting in their bunks. "We should probably let them know their secret is not safe from HR."

"What secret?"

She looked at me like I was not serious. She laughed and patted my head. "Ask your good friend, Amanda," she said.

Confused, I did not know what to say. It took me a tremendous amount of time to understand what she meant. I had never lain with either a woman or a man. When it occurred to me, I arranged a meeting with the two young men after official shift. They were both in their fourth year of service, lean and strong from years of hard work. They were good-looking young men, and they were nervous about being in this meeting, with their commander, together. They were afraid that I knew. I played them the tape of their sojourn into a closet for thirteen minutes. I fast-forwarded through the long pause, saying nothing, but pointing to the time stamp.

Abashed, they looked at each other with mortified faces, one grinning a little and the other not. I told them only that they needed to be more discrete.

I told this story to Amanda in our endless written communications. She got hung up on a particular detail and did not allow me to finish my story.

*You have never . . . Really?*

*When would I? On the boat with my mother and father? In War College where I could get in trouble for building relations with someone I would be leaving behind? Or up here, where there are four women out of nearly fifty men, two of them my direct subordinates?*

*That's awful. I feel terrible for you.*

Lust, oh, confessor, does not feel sinful at the time. I think there is a difference between harmful sexual attraction, like what I felt toward Sergeant Adebayo Anderson, and what I felt for Amanda. For the other women and men of the station, I felt nothing.

I spent a great deal of time with Sergeant Adebayo Anderson in my role as quartermaster. In fact, we were probably co-quartermasters, and all success I achieved must be attributed to her careful guidance. She handed me staffing reports that I did not quite understand. I signed them and got the work moving, then asked what I had signed and listened to her explanation. The only time I left my little desk was to join a work crew, when no other hand was available, and while I worked scraping and irradiating bulkheads, and checking the decay of wiring networks, I dreamed of darkness and stars. I came to fly, not scrub bulkheads with biotic technicians and repair clogged pipes. My only joy, then, was when Sergeant Anderson and I would finish the shift and send the workers on home, and we picked up the lingering jobs on the board together. It was pleasurable to be in close company with her, and to work together on wires and pipes and insulation lines. She was a calm, easy presence, and I felt her physical strength beside me like a dark star's radiant heat.

For months, we pushed on, and I saw the enlisted quarters for the first time through a work crew. I had known, intellectually, the conditions they lived in, but I did not realize how spartan it was until I saw it firsthand. My humble quarters with a bed and a desk and a private bathroom were a palace to the long communal room. Opposite of the hangar bay, the enlisted had cots with cubicle walls in a long row. On one side of the room, potted plants and algae tanks under lights improved the air quality in the large chamber, with a fan constantly blowing over the greenery into the main room. Women were sealed off with large curtains, though, and the fresh air never reached into their side. They had a cot and a locker. The male showers were all behind a wall on one side, and the female showers were all behind a wall on the other. It wasn't a very sturdy wall, and curtains and bits of scrap metal had been rigged to reinforce female privacy behind their section of the long room.

Sergeant Anderson was with me to escort me into the female side to check a bulkhead wiring issue underneath the female showers. Men were not permitted past the barrier without an escort—not even officers.

"This is where you live?" I said, pointing to the long cubicle walls of men, where everyone was playing music on tablets too loudly, watching approved media on large screens that rolled around the floor like cubicle walls to whomever got the screen first after shift.

"We have most volleyball practice here. The ceiling is as high as the garage, but there is no danger to mission equipment. We actually came up with the wall to the women's side on our own. When I first got here, it was not done that way, but it has helped us to stay sane with all these men."

A thought occurred to me, then, regarding supply closets, and the lack of cameras in many of them. It did not involve volleyballs, or anything salacious.

I went, after that work detail, to Wong's office, near the prison cells where I would soon be spending much of my time. "This is unexpected. What can I do for you, Lieutenant Aldo?"

Pulling up a map of the station on my tablet, I flagged a few supply closets where members of my staff had been sneaking off for some time to themselves, away from working cameras. I handed them across to Wong. Sealed rooms, presumably, but a little bit of minor locksmithing could open nearly any supply closet. It was part of their design in cases where maintenance had to get through, or there was some sort of emergency. The old ship was easier than the bubble attached to her hull on the other side.

"I want to open up some rooms, very quietly. I don't think Q needs to worry about what happens in them, considering that I will be in charge of their maintenance, and you will be in charge of door security and smoothing over HR. Thoughts?"

"Who are they for?"

"I want to give sergeants their own rooms, like us."

"Just the sergeants?"

"For now," I said. "I don't understand why we can't expand our living quarters a bit. We could give the enlisted roommates until they reach a certain rank. They still have no privacy in the showers, but at least they can close their eyes behind a door and have a little privacy."

"You know we are being recorded."

"I don't think what I am suggesting is particularly subversive, or corrupt. I am not considering any bribes or favors. I want to improve morale, reduce suicides."

"So do I," said Wong. "Nobody cares about clones except clones. A level of self-attrition is expected. It's in the manual. They do not test the psychological fitness of enlisted personnel for conditions like this. You and I were tested."

"My background was unique. I was raised on a boat on the Pacific gyre. It is not unlike close quarters here. You?"

"My family lived in a small apartment complex, with three families per unit. I shared a room with six other boys until I left for War College in Beijing. It is part of why we are chosen, yes? We have thrived in difficult living circumstances."

"I didn't know that about you," I said.

He shrugged. "We have never been good friends, Ronaldo. The past is a galaxy away. Let's go open some rooms and improve morale for soldiers here. We can set them up for female enlisted first. I don't care about the sergeants. I care about the women. Two sergeants are women, and the other two women can share quarters behind a door that locks."

Together we selected the rooms least likely to draw the attention of other officers. We quietly put cots from old storage in them, and extra footlockers. The sergeants would each take a room. The two other enlisted women would share a private quarters. Wong insisted on one extra room, in case we needed to buy anyone's silence with a private room.

Upon completion, we quietly went up to the enlisted quarters, entering from the women's side after a polite knock.

The women there looked up, confused. Wong winked and pressed his finger over his mouth. He gestured for the women to follow us. I mimicked him, to encourage silence, with a finger over my mouth. Wong went looking for the ranking male sergeant on the other side, to let him know what was going on, and I opened the first room, pointing at the enlisted women. There were cots for them, with privacy screens created with boxes of ancient supplies. Once the door was closed, I spoke in a hushed tone.

"This is the best we can do. You can get a break from the men for a while. If Q... I mean, the admiral finds out, it's probably over, so keep it quiet. Sergeant Anderson, we are going to quietly upgrade you and Sergeant McAvoy to your own private quarters. It is odd in a station this big and empty that ranking enlisted soldiers have no private space."

Adebayo had a look of shock on her face. "The admiral does not approve?"

"The admiral might approve if he knew about it," said Wong, coming up the hall. "I'm certain HR would approve considering the circumstances. Why bother over trivial details like this."

"There are no explicit instructions against it," I said. "Wong and I will get blamed, not you. I will show you your private room, and if you do not wish to stay in it, I will not be offended."

"The biotic crew is already pushed to the limit," she said. "These are more rooms to monitor."

"I have already figured out the scheduling issues. It will be fine. We merely scale back one of the storage closets to a monthly check instead of a weekly, and move all the supply to another closet. We fill these rooms in that open spot instead. Private Giles, you can sweep the rooms yourself, yes? They are low population, low impact?"

"Yes, sir," she said. "Thank you, sir."

"Sergeant Anderson, I appreciate your dutifulness. Have you ever had issues in the night with the men? I understand that sometimes it is hard to find real privacy."

She trembled and looked at her hands. I realized she was about to cry. I had not expected that. "Do not show me this so it may be taken away. Do not do that."

She left and went back to the women's quarter, alone.

That weekend, we had our third or fourth attempt at a water slide. It was rare to see the soldiers smiling, laughing, and I wondered what it must be like to see letters from their families, describing vacations in verdant lands, and marriages and children and this circling place, so far away from anything they remember, all gunmetal gray and fading plastic. The huge sheeting ran from one end of the hall to another, with biotic vacuums running to redirect the liquids into the pipes with the ancient soaps we used for extra lubrication. The man with the highest and fastest completion rate got the first run. Griggs, our engine man, was a hard worker, though I found him loathsome. He cheered and pounded his chest. He took a running start and dove, sliding as far as he could down the hallway. "Mark his path! Mark his path! Winner gets first run next time!" He slid deep past the vacuum rigs, dodging them as best he could while flopping on his stomach. He slid on, into the hallway as far as the soap would send him. To great cheers, we marked his spot in erasable wall marker. Next man had to try and beat the distance. It was goofy and wild and the enlisted cheered each other on. The cleanup afterward took an hour with all hands on deck. I took the numbers from the next three days of work to see if there were any improvements in completion rates. The first day, the work was slower. The second or third, it was as if nothing happened, and everyone continued on. The military could not measure joy.

This was at the same time as the new admiral's continuing effort to improve morale. The admiral brought Brother Pleo up on a direct data line for video confession and private meetings with any who wished to discuss their situation, theologically, ethically, etc., everything helps. I managed to skim time off the data line to actually see Amanda, and let her actually see me.

Amanda connected with me in the monastery's underground garden, under a vitex tree, bathed in red and green light. She was more beautiful than I remembered. I felt a great disconnect between this person I was seeing and looking at, and the person I had been writing every week.

"Hello," she said. "I see you."

"I see you," I said. "You are more beautiful than I remembered."

"Oh, stop. I just got off shift in the orchard. It's dark. I'm sweaty. It's nice to see you, Aldo. I don't even have a picture of you. We should exchange pictures."

"We should," I said.

We sat in silence, uncomfortably.

"So . . ."

"So . . ."

"Any exciting adventures in the stars this week?" she said.

"It is all quite secretive, I'm afraid. I've started a cabal with Captain Wong. We are recruiting. All very top secret, unless you're in the cabal."

"I'll pass. My father sends his greetings."

"The lighting is so strange. Has Brother Pleo been holding his confessions in that weird light?"

"He thinks the sight of the tree is soothing," she said, giggling. "But the purple glow is definitely not. You should alter the light of the confession room. Put in some yellow or green or something. Make it look different."

"I will put in a work order immediately."

I recall asking her about the desertion that nearly ruined me.

She was coy about it. "If Jensen had remained there, in her posting, do you think she would have been effective?"

"Define effective. She would have performed her duties adequately, I believe. What have you heard about her? Is she well?"

"I believe so," she said. "I've asked around, like you wanted. I hear that Jensen got a job quickly, and her boss is very rich. She's out in one of the isolated houses, where someone can afford to build away from the monastery. Ex-military, for sure. They would probably know she's a deserter."

"Do I know her employer?"

"Probably before your time," she said. "I don't know exactly who it is."

"I don't think Wong is going to spend much energy interrogating you, relax."

She snapped her fingers and pointed at me. "Hey, I'm on official business, by the way. One of my tasks is to negotiate some sort of mutual newsletter for both the station and the planet, to keep everyone connected to the news. Births and deaths, marriages. Stuff like that."

"We have only deaths up here."

"We could just send you our newsletter and you could forward it."

"I can do that."

"If you happen to hear about Jensen's births, death, or marriage, I'd like to know that regardless. I'm due for a downcycle someday, if we can clear the taskboard enough. I want to talk to her."

"Sorry," said Amanda. "I can't let you spend any downtime with anyone but me. Come down. I miss you. It's no fun windsurfing alone."

"I miss you, too."

Of all my sins, perhaps the greatest is what I did to Amanda, in the end, when I betrayed her. I don't think forgiveness is possible for that.

It wasn't long after our friendly conversation that I felt the betrayal of lust for another, in its great sinfulness, unexpectedly. I was on a low deck, wearing leg braces, and prepping to dive into a tank to help Sergeant Anderson with a clogged pipe where some new biotic infestation had manifested, suddenly. We were going to blast it with acid and run it through so much algae the otherwise harmless plaque-causing organism that had evolved here would be dead and devoured by the natural systems of cleaning supplies, algae, and high heat. We were out of crewmen, who all had critical maintenance and no time for an emergency biotic infection in a pipe. Instead of reaching out to Wong or Obasanjo to borrow a crewmember, I grabbed Sergeant Anderson and took her down to the low decks to find and clear the clog.

We strapped braces to our legs to handle the gravity. We had back braces, too, because we'd be doing lifting in the high-gravity environment. She got her gear on first and looked up at me with a bright smile. "Race me!" she shouted, jumping to her feet and taking off. I was slower; I chased after her. She dove into a pool of clean water, laughing and kicking into the huge pipes, swimming underwater from one tank to another.

I dove in. The pipes were wide enough for me to hold my hands at my sides and not touch the sides. There was room enough for racing. The water was clean, too. This was our reserve, and it was supposed to be kept as clean as distilled. I swam into the pipe from tank to tank, coming up for air in each tank, while she was out farther ahead. The water was thick and heavy in that gravity, like swimming in a goo, but it was pure H2O. I opened my eyes underwater, seeing her swimming out ahead, her legs kicking hard and her arms churning. I had forgotten the joy of swimming, but my body remembered. I reached the last tank far behind her, gasping for air. She was smiling.

"About time you caught up," she said, leaning on the edge of the last tank. The water made her clothes cling. She had little hair on her head, close-shaved as she was, and her legs floated toward me, kicking lightly to keep her in place.

I didn't know what to say.

"You did not catch me," she said. "You will not stop me swimming back through you, yes? I will pass through you and you will be unable to stop me."

"I will not stop you," I whispered.

"I want you to try."

"I will not, Adebayo," I said. I got out of the water, my hands trembling. "I can't stop you. I'm powerless against you. I respect you."

She lingered there, smiling her mercurial smile. She was as bad as Wong with her stupid grins. Without saying another word, she climbed from the tank. She helped me set up the flush to send the water back into the recycling network, to be refilled from the pipes we just repaired. We were going to have to flush the tanks, whether we swam in them or not. Nothing is ever wasted.

We did not speak about this moment for a long time. I noticed, as well, like a goblin in the back of my mind, that she said very little about her husband, lately.

Sergeant Anderson refused to budge from her bunk in the common quarters, with the sheet separating women and men, and she did not help me keep the new women's quarters clean. I went in, myself, sometimes with Private Giles, others with Private Detkarn, to sweep and clean the biotics and pass them along to the station technicians. I learned very quickly that Detkarn and Wong were having an affair. He was in her room, half-dressed, when she came storming in. She threatened him, jokingly, with the hot water hose, and bleach. Laughing, he dressed quickly, and escaped. He paused in the hallway and saw me.

I had my eyebrow raised, and nothing else.

"The military rules of the interior planets are not always so useful to us on the frontier," he said.

"I don't know what you're talking about, Captain Wong. I was busy calibrating the machines for the biotic sweep of this storage closet, and I don't know why you're in this hallway. Do you need assistance from me, Captain?"

"No, thank you, Lieutenant," he said.

He left quickly. I said nothing to Detkarn. She didn't seem to realize how concerned she should be to fraternize with an officer. It could end their careers, if the admiral didn't like it. I was not envious for her. My heart pined for Sergeant Adebayo Anderson, honestly, even as I was writing letters to Amanda Garcia.

I assumed I was going to be in trouble for opening the rooms to the women enlisted when I was summoned to the admiral's office unexpectedly. I braced myself for consequences.

On my watch, since those first four, there were no more suicides. I saluted and sat down.

"Lieutenant Aldo," said Q. "I wanted you to be the first to know. I'm being promoted out. I've been selected to run a station in the Perseus Arm of the Milky Way. Here, I'll be stepping down into retirement, and a new admiral is being selected to replace me."

"Congratulations," I said. Shock settled in. I had never imagined anyone here would transcend. That it was Q was shocking to me. He never seemed more than just competent, and I knew he had some violations in his early days regarding treatment of the female enlisted. He had to have more ghosts in his record than I did. "What do you need from me?"

"I want to know if you think I should do your performance review now, or wait until the next admiral comes to evaluate you."

"I don't understand."

"I'm demoting Wong. I'm throwing him out, entirely. It was a long time coming. If I do your performance review now, I can promote you into his job."

"I'm an AstroNav. I don't know the first thing about hand-to-hand combat."

He shrugged. "If you just want to study the maps, that's fine. He monitors door locks, for the love of God, and maintains readiness to investigate. I need somebody to step up and take over the job before the new guy comes in. Wong and Obasanjo both are terrible influences on the crew. They need to go. Would you prefer Obasanjo's job?"

"Am I being recommended for transcendence with this promotion?"

"No," he said. "You're interim. You're just interim until the new guy gets in. I don't have the authority to transcend you, or even promote you in full."

"In that case, neither," I said. "I'll wait until your replacement comes for my review."

The admiral looked at me hard. "Listen, my advice is don't get caught up in transcending. Let it go. It will happen or it won't happen. You know why it's done that way, don't you? You know the real reason? Colonies can support their own officer corps, most of the time, eventually. They don't even need us coming from Earth, or anywhere else. They don't need us spinning around the galaxy chasing promotions."

"It keeps us connected," I said.

"Exactly," he said. "It keeps us biologically as well as culturally connected. This is how we stop the island effect with our roving genetic populations, and maintain everyone's core humanity. We keep shuttling in humans that can add genetic material from the home planet to the colony, and from colony to colony. It slows down the island effect. So, don't worry if you aren't recruited for that purpose. Even if you are chosen, the real you remains here the whole time. It is only a copy of you that goes. Focus on here, right now. Help me make this station better."

"I already have," I said. "I set up the female enlisted with separate barracks with help from Wong, without your knowledge. I did it because they are besieged and have no meaningful privacy, and do not feel like the officer corps respect their desire not to be the object of desperate leers. I have maintained mission readiness while permitting my staff to blow off steam, improving morale. Suicides are down on my watch. None since the first four which was just before I implemented my new policies."

He pressed his fingers against his temple. He closed his eyes. He took a deep breath.

"Lieutenant Ronaldo Aldo, I am going to do your performance evaluation right now, after which you will take over for Wong, who has been having an affair with someone in his chain of command. Do you understand how badly this is going to go for you that I am putting you into the position of the worst officer in the entire station, simultaneous to your duties with the quartermaster's role? You will never sleep a full night again, if I have my way. You will work and work until the next admiral takes pity on you. I am doing this to you because you're an arrogant little shit, and you think you're better than everyone else. You think you deserve to transcend, and you don't. You don't deserve the promotion to captain I have to give you to get HR to let you do two roles at once."

He stood up and walked around to the door. He opened the door. "I will send you details with your new priorities in the morning. Don't bother telling Wong anything. He will be sent planetside shortly, with just a dishonorable discharge unless I can dig up some real serious recent dirt on him in the next twenty minutes. Get out of my office and let the sergeant know what's going on. Interesting times," he said, drifting off into muttering to himself.

He was telling the truth when he called me arrogant, and I knew it. I liked hearing him say it. I had done a good job. I had done the best job of anyone I knew, and if that made me arrogant, so be it. I felt the call in my heart to escape my way, not theirs, and figure out the rest of the plan that was slowly coming together in my secret mind. Drifting debris, and me in charge of labeling it. Old equipment, and me in charge of repairing it. I just needed to figure out the human aspect of the plan, connecting the technology to the situation. Also, I needed the guts to do it. And, when Q called me a jerk for trying to help my soldiers not kill themselves, I started to feel brave enough to really do something. This was probably the moment that I began truly wanting to blow up my world.

———————

Come down for Easter, Amanda said. Demand the time off. It is a big festival, with music and dancing. I have vacation time accruing, after all, and nobody cares if the AstroNav hops planetside for a time, she said.

The departing admiral responded to my vacation request with a harsh negative, considering my expanded duties.

The incoming admiral changed all of Q's orders before she even arrived. Wong was quietly reinstated. Other personnel changes were put on hold. The new admiral even wanted me to cycle down to the planet, and run diagnostics on the communications interface between the monastery and the station. I would combine it with a supply run, and Obasanjo promised me I would be there for at least three weeks. Amanda was excited because that meant I'd be down for Easter.

Obasanjo pointed out, quietly and in person, that the resupply and the rotation of the station above the planet meant there was going to be a launch window problem even after resupply. If I stretched out the diagnostics, I could make my time on the surface last a month. I was assigned an enlisted aid, Private Chet Detkarn, but Wong told me, in private, that she would probably not be much help to me with her other duties on the surface. I didn't know what he meant by that, and he told me not to worry about it; the new admiral had something else in mind for her.

Not much of an aid, at the monastery, she disappeared as soon as we landed, off into the dunes with two men from the village.

I met Brother Pleo again. He had a smug smile on his face. "How have you been, Ensign?"

I offered my hand and he shook it. "If Detkarn deserts I will hurt you," I said. "I will hunt you down and plant a full transport on your spine."

"I'm sorry you feel so afraid. We are a peaceful planet. Please don't abuse our trust with shallow threats. Allow me to show you to your quarters."

I had no intention of staying there. "I'm a captain now, thanks. I have arranged my own housing. I will be back in the morning to correct your technical problems."

He laughed. "Suspicious much?"

"You really screwed me, Brother. I got a lot of heat for losing my corporal. We shut down the downcycle to a crawl over what you did to aid her."

"We also saved your sergeant's life, Captain. We are actually trying to help the station with your suicide problem. Thirty percent of all personnel stationed to the Citadel via ansible commit suicide before retirement. We feel you need a full-time chaplain. Our methods are not your methods. Our goals are the same. We both want the best for the colony and the station."

"Detkarn isn't suicidal, Pleo. She comes back with me or I blame you forever."

"You are overreacting, Ensign."

"Captain."

"Sorry, Captain. We are not enemies. Come and join us for dinner. Break bread with us. Join us at evening prayer, if you like. We are not enemies."

The heat struck like a wall of sand. The hot wind blew up over the walls and jumped down to the ground. I looked up at the sky, where the Citadel star was brazen and relentless.

"I will have to decline the invitation."

I passed through the thick stone walls. I walked through a newly planted jujube orchard and manipulated the windbreak gates to get through into the sand dunes that flowed through the alleyways and roads between the buildings. Robots—they looked new to me—moved like sidewinders over the ground, rolling and sweeping the yellow sand off the streets, and back away into the wider world. I knocked on what I thought was the Garcia family door. There was no answer. I picked up my phone and called.

"Amanda? This is Aldo."

"Aldo! Are you down!"

"I am. Where are you?"

"We're out on a job. Listen, the door shouldn't be locked. Go in and get some water. We'll be there soon."

The door was locked. I knocked again, and no answer. I thought of calling her back, but I didn't feel comfortable calling her with this. Should I call her over this? I didn't want to call her. I walked down the street, listening close for any sign of life among the doorways and closed windows.

I knocked on a door, feeling the heat push through my uniform like some kind of damp furnace. No one answered. I tried the door, and it opened. I slipped inside. I was no thief, only trying to get out of the deadly sun. I sat on the cold stone just inside the door, panting and looking around for any sign of water. My eyes adjusted to the dark room. I saw a man looking up at me from a cot. Next to him, a woman I did not recognize. The man, though, was someone I knew.

"Were you looking for me, Ensign?"

"Captain," I said. "I'm a captain now. No, sorry. I was trying to find the Garcia house, and I got lost and now I'm here. I'm sorry to disturb you. I didn't change into appropriate clothes in the monastery. I thought I would be in a friendly home in under a minute."

The woman rolled over and blinked at me. "Whatever you want, just please shut up. I'm exhausted."

She was visibly pregnant. I cocked my head at that. I apologized.

"They're probably digging out the northern trees. We got swamped by sand. It broke some of the windbreaks."

She pushed at him from her cot. "Jesus Christ, Jon. I am so tired. Please shut up."

"Sorry," I said. "Amanda said her door was unlocked. I may have gone to the wrong house. Do you know where hers is?"

Sergeant Anderson looked up at me with this dead tired expression. "Man, you have got to be pulling my leg, Captain. I'm not in the service anymore. Get some water and go upstairs if you want to access the 'net. We're sleeping. Keep it quiet. Or leave. Whatever."

"Thanks, Jon," I said. "You know, your wife is my right hand. I'm the quartermaster. She's indispensable."

The other woman looked up at me, startled. "I don't even know you." She rolled over.

He looked at me. "Upstairs," he said. "Now."

"Oh, God, he doesn't know . . . ," said the woman. She rubbed her stomach and reached for a glass of water. She sat up to drink it. A weedy, sallow girl far too young for him. Her stomach was huge. She had to be close. She moved awkwardly around her own belly, like a counterweight in a physics problem she could not cleanly solve.

Sergeant Anderson led me up, and I realized quickly why he was sleeping downstairs. The room was much hotter closer to the roof, where the sun undoubtedly challenged the limits of the air-conditioning units that chilled the interior along with the natural cold of the basement. He reached to a wall tap and poured a glass of water. He handed it to me. It tasted gritty and warm and disgusting. I could barely swallow it.

"We're divorced," he said. "She doesn't want anyone to know. It would dishonor her."

"What?"

"I don't exactly stand in any position to stop her from telling anyone about it," he said. "I'm out, remember? I don't ever have to go back to that miserable dreidel."

"I don't understand."

"It would dishonor her among her peers, Captain. Please, exercise discretion. It isn't something she wants anyone to know."

"She's within three years of honorable discharge. What will she do down here?"

He poured himself a glass of water. He drank it slowly. "You know, I don't know. It's not really up to me, either. It is what it is. We're divorced. We've been divorced a long time. Two years. Maybe three. How long has it been since I was dumped here to die?"

"To live, Sergeant. I wanted you to live. You would have died flying if I hadn't had the tech check you. You have something to live for now, don't you?"

"I do," he said. "Thanks for nothing. Stay here. Drink some water. I don't have enough food for you, so you're going to have to wait until the Garcia family gets you. Don't be a dick. Pay them for it. Food is scarce. We don't have a huge storage locker of old amaranth bars. Hell, you should try and trade those down here. We'd eat the shit out of those horrible sticky bricks from a hundred years ago."

"Thanks. I'll let Obasanjo know, if he's still around when I get back."

"I'm going back to bed. Don't make a lot of noise. We're exhausted from the storm around here. Everyone is asleep who can afford it."

I sat in the hot room, feeling the pressure of the heat from above, and the cooling system up from below. I sipped water from a tap in the wall with clean stone mugs beside it. What else could I do until Amanda got home? Also, I confess that I snooped a little. I pulled up their tablet and pretended to be searching for maps of the city, but I was also just vaguely scanning the file names and categories. Sergeant Anderson, up in the station, was still writing letters to her husband in the night, I thought. She was still in love with him, I thought. I closed one folder before I could become privy to anything too embarrassing. I saw enough. The date on the file was recent enough. Is it a sin to snoop? It is probably a sin to lie about snooping.

I sipped water, and spread out on the floor to rest. I was off cycle, definitely, and the day lengths were different here than on the station. I rested, and waited for word from the Garcia family.

When my commlink rang, it wasn't Amanda. Obasanjo called.

"You're on the ground, right?"

"I am. What do you need?"

"I need you to tell me something on a secure line."

"Tell you what?"

"Who is in charge of the monastery. Go out and tell me who is running the place now. Pleo is stonewalling me."

"I'm not at the monastery," I said.

"Where the hell are you? You just landed, right? They're charging us room and board for you and Detkarn!"

"Neither one of us is at the monastery."

"The goobers. They're probably just so busy with Easter."

"What are they doing to you?"

"I'm trying to reach the person in charge, but it doesn't look like anyone is in charge right now. No one is returning my calls. It's a new tactic, and it's pissing me off. I'm going to have a nice, long chat with the monastery about housing costs as soon as I get them on the line. Excuse me, Captain."

When darkness fell, Jon Anderson's wife woke up, and came upstairs. She was frightening, with wild hair and dark eyes. "You're still here?" she said.

"I'm sorry to intrude on you," I said. "I don't believe we were formally introduced."

"Maia," she said. "I'm Maia Anderson."

"Captain Renaldo Aldo."

"I don't want you here, Captain. You and the Garcia trans-girl can go jump off a cliff. They're only interested in you for land, you know. They want to own as much as they can get."

"I find it hard to believe there are no other ambitions in anyone's heart on a planet as challenging as this one. Isn't Easter upon us?"

"Happy Easter. Did you sacrifice anything for Lent or Ramadan or whatever?"

"I have sacrificed enough just coming down to the dunes, haven't I?"

She laughed at that. "I was born here. In this very room, in fact." She pointed to a corner where an emergency medical station was not plugged in.

"I'm sorry you have never seen a coral reef," I said. "I am sorry you have never stood in the shade of a tree in spring, and heard the mockingbirds and pigeons in the branches, singing. I apologize for interrupting your sleep."

"I have a lot to do, Captain. Jon's already gone off to work on the moisture vaporators. I can't afford to feed you, and you've already taken a lot of water out of our system."

Politely, I gestured to my tablet. "How much do you need for the night?"

She gave me a price for the water that was high, but I paid it, gladly. I needed friends, not enemies, on the ground. I had enough enemies in this world without alienating Jon Anderson's new wife.

Outside, the colony lamps were lit, and I followed them back to the monastery.

Inside, a brother I did not know was busy sweeping and clearing out the entry hall. He looked up at me with confusion. "It's too early for the festival, sir."

"I'm military."

"I know that," he said. "That's why I called you 'sir.'" He placed the broom aside and held out his hand. "I'm Brother Benedict. Nice to meet you."

"Captain Aldo. I was just talking with my colleague, Lieutenant Commander Obasanjo. He is having difficulty reaching the person in charge of the monastery. Where is your abbot?"

"Oh, he retired. We haven't picked a new one yet. Sorry.

Have you had breakfast? Come on, and join us for a meal."

I took his hand and shook, but I was confused and did not go with him. I held my ground where I stood. "What happened to the old abbot?"

"He retired, I told you," said Brother Benedict "Come on if you're coming. You're lucky I was here to show you in. I was just trying to get ahead of the festival preparations. Ash Wednesday is tomorrow, you know."

"What is the festival, exactly?"

"How familiar are you with the traditions of Old Christianity?" he said.

I shrugged.

He talked while he led me to the cafeteria. "Well, look it up after breakfast. It isn't obscure. Some of the brothers from the Mohammedan traditions and the Baha'i heresy seek to undermine it with other symbols, but it is important to have festivals, and it is the holiest time of the year: rebirth. Soon the jujubes will sprout new leaves. Soon, the amaranth stalks will set flower. All life begins in spring. All rebirth. Will you seek baptism?"

"Probably not. What is it?"

He laughed. "Like a bath for your soul."

We reached the cafeteria, then, and I sat down with Brother Pleo, who was smirking at me. "You're back," he said.

"Duty calls," I replied. "Apparently, you're charging us a hefty fee for use of this facility, and I want to make sure you only charge us for what is actually used. Private Detkarn, has she appeared since arriving?"

"No sign of her. Do you think she might have gone native?"

I did not respond. "Brother Pleo, who is in charge here? Who has the authority to negotiate with Obasanjo? Don't stall for time. Just tell me."

"No one does, right this second. The abbot just retired two days ago. There's no new abbot yet. We have to wait for word from the central church."

"And . . . ?"

"And, what?"

"Who is authorized to negotiate in good faith with the station?"

"Until the abbot is selected? I don't think anyone is."

"Emergency circumstances. Special circumstances. You have called me to fix your lines because you need them operational to get word out to the central church, yes? So, I'm stuck down here even afterward until negotiations complete after the work is done?"

"You make it sound like a dirty plot on our part."

"Detkarn, then. Is it she who needs the time?"

He shrugged. "I can only imagine that the task she has beyond our repair is very important to whomever caused the damage to our little wires and machines."

"What does the monastery even want that Wong can offer you?"

"You would know if you looked closer," he said. "Aren't you moving up in the ranks?

I snorted. "Promotions don't feel like promotions, most of the time. If I'm not careful, I'll get promoted to abbot."

After dinner, I joined the brothers for evening mass. It was peaceful and cool in the church hall, and the singing and chanting were relaxing after so much confusion. I considered, for a brief moment, what life must be like to be one of the men making such music. I sat in the far back of the room, observing the ceremony and listening to the chanting. It was a nice break from the confusion and stress that was omnipresent in that period of my life. It was there that Amanda found me, at last.

She slipped into the back of the room, and gracefully descended into the pew next to mine. She placed her hand over mine. "Hello, Captain," she said. She kissed my hand.

She led me from the service into the long halls of the monastery, into the kitchen. We were alone there, but she seemed to know her way around without help. She prepared a noodle dish with vegetables. She spoke of the difficulties of the sandstorm.

"It would have swallowed the orchard," she said. "We dug it out, but time will tell if the trees survive. We might lose some. Dad is already setting up rooting hormone for replacements, just in case."

"More red date?"

"Pistachio, this time. The water will be here next year to support new trees. We are expanding an orchard on our own lands. If we had more people in our household, our allotment would be higher. I am supposed to marry as soon as I can find a suitable partner."

"How romantic," I said.

She shrugged. "How many suitable partners are there here? Be realistic for a moment. It was hard enough transitioning here. Stupid people still call me Jeremy."

Looking at her, I made the rash decision I had avoided for so long. I sought the man she was born as inside the body and lines of the woman she became. It was a mistake. Once I saw, I couldn't let go completely of the straight shoulders and hips, the broadness of the chest.

"We have to face facts. There's a female shortage around here, and I am at a loss for men, too. I am something else, to them. But I have only ever been a woman to you, haven't I? I am a woman, to you, aren't I? Inside of myself, I have always and forever been a woman, and the med tech backs me up on that."

I touched her hands. I picked them up. They were hard and strong and weather-beaten, but she was right. To me, they were a woman's hands.

"I don't need to spell this out, do I?" she said, pleading.

I leaned in close and roughly kissed her. I felt the pressure of it on my face, where our clean-shaven skin pushed against the sweat and smoothness. I felt, at first, a fluttering in me, as it was happening. I felt a crazy nervous energy wash over me. What I did not feel was lust.

"Amanda," I said, pushing her back. "Amanda, please, not here."

She let me push her. We returned to the meal in silence.

"I am sorry we weren't here to greet you when you landed."

"There is plenty of time for greetings," I said. "Once the orchard is safe, there is plenty of time. You wish to marry and expand your allotment?"

"I do."

"Do you wish to marry me?"

"I do. I really like you."

"I like you, too."

This sin, then, was perhaps my worst. I felt no lust in my heart for this poor young woman, but I believed that I was lost here. I was drifting without an anchor, missing everything that made life pure and good. I did not know what else to say. What I said was: "We will arrange the wedding soon enough. I can't marry until I retire without a dispensation. Perhaps the new admiral will allow it. The ice comet is coming soon. I don't have anywhere to keep you, and I want to have a home when I retire, don't I?"

She laughed. "Darling husband, you know I already have a house and land, right? I'm keeping you, not the other way around. I'll show you after the festival. You can buy some land adjacent to mine. How's that sound?"

I guess it was good. I don't know how it sounded. I felt like the most foolish, useless creature in the whole universe. I decided it wasn't any good. "I want to live in my own space. I want to be my own man. I've been cooped up in a room up on the station, cameras everywhere and recording devices. I want to be my own man, in my own little house. You can have your house, and I'll have mine. We'll travel between them. How does that sound?"

She placed her hand on mine, and it was hard for me, right then, to see the hand as my wife's hand. I feel terrible about what happened between us, and I hope she is happy.

"I have to work tomorrow," I said. "I have to do what I came here to do. The house can wait. Everything can wait. I don't know what to do about anything. I feel useless here, like an extra part glued onto the side of a wing that would fly so much better without me."

She leaned into me. She touched my cheek. "Don't be so seriously depressing to be with." She leaned over. "I want joy. I want happiness. I want a good, long life with someone I love and I want to be cherished. Why don't you try touching me, already? Come on. Give me your hand. I'm a real woman. I'm right here, and I want you. I can't believe you need me to hold your hand through this."

Confessor, I will spare the details of my time with Amanda. She is a beautiful woman, and I was a fool to fail to love her.

We took from each others' bodies, and I felt foolish doing it. I had never been with a woman. It had been years since I even considered the mechanics of the situation. In the hot room, in the windowless darkness, I looked down upon our bodies and felt ashamed that I wasn't any good at this thing that everyone was supposed to know how to do.

Afterward, I felt empty. All that buildup, all that imagination wasted picturing this, and it was such a slight thing, and I was sweaty, and sleepy, and ashamed of what I had done to this poor girl I did not love.

When I woke up, I went to the monastery to work on their machines. It was a simple, brutish job, and the tablet I carried walked me through everything step-by-step. Brother Al-Malik came by from time to time to offer me mint tea. I always accepted it. My body could not seem to retain any water. It was so hot, even at night, that I was drenched in sweat after just an hour or two. I joined the brothers for lunch, when they called to me, but I knew I hadn't done enough for one day. I was supposed to have Detkarn helping me. I left a message for Obasanjo about that, and mentioned that Detkarn had ditched me. I wanted to look for her instead of finishing the job.

He told me to forget about Detkarn, and take my time. He said it would give him leverage to negotiate as long as I was working slow. I was to let him know if I did get close to finishing.

Amanda came to me nearly every night. I grew accustomed to her skin, her body, her lust. You know this, however. You remember because you were in the monastery and sang matins while I sinned in the night with that beautiful girl. At her house, her father was conveniently absent, off at the new fam-

214 • Joe M. McDermott

ily compound where he was working on their new orchard. He came by from time to time for meals, shaking my hand and saying nothing about what he had to know was happening with his daughter. He was warm and open. He offered me every comfort. He refused payment. He treated me like family. I am sorry for him, too.

Confessor, the strangest thing that happened to me was when Brother Pleo came to me after the second week I was there, after I had been laying cables along the outside wall of the tower, attached to the building with magnets while dust blew up and all around me, sticking to my skin, making me truly miserable with its combination of hot sand and cool night air. I sat at the dinner table, feeling the grit everywhere it had pushed through my protective layers into my damp skin. I was going to eat and wash up and make the journey to Amanda's house to sleep in her arms. Brother Pleo came to me, and he sat down across from me, and he handed me a glass of water.

"Can I help you, Brother?"

"You look like you aren't drinking enough water, Captain. Drink some water. I promise I didn't poison it."

I took the water. I sniffed it. I put it down. "Why are you being nice to me?"

"I wanted to take you somewhere interesting. Would you like to visit your lost corporal? You know that I know where she is. The wires can wait until tomorrow. Honestly, you look exhausted."

"Where is she?"

"Safe from your military, and they know it. Honestly, as small as we are down here on the planet, if your people wanted to come down and take her, she'd be took. We don't have any firepower here. Our only leverage is food."

"I'm going to report that I found her."

"Also, that you can't accost her by yourself, which is fine. No one is coming to get her. If someone does, she will move before you get here for her. Look, can you just accept that maybe no one is out to get you here? We actually want to be friends with you. You're an important man on the station, and we're honored to host you here. Relax, Captain. There is no war here. We're all going to be fine."

I drank the water. "Let's go now," I said.

Brother Pleo, accommodating, led me to the very Osprey that had vexed me the last time I was on the surface. He gestured for me to strap into the passenger side, and sat down next to me. He plugged the coordinates into the machine, and let the autopilot take over. He looked very pleased with himself. I admit that I fantasized acts of violence and depravity.

"How long is the journey?"

"Not long," he said. "It's windy tonight. It might get a little bumpy. I'll need to take the controls if they do. I don't think you've been trained in Ospreys in a long time."

"Not since Earth. Why are you being nice to me?"

"This may come as a surprise to you, but we do try to be very nice people. Men of the cloth try to help our fellow men and women. You know, you look like you need some help. When I see you, you look miserable."

"I've been climbing over your walls in the heat and sand. I am miserable. I could use a qualified tech to help me, and Detkarn is off doing who knows what for Commander Wong."

"I'll see what I can do to make your life less miserable. You haven't bought any land, have you? I haven't seen your name listed on any maps. Do you plan on retiring?"

"I do. I'm waiting for the ice comet to melt so I can see where the water goes. Why should anything I do matter to you?"

"I want to know why you're miserable, so I can try and help you work through it and find peace in God and peace on this planet. I am concerned you are a suicide risk. Thanks be to God you have a boyfriend."

"Girlfriend."

"Jeremy. Amanda. Doesn't matter. We're happy for you both. What do you believe?"

We soared over dunes in a twilight darkness. The horizon glowed purple and gold where the sand kicked up. It was beautiful and stark. It reminded me of the ocean where I grew up. I miss oceans.

"I never really stopped to consider belief. I believe you are telling me the truth that you want to help me. I don't know if you are the one who can."

"What do you want out of this life, then? What is your greatest desire?"

I thought hard. "When I was a boy, and I had a birthday party, my mother would tell me to blow out the candle and make a wish. She said that if I told anyone my wish, it wouldn't come true."

"It doesn't count when you speak with your confessor. We pray with you. We reveal nothing. We keep secrets. We are here if you need us."

"Thanks," I said.

We flew out past the canyon, with the towerlike rock, and beyond across the vast, sweeping sands.

He pointed to the dunes. "The ice comet is going to come down, probably, on this plain. It is a very low elevation. Someday, this will be our ocean."

"Someday, but not today."

"We must always imagine the future. Without it, we would have no hope, Captain. It is a way of keeping people feeling hope. Is it so hard to imagine an ocean here?"

"It is an ocean now, in a way. Were you born here?"

He shook his head. "Most of the brothers are retired military men. My mother was a biotic. She taught me her work. My skills are very useful in terraforming. We need diverse soil."

"What use is an AstroNav outside of the service? I am just an overqualified network technician here. Good thing I've been quartermaster. I've gotten serious about plumbing."

"I'm sure you will thrive in retirement. When officers retire, they have so much money. It's obscene. We have so little here. Someday the economy will improve to beggar all of you. We are headed to a retired officer's compound now. She has been retired for almost forty years."

In the distance, a speck on the horizon slowly transformed into a dome of clear material, with shade cloth spread over it to diminish the force of the sun.

"She will have to move when the ocean comes," I said.

"She retired full admiral. She is a prominent donor of our little monastery in the sands. We do not tell her what to do. I advise against telling her what to do, Captain. Be polite."

"She outranks me. I get it."

The flyer landed by itself, a good distance from the complex.

"We park here because the complex actually is underground now. The sand buries it."

He led the way to the entrance, in the shaded dome, where air vents pushed away the sand enough to reveal the doorway.

Inside, a series of hydroponic pipes grew vegetables and grains, while a few weeping jujube trees waited gracefully for a breeze from the door to make them dance.

"There are individual holdings all over the planet, where wealthier officers retire."

An intercom buzzed. "Brother Pleo, that you?" Over the line, she sounded old and impatient, with the kind of barking precision that is the hallmark of experienced and competent commanders.

"It is. I brought you the aspiring AstroNav."

"Name and rank?"

Pleo looked over at me. Oh, I was supposed to answer. "Captain Ronaldo Aldo, ma'am. I am looking for a lost corporal."

"Come on down and say hello."

A trapdoor unlocked, and a stairwell descended into the structure. I followed Brother Pleo down into the darkness. My eyes slowly adjusted to the spacious dark. Water tanks lined the walls, filled with fish. Furniture, as well: couches and tables. Everything was empty, though. A door opened down at the end of the hall. Private Detkarn called out to us. "Come on, then. The admiral is waiting."

"I feel like I have been lied to by a great many people," I said.

"More that you never asked the right questions," said Brother Pleo.

"I have been doing here what you are doing for the monastery," said Detkarn. "Wong arranged it."

"Of course he did. Is she pulling Wong's strings, and everyone else's?"

Brother Pleo placed a hand on my arm. "You are a guest here, Captain."

"I just want to know who the boss is."

Detkarn smiled and nodded noncommittally. She waved us down. "The admiral will see you in the dining room. She sent me up to fetch you."

"Admiral," I said.

We descended into the complex down two flights of stairs and across a room full of laboratory equipment until we reached this dining hall.

At the end of a long table, in a dark room, a woman as dark as the room with a shock of white hair like bleached cotton stared at us. She did not smile, nor did she stand. She gestured for us to come closer.

She was in a wheelchair. She was eating a sandwich of some sort, and drinking jujube tea. She took Brother Pleo's hand and clasped it, firmly. We sat down at chairs there.

"You're the quartermaster, yes?"

"For now," I said. "I was supposed to be an AstroNav, but I got promoted when the admiral shot himself. There is no AstroNav right now."

"I have been asked to come out of retirement. Did you know that no one wants to come to our lovely outpost, even if it means sending a clone as a full admiral?"

"I don't know anything about politics. I just want to bring my lost corporal home to justice."

"You can't have her," she said.

"I didn't catch your name, Admiral."

"Khunbish. Ahn Khunbish. I am ninety-three and I am in no condition to come out of retirement, even as interim. I have told HR as much. They keep pestering me. We need new people, badly. Our genetic diversity cannot support a large colony. We will never get up to fighting strength without more diversity. There are less than three hundred people here. When the first settlement was started in Mars, there were five hundred engineers in the first wave of settlers alone. We need more people. The ice comet will be here in months. We can support more."

"Didn't the first Mars colony fail?"

"Don't correct me. Do you have any idea how old I am?"

"Ninety-three?"

"More than that, I mean. Terran time. Gravity is low; time runs slow on this edge of the Laika. I was born before the war, Captain. I was in the ship when it was fighting. I was in the last battle, shooting rail guns and mines at enemy ships. This was before ansibles could be used to clone anything. We survived out here in a ruined hull long enough to build the technology that saved our butts and let us crawl to the nearest habitable world. I was just a raw recruit, but I survived and I promoted up and out. There are seven of me out there. The ansible is the most important thing in the world, and the military hoards it while the colony flounders. Brother Pleo knows what I am talking about. The colony is the key. Suicides go down if the colony is a haven for wayward souls. We have discussed this a lot."

"We have not, Admiral."

She nodded. "Of course, of course. I'm just an old fool. Don't mind me, young man."

"You have fresh food and water; we have the ansible. I am stuck down here while Obasanjo negotiates contentiously without any other source of food. I am not political. I do my duty."

"The colony is more important than the station," said the admiral. "You have to see that."

"Like I said, I am not political, Admiral. Brother Pleo said I could come here and see my lost corporal. I want to try to convince her to come home, face the music, so to speak."

"Good luck with that. She will be here soon. I was looking over your service record. Don't bother asking how I got it, because I have it. You aren't going to promote out. You understand? The military will never promote you out. This is it, for you. HR is not impressed. At least, your commanding officers have always said bad things about you, and HR doesn't care if you deserve it or not. There is no appeal out here. The Garcia boy, you are with Jeremy?"

"Amanda," I said.

"She's post-op?"

"Yes," I said.

"Good kid. Smart kid. Smarter than you. Hard worker. Right. You like being quartermaster?"

"It doesn't matter what I like," I said. "I serve. I obey. In a decade, maybe, I can retire and build a beautiful house like yours and live in peace."

"You don't like it. You want to fly a warship. Not with your record. No, not with your record. You're lucky to get supply runs. Death and desertion on your watch. Lower suicide rate, though, since those three or four out the airlock, and you have been trying to improve morale. Picking up extra shifts with your staff sergeant so you don't blow out the staff. You seem nice enough. Detkarn says you try to help the women survive the men. Q is no leader. He's just a technician in over his head, writing to the Terran council like he knows what is important here, quoting scripture at bureaucrats like a fool. HR keeps pestering this old lady. I knew what was important. I didn't waste their time. Well, let's go find your lost corporal."

Her tea and sandwich untouched, she directed her chair with a switch to lead the way deeper into the complex. The chair was surprisingly quick, and I had to walk fast to keep up. Brother Pleo stayed behind to eat the sandwich and drink the tea. He waved to me and smiled.

"I am going to accept command, you know," she said. "When you finish laying cables, I go up with you to take over for Obasanjo and Q." The halls were cool and dark, with low-energy lighting along the floor. There were too many rooms to count. "Q's transcending because he has a good blood type. It will make the retirement order sting less. Good technician, terrible admiral. Obasanjo has got to go. He's worse than Q. Okay, here's the nursery."

A door opened without warning, sliding gently away from me. Inside, it stank of talcum powder. There were seven cradles, with seven babies sleeping in them, all under plastic oxygen hoods, hooked up to machines. "We lost one. Orhan died the first week. The rest are going to make it. These are my children, Captain. These are what I am leaving behind to go clean up the mess you officers are making of the station and the precious ansible."

The corporal was there, watching over the babes. She was visibly pregnant, though not so far along.

"You came to get me," she said, to me.

"It is my duty to try and recover you to the station for justice. Come home, Corporal."

Jensen pointed at the babies. "Two of these are my girls," she said. "Go jump in a lake, Ensign."

"I see my persuasion techniques are ineffective. It will be hanging over your head your whole life. Any military person could swoop in and take you up to face court martial. It isn't a serious charge, and it won't be if you have a good friend in the admiral. Come up and get a clean slate," I said.

"My wife won't be facing court martial," said the admiral. "She's going to be more mother to my own children than I will ever be, at my age. I will be just a memory to these darling babes. I was lucky to find a willing womb in need of shelter. Jenny, be a dear and harvest more greens before you come up. I can't touch the damn sandwich. Too heavy."

"Sure thing, Ahn," she said.

"Does HR know about this?"

"Does HR care about one damn desertion? I can pardon her as soon as I have official stationery. And I will. You have seen her. I have seen you. This meeting is over. We will talk again when you fly me up to take command."

"I have no reason to disbelieve you, Admiral, but at the moment, I am going to have to call Obasanjo and Wong and file a report and set the location."

"Your duty," she said, rolling her eyes. "I was beginning to like you a little. Now, I think you're the idiot Wong says you are. You won't have a signal this low. Go on up top. There's an elevator at the end of the hall that will take you to the green roof. I will open the door for you."

Up and up, then, and in the green, I walked among trees and plants in a climate-controlled dome, cool and refreshing in the shade with such terrible heat outside on the dunes. I couldn't imagine a world full of green if I tried. I had seen nothing but gunmetal corridors and sand dunes and rocks. To imagine a future of green grass, green trees, a breathing, vibrant world, was to imagine a fantasy.

Still, the ice meteor was coming. I logged in while I waited to estimate the cost of this very domicile, and it must have been built slowly, top level first, and it must have been too expensive in energy and exchanged food to sweep out the sand that was burying the entryway on the other side of the dune.

I messaged Obasanjo and told him that I met the old admiral, and she seemed to think she was coming back on duty. He didn't know what I was talking about and thanked me for the news. I think he forgot about it. He didn't mention it later on.

Brother Pleo came up with a sandwich and a thermos of tea for me. I ate in the Osprey.

"What a strange woman," I said.

"She is very influential. I am not surprised she isn't mentioned much on the station. It wouldn't suit her goals to be so overt."

"Maybe she should be talked about more."

"I thought you weren't political. Do you take a side in the ongoing battle for the ansible between us and the station?"

"No, I don't care who is on top. It seems pointless as long as we all survive and the enemy doesn't come to make war on us."

Back at the monastery, I had two more nights to lay cables and sweat and scrape against the sand on the outer walls, and then everything stopped for the Easter festival.

Much of the festival, I was with Amanda and her father.

There were booths with foods I had never had before, most of which did not compare to my memories of Earth, but they were better than I was accustomed to on the station. I was polite about it. There was a drum circle for a while, and dancing in the spotlights. There was a swimming pool in the center of the monastery. It was shallow, but it was cool and refreshing and we could all just jump in and wade into the water to our knees, splash and dance to the drums. That night, with Amanda, I fell asleep in her arms, and for just a moment, a fleeting feeling that burned away in waking, I thought I could be happy on the Citadel. Three days of high mass started on a Friday, and half the day was spent listening to music and stories from the pews, of all the chanting and storytelling of the monks. Christ is risen, alleluia, etc. The other faith traditions among the monks injected their variations, but it all revolved around a risen Christ. I fell asleep during two of the ceremonies. The first time, I was kicked awake by someone behind me. The second, I was allowed to sleep in the back of the room, and I woke up alone in the dark, confused and sore. I stumbled around until I realized where I was, and why there was no light. I found my way back into the main hall, then, and found a brother who could direct me to a place to get some food. Afterward, all the stalls and shops and music faded into the dust, and tired people went back to work surviving. I don't know what to think about the festival. I had too much to think about. Amanda enjoyed it, and I was happy to make her happy for a little while.

Work on the wires went slow, by myself. Detkarn returned from the old admiral's house in the dunes. She helped me, then, finishing the task at hand. We laid wires and cables, which were thick and strong against the winds and dunes, a technology older and sturdier against the storms than the wireless connections that kept dropping in and out with the sand and strong winds.

I told Obasanjo that I was almost done, when I had about a day left of laying wires.

"Good news: We got a new admiral coming in. I don't know all the details, but watch your orders. Q is pretty freaked out, but I guess retiring early is weird. I've already shipped him out up the ansible. Apparently our metrics still suck, so they're re-

226 • Joe M. McDermott

tiring him, and they're bringing in someone else, even though
he did well enough to transcend? I don't know. HR never
makes sense."

"It's not his fault. Anybody could be in charge and metrics
would suck."

"Whatever's going on, nobody likes it. Have you heard anything?"

"Maybe, but I don't really know what's going on. I've been
crawling all over the monastery putting wires in every room."

"You're useless to me, Ronaldo. I hope you had some fun.
How was Easter?"

"I slept through most of it. I was tired. The music was nice."

"What a wild boy. I hope the colony survived your shenanigans."

"I found our deserter. I've got the report ready, but I don't
want to send it to Wong."

"Corporal . . . What was her name? The woman?"

"Yes."

"Why bother?"

"She needs to be brought to justice."

"Not really, though. If she comes back, sure, but who cares?
I'm just glad she didn't kill herself. Go AWOL if you can secure
a hiding place. It's not a bad idea."

"You're on a recorded line, Lieutenant Commander."

"Who's listening? Wong? He doesn't care. HR has heard me
say worse to their faces. I've got to go. Orders came down and
we're really opening up the ansible to the colony. Ice meteor's
coming. They need things. Lots of things. No one cares about
us, floating in space, watching for the return of the enemy. I
don't even care about us, and I'm the ExO."

"I find your casual attitude upsetting to my morale. I'm

hanging up now, in protest of your terrible attitude. I have faith in my superiors. Hooray for the mission."

"Bye!"

I hung up on him.

When the orders came, I was genuinely surprised to see them, even though I had an early warning. The retired admiral I had met was going to be our permanent interim commander, set to replace Q's interim.

She was in a wheelchair, and needed regular treatments for her kidneys, but she was not cowed in her old age. Later, when she came to me in my little cell, she was not cowed. She only came to me once after my great crime against the ansible network. She said one word to me, with such disgust in her voice. *Shithead.* Then, she left me to wait for justice in my cell.

———

Flying up, the first thing that happened was Q was angry for no apparent reason, and Captain Wong remained in uniform, taking over as both quartermaster and security, with staff sergeants to do the heavy lifting for his dual role. Obasanjo, smirking and amused by the situation, was retired early. He would go to the planet surface on the next available transport. In his stead, I was promoted to ExO over Wong and Nguyen, the last remaining officers. The new admiral explained to me that in this role, I would mostly be overseeing ansible transfers, and that negotiations with the surface would be done by her, directly. She had better relationships with the monastery, anyway, and I did not disagree with that, nor had I any desire to take over the contracts with the monastery. The ansible transfers were challenging enough to a newcomer, like me. I also was put in charge of overseeing most personnel issues, as a sort of backup officer to mediate between officers and their subordinates, and making suggestions for promotions. In that role, I only actually performed one task: I received the official resignation letter of Wong from the role of quartermaster, within weeks of his expanded duties, and I suggested replacing him with Sergeant Anderson in full, promoting her to a warrant officer sergeant to hold the budget down during the transition to the ice comet's arrival. This suggestion was approved, despite Sergeant Anderson's stated discomfort with the role. She was the best person for the job, and she had no choice.

The last thing Q said to me when I got back to the station was this: "You keep telling everyone how you're not political, and here you are, ExO right behind my back. I was starting to like you, Ronaldo. I was foolish enough to like you. Shows me, you selfish little turd." We were in a brief staff meeting, where the admiral introduced herself, and announced her changes, and asked us if there was anything anybody wanted to say about them. Nobody had anything to say to her face. She rolled away, and we sat in silence for a moment, and then Q turned to me and told me off. I suspected his early retirement was going to be quieter than Obasanjo's public fall from grace. But I was wrong. Obasanjo was as indifferent to dishonorable discharge as he was to the line rituals in the cafeteria. Obasanjo had been very political, apparently, and his side had lost. He took it gracefully, and with an easy smile.

To the old admiral, the only thing that really mattered was the colony, not the war. If war ever returned to us, in the tiniest thimble of the tiniest galaxy, we would best be prepared with a robust local economy to support an independent army. The ice meteor was arriving in a matter of weeks, and the amount of life possible on the planet surface would only increase after the impact. Building up the colony, and improving it, was deemed the most important job for the ansible. We would be running on our old equipment, never upgrading. We would minimize the introduction of new staff members. We would focus, wholly and completely, on pulling in machinery and equipment to build up the infrastructure and agriculture on the world below.

I still recall the very first thing I arranged in the network: six young olive trees. They came from the Proxima Centauri colony, a young installation carved into the side of a series of stitched-together asteroids and lesser moons, where a clear dome opens and closes daily in a locked orbit. I remember when I was taking tests with my cohort in boat school and reading about this colony, a technological marvel. I placed an order in the system, and heard word from their ansible administration team that they could deliver, if I could locate for them some ancient replacement parts. I arranged a quantum cloning of biotic-infused water to a new colony, which arranged a transfer of biota to another colony, which—in turn—set up a transfer of the replacement parts to Proxima Centauri. Every colony runs on the ansible network, and the data line is only so large. During a transfer, only colonies that take the transfer can have their line open. The vast amount of data clogs the network, slowing down everything. Negotiate and bribe and cheat and steal, then, to get what we need. It was enough to drive me mad, the daily quest to find what I needed in the network before someone else did, a raw and openly corrupt marketplace with extra seedstock and earth alcohol running underneath the surface. I did manage to get some whiskey, but it was too valuable to drink, and I brought it to the admiral, directly, without scheduling an appointment.

"This isn't a good time," she said, looking up at me from her terminal. She had on video display three different men. I recognized one of the brothers from the monastery, and two men from different colonies with what appeared to me to be very strange hair on extra-ansible communications—lightspeed quickconnects that ran only as fast as light. Their responses were going to be very slow.

I held up the whiskey. "From the ansible. It's too valuable to drink." I placed it on her desk.

"What am I supposed to do with it, Captain?"

I shrugged. "Hide it from the rest of us in case of emergency."

"What emergency requires whiskey?"

"Supply emergencies," I said. "This bottle can get you almost anything over the ansible quickly. Everybody wants good Earth whiskey."

She flipped off the monitors. "That's new. Illegal, too. Think HR knows?"

I shrugged. She took the whiskey and slipped it under her desk. I didn't tell her about Admiral Diego. I'm sure she knew enough about him. If she ever found his secret stash, she never said anything.

That night, I sat in the observatory, trying to unpack the noise in my head from all the shouting faces across the galaxies demanding things and calling, looking for things. Negotiations were handled primarily with lightspeed quickconnects, so it was all recorded messages being transmitted and frantically adapted around. Master Sergeant Anderson was there, by herself, waiting for me.

"Hello, Chief."

She nodded. She looked pensive. Her hand was shaking. "Are you alone, Captain?"

Confused, I looked around. "I am. Chief, I was asked not to speak about something, and I respect that request. I am not interested in getting involved in any personal issues, and defer to your preference on the matter."

"And his," she said.

"It was my understanding that it was your preference. Is it not? What do you want me to do?"

"Nothing," she said. "Everybody's getting sent down. Word will be back here any minute now. People will know I was not being honest about my relationship with my husband. They will want to know why I did it."

"You don't owe me an explanation, Adebayo," I said, almost whispering. "Is there anything I can do to help your situation?"

"I don't know," she said. She started to cry, but choked it down.

I was struck by her in the starlight, flummoxed by tears and emotions that were as mysterious to me as planting a garden in the dunes. I didn't know the first thing about a woman's tears—about anyone's tears. That made me sad. I realized, naturally, that I had been sad for many years and I had never cried about it. I just endured it. Thinking about it made me want to cry, that I hadn't. Here she was, this beautiful, strong woman in tears because soon everyone would know her marriage had ended and she hadn't said anything to anyone about it. I was selfish. I was thinking so selfishly. I did cry, but I cannot say that I did it for the right reasons. I was sad for her. I was sad that she was sad. I was sad for myself, that I had endured so long here, risen up to some sort of ceremonial second-in-command position that felt as meaningless as anything I had ever done. Our miseries merged into a moment. We reached for each other, then, and we floated together, drifting away from the walls.

Our time together was going to be very short, both here and with what adultery there was to come. Soon after we finished crying, she pulled away from me, and I lingered in the smell of her tears on my shoulders, floating in space. I thought of Shui Mien, of Amanda Garcia, and of my mother. The smell of the saltwater is the smell of home—the sea spray smell of my mother at the helm while my father was working on the satellite lines. Her body was hard and strong—I mean Sergeant Anderson's body—and I had to really think awhile on how it was that the strongest person I knew was so fragile underneath her uniform. She couldn't even face her own divorce.

We held together and wept together. When it was done, her body trembled in mine like a child's. I didn't know what to do. I felt awful. Crying didn't help. Her smell was intoxicating to me in my despair. I loved her beautiful skin, the smoothness of it and the darkness of it, like staring across a black horizon on the exterior walks of the station. I thought hard not about how to help her feel better, but about what I could do to make my own mood improve. This was selfishness, I confess. I should have thought harder for Adebayo, and what was actually best for her soul.

———————

I know, when it all comes down to it, the great confession of my sin is not carnal, or even personal, but material. My criminal scheme wasted resources that other colonies needed, that did not belong to me. It was already born in my brain, lacking only the application of the human scenario that could make it so. I was going to commit a grave act against the limited resources of the many colonies, a violation of the trust placed in me as an officer. It was the only thing that would make sense to me after years and years of miserable work.

The idea for the human solution to my technical problem began when I was sitting over a bucket of my own body filth.

With the loss of so many maintenance techs in preparation for the ice comet's arrival on the planet, parts of the ship would bend and break and remain unrepaired for weeks. The facilities on the officers' deck were backed up and broken and on a list of emergency repairs that included oxygen systems and the power converter for the kitchen ovens. We did our business in buckets, for a time. And we were expected to manage our own buckets. I was issued a bucket that I would use to carry my own waste down to the bottom-floor algae tanks, where I would put on the leg braces and walk the bucket to the right tank for deposit. It was my personal bucket for the duration of the plumbing emergency. And, at my desk, I was being asked to fill in as the AstroNav while simultaneously working on the negotiations for transfers, because the ice comet had every available terminal preparing for the dangerous contingency situations of slowing down a comet to land and melt in the middle of a large plain on a desert world without kicking up a dust storm that could last a hundred years or more. I felt underutilized in the process. I was the most qualified person, the most experienced pilot in the entire Sagittarius galaxy, where the pool of candidates was notoriously slim. The admiral, instead, was personally leading the team that was coordinating the gentle descent. Drones attached to the comet, and accumulated upon it, all pushing at once to redirect the energy into the slowest possible descent. A large hole was dug out and covered in concrete to let the comet land where it would have something holding the dust down. The drones would first redirect the comet into a gentle orbit, then switch to total slowdown. Once gravity had the right trajectory and velocity, the drones would break off and return home.

And me? I had nothing to do with it. I was watching planning progress from a side monitor while working on negotiations. I was smelling my own filth in the broken station. I was lonely and exhausted and got a message from Wong to make sure to review emergency protocols because the admiral was ninety-two for goodness' sake, and there was more to taking command of the station than I knew. In most cases, it was a simple transfer of authority, like when Admiral Diego shot himself. In some cases, it wasn't. I read more of the protocols. What the ExO did if there was a situation that incapacitated the admiral, and damaged our signal line, and was an imminent threat to the station was fascinating to me. If the attack was bad enough, or sudden enough, the message needed to go through. Complex data and interpretation of the data and intelligence was needed. Ranking officers should, in an emergency of imminent death, push an emergency signal through all the ansibles, overriding all other signals. Sometimes, if the data merited a human interpretation of events, they would send someone through the signal.

Carrying my bucket downstairs, a thought appeared in my head. This plan I had considered and plotted for years was actually much simpler than I had anticipated because of the human problem of maintenance technicians on the surface, and the ice comet distracting everyone. If someone could do it, someone would, eventually. It might as well be me.

It was such a simple first step, too. I opened an old file in the AstroNav system and found one of the farthest of the probes in the darkness that extended out from the Sagittarius galaxy into the unimaginable void beyond. I searched for the things I had been mentally cataloging for nearly a decade. These things could be misconstrued as heading toward us on a militaristic sweep. I slipped into the back of the probe's system on its slow, single-atom ansible connection. It was such a small probe, no larger than a cup of tea. It was old, too, likely sent off as soon as the battle was won, after whatever enemy ships might remain in our shared sky. I found a dead world there, hurtling in the dark, a huge block of metal and stone and black and chlorine ice spinning through the void between galaxies for a thousand years from some forgotten, lost star. An astronomical curiosity, truly, and worthy of close study for that alone. But, also, it was aimed toward the Milky Way, and would someday fall into the gravity of her spectral palm. I surged the little sensors from the back, and it set off an alarm in the AstroNav system. An EM pulse it was not, but the old sensors only knew they had felt a surge. I had spent enough time staring at the codes and interfaces of all these old machines, I could fake a surge. The probe died, going dark and taking evidence of the surge with it. The alert system can be easily accessed and tampered with by an accredited officer to prevent any anomalies and mistakes from entering the ansible network beyond one station. It could easily also be used to delete evidence that the officer was tampering with the probe short of a full archaeological investigation. In moments, my plan was in motion.

I called the admiral directly.

"Can this wait, Captain?"

"Probably not for long. There is no cause for alarm yet, Admiral, but you need to know and I am about to send you a re-port on it. A probe got flashed by EM."

"What?"

"There is a large object out there unaffiliated with any orbit trajectory, as of yet. It's a little larger than Charon, actually, and it just surged a probe."

"ETA?"

"We have time. It did not appear to be on active thrust. Sublightspeed. Even at lightspeed, we'd have time. If a probe was truly hit, they're probably going to pick up the pace. If it's them. It might not be them. The probe died before it could know what it was. It might be an anomaly, or a busted probe."

"Are they back or not?"

"We don't know," I said. "We know a probe was hit with an EM pulse that surged it. That is what we know. Deep space is . . ."

"Well, it is a weird place between galaxies. I've lived here longer than you. I know that. We still need to check it out."

"I recommend a full sortie, Admiral, to check it out for ourselves, and let them know, if it is them, that we know they are coming and they should turn around."

"Our galaxy," said the admiral. "Plenty of galaxies out there. Leave ours alone. Right. What was I doing? Okay, I want that report right now, and set up a trajectory based on known speeds and possible lightspeed intercept. I will check it. We need to get the ice comet down and stabilized. We need to get that done, first."

"We have a month even at twice lightspeed, and they weren't going lightspeed when they surged us, if it was them."

"Anything else it could be?"

"A piece of wreckage, perhaps, with an old defense mechanism that still works? A magnetically overactive anomalous object that found its way to our probe in the gap of space? A free-floating pulse or mechanical issue in the probe and we are placing an interpretation upon events from limited knowledge."

"Captain, when I left Earth on this ship a thousand years ago . . . God, so many of us died, Captain. So few survived the battle, when it came. So many died after the battle, too. I hope to God it is some anomaly."

"We will know when we know, Admiral."

"I am the only person in this galaxy or the next who has actually flown in wartime, Captain. I am going to take the ship out, and you are going to stay behind and build me another in case it is the enemy. I will pass word up the chain. We are the vanguard colony. We are the tip of the sword of mankind. We will not let them back into the colonized worlds."

"We don't even know if it's them yet, Admiral. We just don't know. Why risk your knowledge?" I actually wanted her to go, for once. This was a situation where I win no matter what. I go and I get to fly the warship, finally. I stay, I get to transcend, finally.

"I am going on sortie, Captain. If it is them, I am already ninety-two years old. My children are fine. I pray to God it's not them, Captain. I want a skeleton crew on my vessel, and no one who isn't completely expendable to general ops. We put up a good front, act like we're robust. Maybe they reconsider coming back."

"Deep space is strange. It is too early to start panicking. We have limited knowledge."

"Who's panicking?" she said. "Send me the trajectory and a full report on the flash."

"It would help me compile a report on the flash if any of the scientists and researchers could explain the enemy to me. Nothing makes sense about them. There are so many planets, so many galaxies. Why did they come for us? What do they even look like? What does anything in their weird ships . . ."

"How do they even work? I don't know. No one can explain it beyond rudimentary signals and the impact of weaponry. I am trying to land an ice comet to save this colony. I will read the report and I want you to get to work on the ansible with materials personnel to pull in the parts for a new warship. Work it in quietly, with the colonist stuff. Pretend you're hiding it from me. We need new parts, anyway."

"On it, ma'am."

"Shit. Shit shit shit. Hey, keep this between you and me, right now. This is confidential. You and me. Got it?"

"Yes, ma'am."

"Shit. Shit."

She hung up. I got to work on the plan. Such a simple thing, my transgression. I had never felt so alive. The nature of sin is to steal God's energy, to steal His power to be in control of reality and self. I have had long discussions about this with Brother Pleo since my incarceration. I felt powerful, exhilarated, and in control. For the first time in my career, I had rediscovered the feeling I felt beneath the mesquite tree before my first transcendence. I felt like a future was out there, waiting for me to take it.

I prepped the necessaries, and watched the meteor land with a calm excitement, disconnected from the events on the screen.

Sergeant Anderson asked to meet me for a workout in the low floors, where we had first met. She said that we both had a lot of stress to burn off. I asked her how her crew was doing with the pipes, when I met her there. I had my bucket with me. I wish I could have left it at my desk, not taken it down with Adebayo, but it needed to be done, and appearances mattered.

"There's something different about you," she said. "It's disturbing, actually, and you need to get some exercise and burn it off."

"What's different?"

"You're smiling a little now. It's just a little, at the corners of your mouth. But it is really strange and disturbing."

"Well, I'm sorry it bothers you. I wouldn't mistake it for happiness, considering the situation." I meant, of course, the war I was starting, but it wasn't the war she interpreted. I finished my legs, and picked the bucket up again.

She pointed at my bucket. "It is a situation, indeed. Sorry. We're backlogged landing the ice comet. I'm doing my best. We need to eat, exercise, and sleep or we'll be worse off. Oh, technically, you're here to help me with a job. I brought you some extra tools."

"It's actually a good idea to expand jobs to anyone qualified in their off hours, regardless of specialization. We could post a message board and offer extra data access to volunteers who finish tasks to your satisfaction."

She shook her head. "No, we will not. I have enough supervising already. We cannot afford any meaningful mistakes from well-intentioned amateurs with our systems while so many are on the surface. We do our best and triage jobs. Let's go for a walk."

We went to the open cistern for sewage. The contents did not smell once it was thrown into the cistern. There were powerful biotic agents developed for station use that took care of the smell, mostly. It smelled musty, human, like sweaty sheets left unwashed. It was not a wholly unpleasant smell compared to how a one-thousand-liter tank of fermenting human filth should stink. The buckets stank, but I was going to leave the bucket beside the tank for a cleaning crew to handle in the morning. I was spared the indignity of hosing out my bucket. Clean buckets were lined up next to the dirty ones. It reminded me of places I had seen as a child, filthy under-cities where my family's boat would occasionally find the shadow of airports and train stations along the shore. The illegal slums were cheap places for harbor when Dad wasn't finding good contracts, and Mom couldn't get a buyer for her design work. I had thought War College would take me away from the filth of life.

But, inside of me, I knew I was going to transcend. Knowing this, I could feel a hope that I did not see in Sergeant Anderson.

"Why did you keep his name?" I said.

"What?"

"I'm just curious. It's not really any of my business. You could have changed your name back. You don't owe me an explanation if you do not wish to give it."

"Ask him. He is the one who took my name. Before we married, his name was O'Conner," she smiled, sadly. "I think he got used to everyone calling him this name, and he was a clone, anyway. Our lives actually began here, together, not somewhere else. Memory is just the story we tell ourselves. That is what Obasanjo said, and I think there is a truth in it. Even if Jon and I are no longer together, we were together so much and formed so much of each other's place here. That is what I think. I will have to ask him when I see him again."

"Oh," I said. We stood there, in this long pause. She looked away from me, to the tank. I looked at her beautiful face. I remembered my time with Amanda, and I could not deny my deeply felt pull toward this sad woman, with her body as muscular as any security officer and the tenderness of a long sadness at the edges of her smiles. I would be eternal soon. I was already a sinner. What pain I might cause Amanda was, to me, an inconvenience. The woman I wanted—the life I wanted here on this planet—was with Master Sergeant Anderson. I took her hand in mine, lifted her palm up to my face, and kissed her wrist. She did not stop me.

"I see," she said.

"I do not mean to offend you," I said. "I do not mean to cause you pain or ask anything that you aren't willing to give."

"It is not to be, but perhaps," she said. She looked down the curving architecture away from me. "It is possible that I could be convinced, Captain. You are in my chain of command, are you not?"

"I am in everyone's chain of command. Please don't hold it against me. We can keep things quiet for a long time. There's plenty of time."

"There is," she said. She pulled her hand away. "No need to rush anything, Captain."

"Of course not," I said. Inside, my heart was beating so fast it was dancing. I felt so alive. We raced each other to the other end of the station, laughing all the way. I lost. Of course I lost. She often walked down here without bracers to build strength. She did push-ups and pull-ups here, where gravity was hard enough that a single, clean pull-up was a challenge. I was only there to place a bucket down until the pipes were fixed.

Uplifted with the endorphines of exertion, we extracted

242 • Joe M. McDermott

ourselves from the braces at the elevator door.

"When will I see you again off duty?" she said to me.

"Tomorrow?"

"Tomorrow," she said. She nodded. "What will we do tomorrow? Do you have a plan to win my heart, Captain Aldo?"

"I will come up with one between now and tomorrow."

"Make it three days. I deserve a decent plan, Captain."

"Aldo," I said. "Please, just call me Ronaldo."

"No. Not while we are here, where people and algorithms and HR are listening. Not here. Not where it can be accidentally overheard. I've done this before. Trust me."

I was promised to another, of course, and I was betraying her trust. I was also lying to the admiral about the identity and origin of an object in the dark space. I was staging my system for a false alarm that would trigger my emergency message to reach the many, many ansibles and reroute them for my disbursement into the network. I needed to be ready to move fast. I needed to distract the network security officer.

Leaving the low floors, I went to the NetSec offices next. I knocked on the door, to see if he was in.

"Enter," I heard.

My entry was met with a cold, hard glare. "What do you want?" he said.

"No salute?"

"What do you want, *sir*? I'm very busy."

"Are our networks under attack?"

"Always. There's enough free-floating viral shit out there to wreck our network for a hundred years, and enough archaic code ghosting through the network . . . Man, I'm the hardest working officer on the ship and no one even notices. What do you want?"

I closed the door behind me and sat down. "We need to discuss something that needs to stay between us. I'm preparing a mission for the admiral as soon as the ice is down and secure. General crew doesn't know about it. I'm not supposed to tell you about it, but I think we're going to need you in the loop. As you say, you are critical to our survival."

He closed his computer. "You have my undivided attention, Captain."

"I'm AstroNav. I've always been AstroNav. I got a hit on something dark and mysterious heading our way. It doesn't look good. Admiral is going to fly out a recon. Code tech has changed a lot since she was flying. I don't want any chances. The enemy has to have been as busy as we were."

"If it's them, we don't even know what they'll hit us with. I don't have the tech to set up an ansible in. You have the keys to the factory, not me."

"I can get you the tech in a matter of hours, but there isn't enough time to install it without raising suspicion, nor is it safe to hand an ansible to the enemy on a scouting ship. Look, it's probably not the enemy. But, if it is, we need to know fast, and get back fast, and I'll spend the rest of my career pumping war supplies through the ansible, and stocking up on noble gases."

"Would the admiral take me along?"

"You're the best data guy we got. We need someone who can see the signals right away, if there are signals, and analyze the data. How up to date are you on enemy data lines?"

"I'm rusty," he said. "I don't have time to upgrade, either."

"You're the best we got, though, right?"

"Right."

"You will be critical to our success if the scout goes down. You stay here, but I want to set up a lightspeed quickconnect.

We have a bunch of them sitting in storage already, and you could install it yourself on the ship without raising a ruckus."

"That's old tech. I haven't worked with one since college."

"It is old because it works. We still use them for ansible negotiations, and I know the admiral uses them to send noncritical updates to HR. Lightspeed will have to be good enough. You're busy. I can do the install for you," I said. "I want to keep this nice and quiet. People would notice you climbing out of the hole. No one cares about me. AstroNavs who don't get to fly are supposed to pine over their warships."

"You know how to set them up?"

"I did it in college too. We can test the line before we fly. We have time for that."

"We aren't ready for a war. Not out here."

"We don't even know if it isn't just a broken drone yet. It is most likely a broken drone. We just have to be ready because it is our job to take slight odds very seriously. There is no call for alarm. We will prepare. When we know, we will follow orders. There is no confirmation yet. The universe is a mysterious place. It is full of surprises, many more likely than the enemy's return. Can I count on you to keep this between us?"

"Yes, sir."

"Good. I will do the install tonight, and we can test it in the morning."

It is a simple plan. After the test, I would intercept the signal out with a second signal box. Upon the admiral's approach to the object, I would cut the lightspeed signal to NetSec. I would override the AstroNav data to signal an attack with the acting admiral credentials. I would cut the line at the ansible, then, and separate us from the network in almost every way but one. Then, I would calmly step into the chamber and set the emergency signal from my tablet before anyone even realized what I was doing.

I had almost forgotten about Sergeant Anderson. I was on my way down to the ship in dock, climbing down the ladder near the center of the station, when she called me. "Where are you, sir?"

I had forgotten about her. "I am still on duty, Sergeant. I have a special assignment for NetSec before I can take my bucket down."

"We have almost fixed the pipes, today. One more juncture needs repair. We are rigging the new pipes directly out of pre-fabricated drone shells that have gone unused."

"I can't wait," I said. "I'm behind schedule too."

"I see," she said.

"No, don't misunderstand. You can meet me there, if you like. Have you been aboard the warship?"

"I am in charge of the maintenance crew. I have been there. I have checked their work. I have had my fill of the scouting vessel. I find the fascination with its fast weaponry tedious. Contact me when you finish yours, if you can keep your eyes open."

Only after I had offered to take her with me did I realize it was better if I didn't. She would know what I was doing, rigging the old lightspeed quickconnects in series, to cancel each other out. She would wonder about it. I got lucky. I couldn't pull this trick off if I relied on luck. I would have to be sneakier. I needed to conceal what I was doing in the ship. The preflight crew would notice it. I needed to create some sort of protection for my little hack.

In the ship, I opened the control panel with the tool kit plugged into the wall. I quickly installed the little devices, both together no smaller than my palm. I pulled some wires over them to try and conceal them, but I knew that wouldn't work. Then, I had an idea. I unplugged the true one, and used spare wire from the tool kit to rig it out and extend it. I hid the second lightspeed quickconnect as far away as the wire would go, hidden under the tool kit itself, beneath the extra wires there. It was very unlikely that anyone would bother with an old lightspeed quickconnect, as long as an officer told them to leave it alone. It was even less likely, in that scenario, that a lightspeed quickconnect would be investigated out to the wires. The maintenance crews brought their own wires, and these extras in the tool kit were intended for midflight maintenance. As long as there was smooth sailing (and there would be) no one would discover my little reroute on the lightspeed line. I had my tablet with me and put together my simple command structure and rechecked it, before flipping it on and setting up the quickconnect farther down the chain.

The tests went fine, and everything was greenlight. No one seemed to suspect that I had a plan running under the surface of the debris that was floating out in the void between galaxies.

I was almost free, then.

The ice comet had to be secured in gauze and plastics, and all my best crew were down preparing their equipment for wrapping a huge comet for a controlled release of H2O. I got reports from them, and didn't read them. I stamped them and filed them away for HR. I never heard anything back from them about my work. It's odd, to me, that even then, HR said nothing to me. I got everything second- and thirdhand from higher-ranking officers. It created, in me, a deeper isolation when I think of it. No wonder I rebelled. They are a godhead without a body or a voice, like a false religion. Lacking feedback from my mental structures of the world, I pushed hard against them all, to test their worth.

Down on the first floor, with Sergeant Anderson, we were feeling the heavy, heavy weight of the full centripetal force. We had full-body gear on, and climbed through metal storage pipes and heavy equipment, ancient tractors once intended for emergency ground construction but powered by varieties of agricultural biodiesels we don't produce here. We had exoskeletons on, and scrambled through the mess of machines and equipment, playing tag until the timer alarms went off, and we had to get up to a lower g-force or risk damage to our bones and organs. We were laughing.

"How often do you go this low?" I said.

"Not often. It's hard on the body. You'll feel it tomorrow, I promise, but it was something new, yes? A prize, here, where the imagination has no new places to spare."

"How can I thank you for that great prize?"

"You might, and I am only suggesting that you might do this, but you might consider a friendly kiss."

"Only friendly?"

"Well, it is really up to you if it is friendly or not. But it should not be too friendly. Too friendly would be very bad."

"I'll do my best," I said. "You know, I haven't done this very much. Even before I was cloned, I lived on a boat with my mother and father."

"You talk too much, Captain."

Her beautiful face, smooth skin as deep and vast as any expanse of night, I thought of the distance between galaxies, a century at the fastest speeds we can survive, and how these distances seemed so small compared to the space between two bodies; how far I had to lean over, gently and controlled, to place my lips upon hers.

Oh, the mess of life I have made here, confessor. Embracing my sinful nature, I have lost Amanda, and I have even lost Sergeant Anderson. I am alone in this cell. But she kissed me. I had all of her powerful body in my arms. For a time, it was glorious. Perhaps the future will bring me another opportunity to impress Adebayo Anderson, when I am a monk and rise above the temptations of flesh and bone. I want her to respect me again, someday, more than I long for her affection.

I was at my desk, running through my checklists on the AstroNav system, and waiting to hear back from two stations for a series of ansible transactions while the letters were running through. An alert pumped through the tablets about the foreign body entering our system. The ice had arrived, at last. All hands on deck, and we all switched over to our monitoring station to see what we could do, if anything, to help. Meteors don't land softly unless we make it so. Much was lost in the atmosphere, but that was where it was wanted, entering the moisture and water cycle of the atmosphere. Drones would be sacrificed to level out the arrival, attempting to slow it to a gentle crawl. All hands on deck, watching for damaged drones, repairing drones, and getting a transport ship out of drydock to sacrifice it to the water, if needed. Water was everything and hope.

I got to fly the transport, and I got to sit out and wait in the dark beside it, in case the drones couldn't handle the weight of gravity and matter colliding. I raced to the transport, and launched into the night sky. I realized that this was going to be the very last flight I ever took, considering what I was about to do during the admiral's voyage.

The night sky, endless and gorgeous, scattered jewels, and a distraction to me, because I knew it would be my last time flying. I heard the chatter on the channels, where the admiral was leading the drones into the descent, assigning different AIs different jobs, and getting the station weaponry involved, using an antimatter implosion charge, for instance, to lightly thump the bottom of the ice, to hit it where it bounced and slow it down. She missed dead center, and it caused a backspin that a drone team had to redirect. It was mostly done by computer, with calculations too precise to leave in the hands of our human technicians. Sergeant Anderson had her team on standby to repair any damaged drones that flew in or were recovered by other drones. Wong's people were coordinating our heavy matter weapons to control the descent of the ice comet, and spread out the force to prevent the creation of a powerful dust plume. The worst case scenario was the kind of impact that kicked so much dust into the atmosphere that the system's star could not breach the fog and reach the colony. It would drive the entire human population into the station, which is ill equipped for such a population explosion, much less the many problems that would create for supply lines.

I watched the ice meteor go down for two days, riding alongside it as it entered orbit, slowly and slower and slowest until the drones were crushed under the weight of ice, and I was sent back into the ship for the requisition of drone parts for replacements of the ones lost. I'd have to send the flight sergeant out with the supply vessel to acquire enough raw gases and raw matter to put together the necessary components with so many drones lost. Still, the gentle descent was perfect, and the ice was quickly sprayed down with a plastic coating to keep it from evaporating faster than the atmosphere could handle, to prevent any other issues. I understand that it was expected to rain with some regularity now, and there was

250 • Joe M. McDermott

to be an accumulation of enough water in the planetary water cycle for the beginning of meaningful ocean, with another ice meteor scheduled for the next thirteen years.

Distracted by my knowledge of the next mission, I had difficulty focusing on the tasks at hand. What was a drone, to me, when the universe was going to be mine? What did I care for ice comets and ice meteors or descending icy worlds, when I would see Shui Mien again, in one or more of the many colony worlds. I would walk on grassy fields, and sit under a tree and look up at birds, again.

We held a mock funeral for drones that doubled as a celebration. The admiral put pictures of all the lost drones up like lost crewmembers with paper flower arrangements and black pudding and roasted black jujube tea. It was a joke funeral, but it was well received among the men and women. I sat in the back of the room, sipping tea and imagining what coffee tasted like, once, or what the confectionary beverages of Thailand street vendors tasted like, with tea, spices, sugar, and coconut cream.

Part of me was going to know these flavors again, and others that were new and exotic to me after nearly a decade of this miserable station. I sipped the bitter, roasted jujube tea, and I remembered. Memory, this story I tell myself of a time before this station, when I lived on Earth, and saw the ocean every morning from the deck of the boat, was feeding me the very dreams that consumed me during the execution of my greatest sin.

After the party, an all hands meeting was scheduled to announce the scouting mission. I was asked to present my findings to the crew, as AstroNav, and I was going to have to lie my pants off, to everyone, and I wasn't afraid. There was nothing to fear. No one cared about the rocks floating in space, or their activities.

I put together a presentation about what I knew, pretending it was a recently discovered object in scanned space. There were actually quite a lot of free-floating debris in the black that it was easy enough to fool anyone that wasn't closely following the trajectory of various cosmic filaments invisible to the naked eye in the huge voids between galaxies, and the structure and scope of galaxies that together form superclusters, that may even crash into each other, blowing off their gases and rocks in explosions larger than the Milky Way. AstroNavs were trained to calculate trajectories of gravimetric matter all the way back to the Big Bang, and to consider the complex calculations of gravity and the relations of different impacting objects. It was done through software, but there was an art to understanding what is presented in the software, and the training took as long as learning how to fly manned vessels in the odd conditions of free space. I had an object that was absent from prior sweeps, and then appeared. That is what it looked like, to everyone but me, because I had deleted the prior record of the artifact. I was told to bring the crew's fear level down as much as possible. We were not warriors, just military personnel sitting out on a listening post. We did not need more fear.

I stood before the whole crew, then, with cameras playing out to the monastery and colony below. I gave my little speech about the mission.

"Probe X-13343, commissioned sixty years ago, encountered an unknown object in its sector and sent out exploratory signals. It was shorted. Let me be clear: No one in command staff here or back at the Terran sector believes for one second the enemy is returning. There is a procedure in this scenario that we must follow, and we will follow the procedure. So, this is an exploratory mission only.

"Space, as many of you are aware, is very large and lots of things happen out there without any knowledge or input from us whatsoever. Even heavy-duty probe drones break, sometimes. There is no reason to think anything, until we can go out and look at it and see what happened to our probe. This sector is quite far away from the celestial filament. There isn't a lot of gravity to pull off all the stuff blowing around between galactic clusters. Lots of cosmic clutter is floating around there, causing problems. Many crewmembers have had to fix probes and machines damaged from these sorts of things. This is an unknown object that matches traits we look for when we consider scouting missions, that likely coincided with a cosmic event. The scouting mission is not a war mission.

"We will still be prepared for all possibilities. The most likely possibility is that this is something that banged into something else and flew off on a new trajectory where we didn't see it with our probes. The admiral's mission will be to consider the unknown object's trajectory, appearance, and activity to either blast it out of the sky preemptively, or to ignore it. Either way, she is one of the last surviving veterans of the original conflict and uniquely qualified to judge how much time we waste with our old and outdated drones. I'm sure when she gets back, her stellar report will fill us all in on how much time we wasted scanning a wayward rock with our fully armed warship. Any questions? No? Well, orders are going out to terminals now, and those of you chosen for this giant waste of our time when the ice comet mission was a huge success will be missing some of the most exciting things happening planetside in decades: We will literally be watching some ice melt on the surface below. Terrifically exciting stuff out here. No questions, yes? Excellent. We will keep everyone informed of our results."

There was light chuckling, but my jokes were not well received at the time. I'm sure, in retrospect, the humor was not lost on anyone. At the time, I gazed across the cafeteria at a mixture of contained terror, naked terror, and shock. The officer corps looked grim and firm. I had done this to them. I had brought such terror into life from the night for my selfish aim. I am guilty, and deserve the court martial I receive.

That night, Sergeant Anderson cornered me in my office.

"How long have you been sitting on this thing?"

I took a deep breath. Lying was hard work. I had to keep it all straight. "I prefer to focus on the future, not the past, Sergeant."

"We couldn't handle an invasion here. Not here."

"First, let's find out what the thing is. Space is weird, Sergeant. It is a big, black void, and we don't know what we see until we get a good look at it. We shoot at it. If it doesn't shoot back, then we have nothing to worry about."

"Are you okay?" she said. She took my hand. "Are we?"

I sighed. "Come on. Let's go for a walk somewhere a little more private."

I led her to the airlock, and handed her a suit. "Keep the recording device off, okay? Let's just talk, you and me, as equals."

I saw the fear on her face, saw her trembling hands accept the suit. She pulled it on quickly, nervously. I was not afraid. I double-checked her seals and she double-checked mine. It was the most basic thing in the world to a spacer, particularly on the quartermaster's crew, but she had a mistake in her oxygen line, and I had to stop her and try again.

"Oh, my," she said.

"Indeed."

Outside, in the darkness, I oriented myself and looked up into the darkness toward the little rock I had conjured into an enemy ship. I felt it hanging over my head, like a needle screaming toward me.

We walked a bit, around the surface of the ship.

"It's easy to forget how beautiful it is out here when we aren't working," she said. "The last time I was out here, I was carrying so many tools on my back, the devils nearly crushed my oxygen line."

"On other colonies, they build solar sailers, and surf the sky itself. I have looked into it, and it would strain our drone supply too much to monitor human recovery in emergencies."

She stopped in her tracks.

"My recorder has been off for a while now, Captain Aldo."

I turned to look at her through the glass ball, her face lit up from below like a monster's mask. She was afraid.

"I want you to be close to me when the mission is happening," I said. "Listen, there is a loophole in the system. If it is an attack, and we can't stop it, the ranking commander can set up an emergency ansible transfer of data. It doesn't say what that data is, but, in the past, it was intended to be a complete record of the invasion along with a witness of it to respond to direct questions. Stay close. I may need you to handle the transfer controls."

"We'll still be dead, you and I," she said. "Your clone will be fine. What about everyone else?"

I looked up at the night sky. "We can only do the best we can, Adebayo. We won't have long to do it, I'm afraid. If we are under attack, the station has no meaningful defenses against EM sweep anymore. There are too many insulation holes where the station built out over the damage in the hull's shields."

"Ronaldo, please tell me you're joking. You want to just clone out in an attack?"

"Why not? Is it wrong to want to ascend? This is your chance, Adebayo. You can come with me, if it happens that way. We can go together."

"I should report you to the admiral."

"The only breach of protocol and procedure, yet, is my invitation to you to come along, if we are under attack. It is implied that the highest-ranking station member or the commander go alone, except when there are exceptional circumstances."

"I should still report you."

"Do what you like," I said. I looked up. "It's there, coming toward us now, but it isn't on a collision course. It could easily be a rock that bounced off a rock where we didn't see it. It is not a lie to tell you that that scenario is most likely. Only one scenario like this has ever led to positive contact."

"Where was that?"

"Far away, and long ago. Back when we didn't even know what we were fighting. The survivors of the colony sent back their reports, and one of their officers, and it was a turning point in the war."

This was a lie. I was amazed at how easily lies came to my lips. Someday, the truth would come out, and soon.

"Come with me, Adebayo. Please, come with me."

"You sound so certain that we are doomed," she said. "I'll think about it. I'm going back, and I will be turning my recording device back on now."

I stayed out on the hull awhile. I walked up and down, nominally inspecting for signs of damage. There, the very spot my predecessor stood when he ripped his helmet off and died. I walked around it, circling it like a vulture. I knew where it was.

I struggled to remember his whole name, beyond just Edward. I should know it. I should never forget any dead people's names, but I do.

———————

The mission, then, was particular in its timing. I watched the ship fly out for the patrol, and kept a line in to the communication devices, and the different maps and projections. When the admiral got close, I needed to be quick on my feet. I also needed the sergeant's answer.

I went to her in the enlisted quarters, from which she refused to budge without a signed letter from HR, the admiral, or both. With the dimmers on, only the floor pathways illuminated. I had a homing tag set up on my tablet to go to hers, courtesy of the privilege of command, and sought her out.

She was wide awake, sitting in her cot behind a screen of blankets and old towels, with the other women enlisted. She was reading something bound in paper and leather. She stood up and saluted me.

"It's almost time," I said.

"How much time?"

"Two days," I said.

"Plenty of time. Are you wide awake?"

"Completely awake."

"I, as well."

She gestured to me, to follow her. I did.

She took me to a far room, on one of the uninhabited floors with limited gravity. We were lighter there, taking slightly longer strides, able to push too hard against the ground to touch the ceiling. She took my hand out to the edge of the room, and placed it on the farthest wall from the door. She attached me to it, binding me with a rope to an old supply hook.

Then, she pulled herself up, where gravity was light enough we could almost float a moment, at this weird corner of the room, where it must turn higher up than the rest, for some archaic designed reason in the old space vessel.

And, hidden there among boxes and the stale stench of dust and biotic cleansing agents, and lashed to my surprise to a ceiling that helped me float—there, we became one.

Afterward, she held on to me to keep floating.

I assumed this meant she would be with me when I jumped, but this was no answer.

We fell asleep, and I woke up alone, untied, and resting gently on the ground.

Back in my office, I saw a stack of messages, and ignored them all. The only thing that mattered was the jump.

It was nearly time. Thinking Sergeant Anderson was on my side after the night, I called her and asked her to meet me in the chamber for some maintenance checks. I asked her to come alone.

I had my tablet set up.

I had everything ready.

I called NetSec and asked for an update on the lightspeed quickconnect, claiming that I was having issues getting through.

"Everything's fine over here. They're getting close, though.

Another day. Maybe two if the object picks up any more speed. It's fluctuated."

It has fluctuated, and has been fluctuating for some time, but I didn't tell him that. The object has some unstable elements that kick off and contribute to either speed or slowing down as they deteriorate unevenly. It is likely a methane ice with radioactive elements, or some other unstable composition. Regardless, I thanked him, and told him to keep me informed if anything changed.

Sergeant Anderson messaged me to tell me that she was busy.

I messaged her back that it was important that she come, alone.

She arrived.

"Adebayo," I said. I kissed her cheek. She drew away from me.

"What is this?" she said. "There is nothing wrong with this facility, and you order me over here?"

"Just hold still," I said. "It only takes a moment to check the system out, together."

I pushed the first button.

"What are you doing on your tablet?" she said.

"Working," I said.

"It is good to work. It is good to follow rules. It keeps the station spaceworthy. It protects us from stellar radiation. I leave you to it, sir."

"Wait," I said. I held out my hand. "Come with me."

"I will not. If something happens, let me die here. There is enough of me in this universe. I will not go with you."

"Please?"

She shook her head and turned back to her work. "Sorry, Captain," she said.

I did not make a scene. If I made a scene, she might suspect something was up. I lowered my hand. I left her to her work. I told myself that Shui Mien was out there, and a thousand others just as beautiful. I should not be greedy and take everyone with me. I should limit my transgression to a single cell.

This is what I thought, until she arrived behind me. She placed a finger on my back. I paused, in my doorway, afraid to turn around, because I knew it was her.

"What scheme are you up to, Commander?"

I turned slowly. "Come with me," I said. "You'll see."

She crossed her arms and looked me up and down. I was in my cleanest remaining uniform, and my hair was cut sharp and tight. She did not trust the way I was dressed. "Why can't you tell me now? There is no reason to wait."

I took a deep breath. "It will make more sense when I show you, first."

Trusting me, the fool for it, led to a happy glen and a lake, an ocean, an island of sand, and all the great trees of all the colonies. She took my hand and let me lead her in. The glass descended. She looked at me, as the gas poured in, with an expression I am unable to describe in words. It was as if every emotion poured into her along with the gas of the transfer protocol. The gas cleared with the vacuum seal of the line, pressurizing the chamber a little, and all the air whooshed out in a rush.

Then, it was over. There were no spots in my eyes, this time, and no great sense of alienation. I was in the same terrible space station, above a planet where I would go to live and die. It did not feel like it was supposed to feel. I don't know what I thought would happen.

I plugged back into the data lines. I checked my protocol network, and had set up the ansible for immediate, emergency transfer. When the time came, I did not hesitate to push the button on the quickconnect, and then wait for the signal to return, empty. Then, clearing all the protocols, I could send us both across the galaxies of man.

My line lit up, with NetSec howling. Everyone would be afraid. I kicked the alert back into the network.

"We are on alert!" she said, as the war horn sounded. "What did you do?"

I completed the cycle, blasting us both across the two galaxies of human habitation, cloned in every system as the warning harbinger of a war that was . . .

Well, the quickconnect returned after my last blast, and the admiral was on the horn with me, trying to figure out what happened.

"I don't know," I said. "I thought we were at war, there, and I hit the alarm. I thought an EM blast was coming."

"We're fine," she said. "We've gotten a good look at the enemy. It's nothing. It's galactic debris, and it's dead as a stone. It's human, even. It's from the station itself. It's part of the old warship engine crashed onto a methane meteor. Captain, what did you do?"

"I believe I have made a terrible mistake, Admiral."

The ansible reports were flying out of the station swift and fast, carrying our alert, throwing all the transfers off.

"I'm getting lots of urgent messages from NetSec. I'm getting lots of messages about a dataline jam on the ansible."

I never planned my second move. Getting away was all that mattered. I didn't bother to cover my tracks. I didn't think anything of it.

"Let me put together the reports and we'll figure it all out," I said. I hung up.

"You did something awful, did you not?" Sergeant Anderson said. She looked at me with such horror. "You did something evil to me."

I didn't say anything.

"I did not want this," she said. She grabbed me. She punched me, hard. It hurt. I didn't fight back. She called security down, called emergency and rang alarms and arrested me.

She, whom I have transcended.

She had nothing to do with me or my plans. Nothing. It was all me. It was only ever me. I did it for myself. I decided to bring her, because I thought . . .

I don't know what I thought.

I like to think in other colonies we are lovers.

————

Obasanjo came to visit me. He sat down outside the bars of this cell in dirty, dusty clothes. Confessor, he said he was proud of me.

I told him that I was going to become a monk, if I could.

He frowned then. "You have defeated the bastards, and now you're going to surrender to them?"

"I think I have found God, Obasanjo."

"When?"

"After I committed my great, selfish sin, I had a dream. In this dream, I shared the dream with every other version of my self, all of the hundreds of us who were born that day when I overloaded the system with my false alarm. We were all together, in our consciousness, all one soul spread out in so many bodies, all sharing the same memories. We sat under a mesquite tree in San Antonio, together in one body. We looked up at the sun, and I knew that I was looking at God."

"I had a dream I gave the old admiral a good punch in the jaw once. It didn't cause any conversion experiences. I never punched him, either."

"I touched the sun, Obasanjo. I did something . . . Past the branches of the tree, and all the way up to the sun itself."

"Like Icarus, you have fallen," he said. He reached through the bars and held out a sweet stick of pasted jujube and malted amaranth. I took the candy. I chewed. I swallowed. "I wanted to tell you that I always loved you," he said. "I wish it was me that you loved."

"I have always considered you my friend," I said. "I'm sorry I can't be more than that."

"I know," he said. "It's not your fault. You didn't do anything worthy of my infatuation. It is a lonely posting, and that's all. I'm getting married, though, and I thought I would tell you that, just to clear the air. Amanda doesn't want to see you. We are having a party. You aren't invited. Frankly, I don't think Amanda wants to see you again."

"Congratulations," I said. "I understand how she feels. I'm sorry I made such a mess with her. I hope you both are very happy."

"Tell God, if you see him again, that I don't believe in him. I don't believe in anything that would drag us out here to this place."

"I will let Him know, if I encounter Him again."

That day, after he was gone, and the sun was setting, I was taken outside for physical activity. During my exertion period, I was permitted to plant huisache trees in the yard, under supervision of the monks. My imprisonment is not so bad, when I have visitors, and I am able to plant trees.

I regret that I did not apologize to Obasanjo. I knew. I always knew. I think I took advantage of him, a little bit, and abused our friendship with the kernel hidden in his face and voice. I should have apologized to him. I wish to send him a lovely note for his wedding, and I hope, dear confessor, you can let me borrow a pen and something that would work as a formal card.

Memory is the story we tell ourselves, and we believe it is our only story. Memory of us is what we ask of God. What God forgets does not exist, even as a memory's memory. I turn my life over to God, that he may never forget me. For too long, I have felt like an afterthought in the mind of God and history. Perhaps it is my pride, again, but I wish to never to be forgotten by God—to never feel forgotten by God . . . By God, or by anyone.

I can't think of anything else to confess.

# About the Author

Photograph by Angela McDermott

**JOE M. MCDERMOTT** is best known for the novels *Last Dragon*, *Never Knew Another*, and *Maze*. His work has appeared in *Asimov's Science Fiction*, *Analog*, and *Lady Churchill's Rosebud Wristlet*. He holds an MFA from the University of Southern Maine's Stonecoast Program. He lives in Texas.

# TOR·COM

**Science fiction. Fantasy. The universe.**

**And related subjects.**

\*

More than just a publisher's website, *Tor.com*

is a venue for **original fiction, comics,** and

**discussion** of the entire field of SF and fantasy,

in all media and from all sources. Visit our site

today—and join the conversation yourself.